PRAISE FOR USA TODAY AND WALL STREET JOURNAL BESTSELLING AUTHOR JAN MORAN

Seabreeze Inn and *Coral Cottage* series

"A wonderful story… Will make you feel like the sea breeze is streaming through your hair." – Laura Bradbury, Bestselling Author

"A novel that gives fans of romantic sagas a compelling voice to follow." – *Booklist*

"An entertaining beach read with multi-generational context and humor." – *InD'Tale* Magazine

"Wonderful characters and a sweet story." – Kellie Coates Gilbert, Bestselling Author

"A fun read that grabs you at the start." – Tina Sloan, Author and Award-Winning Actress

"Jan Moran is the queen of the epic romance." —Rebecca Forster, *USA Today* Bestselling Author

"The women are intelligent and strong. At the core is a strong, close-knit family." — Betty's Reviews

The Chocolatier

"A delicious novel, makes you long for chocolate." – *Ciao Tutti*

"Smoothly written…full of intrigue, love, secrets, and romance." – *Lekker Lezen*

The Winemakers

"Readers will devour this page-turner as the mystery and passions spin out." – *Library Journal*

"As she did in *Scent of Triumph*, Moran weaves knowledge of wine and winemaking into this intense family drama." – *Booklist*

The Perfumer: Scent of Triumph

"Heartbreaking, evocative, and inspiring, this book is a powerful journey." – Allison Pataki, *NYT* Bestselling Author of *The Accidental Empress*

"A sweeping saga of one woman's journey through World War II and her unwillingness to give up even when faced with the toughest challenges." — Anita Abriel, Author of *The Light After the War*

"A captivating tale of love, determination and reinvention." — Karen Marin, Givenchy Paris

"A stylish, compelling story of a family. What sets this apart is the backdrop of perfumery that suffuses the story with the delicious aromas – a remarkable feat!" — Liz Trenow, *NYT* Bestselling Author of *The Forgotten Seamstress*

"Courageous heroine, star-crossed lovers, splendid sense of time and place capturing the unease and turmoil of the 1940s; HEA." — *Heroes and Heartbreakers*

BOOKS BY JAN MORAN

The Love, California Series

Flawless

Beauty Mark

Runway

Essence

Style

Sparkle

20th-Century Historical

Hepburn's Necklace

The Chocolatier

The Winemakers: A Novel of Wine and Secrets

The Perfumer: Scent of Triumph

WALL STREET JOURNAL &
USA TODAY BESTSELLING AUTHOR

JAN
MORAN

BEACH VIEW
Lane

BEACH VIEW LANE

CROWN ISLAND, BOOK 1

JAN MORAN

SUNNY PALMS

PRESS

Library of Congress Cataloging-in-Publication Data
Moran, Jan.
/ by Jan Moran

ISBN 978-1-64778-117-0 (epub ebook)
ISBN 978-1-64778-119-4 (hardcover)
ISBN 978-1-64778-118-7 (paperback)
ISBN 978-1-64778-121-7 (audiobook)
ISBN 978-1-64778-120-0 (large print)

Published by Sunny Palms Press. Cover design by Okay Creations. Cover
images copyright Deposit Photos.

Sunny Palms Press
9663 Santa Monica Blvd STE 1158
Beverly Hills, CA 90210 USA
www.sunnypalmspress.com
www.JanMoran.com

Thank you for choosing *Beach View Lane*.
As a bonus, I would like to offer you a FREE Love California
digital ebook, too. Simply go to
https://getbook.at/BONUSFlawlessEbook
to download FLAWLESS. Happy reading!

1

*A*s a fresh morning breeze wafted from the nearby beach, April stepped outside to wave at her friend Deb cycling toward her. On Crown Island, locals splashed their homes in all shades of the spectrum, like sun-dazzled gemstones tumbled from the heavens surrounded by a sapphire ocean. Nearby, the Majestic Hotel was the magnificent ruby in the crown and the heart of the community.

Depending on the street, some houses were sherbet-colored, cool and refreshing on a summer's day. Other neighborhoods boasted hot, happy colors, spilling forth like jelly beans. And on another side of the island, riotous shades bled from houses and swirled onto muraled walls in crescendos of color.

Deb eased to a stop in front of April's house. Or rather, it was her mother's home, a pop of deep, rosy pink amidst a neighboring sea of blue bungalows and sunny yellow cottages. Only the towering house at the end of the block stood out in blinding white.

April adjusted the brim of her cotton visor against the sun. "I thought you might have forgotten about our ride."

"Sorry I'm late." Deb rubbed her shoulder. "I took a run on the beach with Duke this morning. Another dog attacked him, and I had to bandage a gash on Duke's snout. He fought me over that part, but he'll be alright."

"Poor Duke." Deb's rescue shepherd-collie mix was usually playful. "It's okay. I've been cleaning up this old bike." April eased onto the seat.

Deb peered at the tires. "Do you have an air pump? Your tires look low."

April slid off and bent down to inspect the tires. "You're right. This will only take a minute."

Her mother had stored bikes in her garage for years and kept them in good repair. Still, salt air could creep into every crevice. Specks of rust dotted the faded bubblegum-pink frame of her beloved old bike, and cracks from the summer heat etched a web across the seat. She drew her hand wistfully across the old handlebars.

"A little air in the tires, and she'll be almost as good as new." April set the kickstand and brought out a bicycle pump. Hitching up her knee-length shorts, she squatted by the bike.

Her closest friend from childhood perched on a gleaming bike, her sun-bronzed shoulders still toned and taught. Unlike April, who'd moved away thirty years ago, Deb had never left Crown Island except for vacations. Maybe that's why she still looked healthy and fit. No mom-shorts for her. She wore slim bike shorts and a tank top that showed off toned upper arms.

April covered hers with a navy hoodie that bore a history association logo. Deb was tall, blond, and blue-eyed—more like April's mother in her youth. In contrast, April thought of herself as fairly average. Her only distinguishing feature was her deep green eyes, which she'd recently learned she shared with a newly discovered set of aunts and cousins.

Deb leaned on her handlebars. "Since you're spending the year here, you'll have time to refurbish that bike."

With a small smile, April said, "I don't think I'll have time after all." She bent to secure the pump nozzle to the tire valve. "Calvin called."

The early morning call from her husband had been a surprise, especially because the genuine regret in his voice was evident. *Darling, I'm so sorry and ashamed for all I've put you through. But I want us to make this right because you and the girls mean the world to me. I can't bear to lose your love.*

These were the words she'd been longing to hear from

Calvin. Family meant everything to April because she'd lost her father as a teenager. Reuniting her currently fractured family and helping her daughters find their true paths—this is what April longed for.

Although, admittedly, she'd heard her husband's words before. Yet, here they were again.

Several months ago, April had taken a leave of absence from teaching history at a university in Seattle, Washington, to care for her mother on Crown Island, an artist colony just off the coast of Southern California and south of the Channel Islands.

A severe case of pneumonia had landed Ella Raines in the hospital, and she needed her daughter. Fortunately, her mother was never to be underestimated. Ella had rallied back, even returning to her yoga practice at home. Having worked as a nurse, she'd also received the best care in the local hospital she and her husband had helped establish fifty years ago.

But that wasn't the only reason April had ditched her summer classes and gone on hiatus. After what Calvin had done, she couldn't face her fellow faculty members. Their eyes were full of pity for her, understandably.

And she hated that. She turned back to her friend.

Deb raised her brow. "Are you sure you want another ticket on that rollercoaster?"

"We have a family," April replied, maybe a little too curtly.

Deb held up a hand. "Just checking in with you."

Instantly, April regretted her defensive tone with Deb. Still, with Calvin's charisma and good looks, her husband could hardly help attracting attention. For the last time, she hoped, with guarded relief. Soon, all that would be behind them.

Deb shot her a look of warning, but before she could say anything, April's mother opened the screen door. As Ella Raines stepped out, her thick, lustrous silver hair glistened in the sunlight like a halo. Her casual, blue cotton beach dress hung on her lean, usually fit frame now thinned by illness, although she was regaining her strength. "What a gorgeous day for a ride. In a few weeks, I should be strong enough to join you for an easy spin on the beach."

Deb's face brightened. "Just in time, Ella. Would you talk some sense into your daughter? She's threatening to leave."

Instantly, her mother's face drooped. "You're not going home already, are you?"

"I was going to tell you, but Calvin called as I was dressing. He was getting ready for a flight for a meeting in San Francisco. After that, he'll catch another flight south and take the ferry. He'll be here this evening." April plastered a confident smile on her face. "I'll ask him to stay over the weekend, but I imagine I should be ready to return with him to Seattle when he wants."

"So soon?" Ella asked.

At the sight of her mother's expression, April quickly added, "I'll be back to visit as soon as possible. I'm sure Junie will want to stay with you." After what her daughter had been through, she needed sunshine and fresh air.

Ella nodded with reluctant acceptance. "You have your life to live, but it should be your best life, dear."

Remorse about leaving her mother poured over April's shoulders, but she was also pleased that Calvin was on his way. "You always told me to fight for what I wanted. Calvin is retiring in ten years, maybe before. He wants to take off in an RV and travel the country, and he'd like to take a cruise every year. Maybe do some volunteer work."

Deb twirled a finger at her. "Somewhere in all those words, I thought I'd hear what you wanted, but they were all about Calvin."

"I want that, too." April lifted her chin, masking the pain in her heart. "He's still my husband. And the girls will be devastated if we don't get back together."

Even though she'd left to look after her mother, they both agreed it was a good time for a trial separation. The truth was, they'd been emotionally separated far longer. Calvin had also left her bed a year ago, feigning trouble sleeping and taking over the guest room.

Taking each front step with care, Ella joined them. "They're not children anymore. They would understand if you had to make a choice. May—I mean, Maileah—has quite the worldly attitude." She pressed a finger to her lip. "I keep forgetting her new name."

"I worry about Junie." Her youngest daughter's husband had died in a freak traffic accident on a business trip to London two years ago. Even though relations between Junie and Calvin were strained, she needed her father.

While her mother acknowledged that, it didn't stop her. "Junie is stronger than you realize, my dear. About your husband —be selfish this time. Tell him what you want."

"I have, and I will." Air hissed from the valve as April bent over to unscrew the dust cap on the wheel, and she could feel the blood rushing to her face. Anger, hurt, embarrassment, and disillusionment swirled in her, but she always harbored hope for a better future. She'd been through so much with Calvin.

April threw her energy into the bicycle pump, forcing air into the tire to fill it to capacity. If only such exertion could fill her marriage with renewed passion.

Her mother watched. "It pains me to see you hurt."

"These affairs run their course." April switched the nozzle and pumped air into the second tire with equal vengeance. Over the years, her husband had slipped up before, but never in their own backyard at the university. And with a leggy Russian woman the same age as their children? She puffed out air at the thought.

"What was he thinking?" she mumbled.

Suddenly, she realized she'd said that last bit out loud.

Her mother seized on her words. "The question is, what are you thinking? You've hardly heard from him all summer."

"Well, now I have." April bit back with a sharper response than she had intended. Worry and agitation weren't good for her mother's health. "I've weighed my options, Mama. I've worked hard for our future, and I'm not backing down when it's right around the corner."

"I'd love for you to stay a little longer," her mother added softly. She placed a hand on April's shoulder. "A few more weeks might give you more clarity."

As April snapped off the nozzle, air hissed out again. Quickly she screwed on the dust cap. "You can't fault me for trying to keep my family intact. You remember the wonderful life we had before Dad died. And what we lost."

"We all have a time, so I focused on being grateful that you were put into my life," her mother said, her lids lowering slightly at the memory. "Your situation is different, though equally painful. At some point, you must decide what you want for yourself."

"Don't think I haven't."

Immediately, April wished she could withdraw her words. A pang of guilt shot through her. The young girl, tucked inside a body now surprisingly over fifty, still longed for a deeper sense of family. For years, she had missed holidays with her father, carving a turkey, setting up a Christmas tree, and shooting fireworks over the ocean. Her mother carried on, but it was never the same. April couldn't do that to her daughters and their eventual offspring.

She put the bike pump away in the garage.

"I'll shut the garage from inside," Ella said.

Deb shared a look with Ella that seemed to say, *I'll try.*

But how could Deb understand any of this? She'd never been married, and her parents and brothers still lived on the island.

"Your mother will miss you," Deb said. "And what will you do if you're not teaching?"

"There might be an opening in the second semester. In the meantime, I can review my research notes for that book I've outlined. Maybe even start writing." However, the words weren't flowing. And before returning to teach, April needed more time to let this ugly incident blow over.

One of her friends had told her that Olga had left the graduate program and planned to pursue her master's degree at another private university. But when April pressed her friend, a professor in that department, she admitted she'd seen the tall, buxom Russian woman on campus. With a mane of blond hair and legs that went on forever, Olga was hard to miss—and presumably, equally hard to resist.

Maybe Olga was only on campus to see friends, she told herself.

"You could write here," Ella said, interrupting her thoughts.

Swallowing her pride, April reached out and hugged her mother. "I know both of you only want what's best for me. But I'm trying to do what's best for my family."

"What a shame they're not the same." When her mother pulled away, redness rimmed her eyes. "A ride will be good for you, dear. The sea breeze always clears my mind, helping me see problems with greater clarity."

Deb nodded emphatically. "I'll take her on the Queen's Flight." She wheeled from the driveway.

April followed, glancing back to reassure her mother. Although she was sure of what she needed to do, her mother's words clung to her like foxtails on the island trails. Once stuck in your hair, they were hard to get out.

Sort of like Calvin Smith.

April inhaled a deep breath of fresh, briny air and instantly felt her burden lighten. Her mother was right about that, too. Rising on her pedals, she quickened her pace to catch Deb.

"WAIT UP." Panting from the exertion of riding and pushing her bike uphill, April paused to peer down the other side. Standing at the high point of Crown Island, she rested on her handlebars, taking in the view.

The morning sun sparkled on the Pacific Ocean, and palm trees swayed in the light wind. From this vantage point, Crown Island shimmered like a rare jewel—so named after a talented jeweler to the courts of Europe, whose specialty was crowns and tiaras. The island was a gift for her service to the crown during the latter part of the Spanish Colonial period in California. From here, April and her childhood friends used to spot whales, sea lions, and seals off the coast. Now, the island contained a bustling village and a sprawling nature conservancy home to more than two hundred species of birds and animal wildlife.

April lifted her face to the ocean breeze that cooled her face.

Ahead of her on the trail, her friend Deb waited. That is, Deborah Whitaker of the Crown Island founding Whitakers and a one-time princess in the annual island parade when they were fifteen. With her stature and poise, Deb could still pass for island royalty, even four decades later. Her artfully tinted blond braid hung between her shoulders. She was the best friend April had ever had.

When April returned to Crown Island at the beginning of the summer to look after her mother, Deb was the first one who called to offer help. April had confided in her when Calvin told her he needed a break from their marriage. Maybe she'd told Deb too much of the ugly side of her marriage and not enough of the good.

When April reached her friend's side, she stopped. "Whew. Wasn't sure I could make it up here."

"I knew you could." Deb stretched her arms over her head in the sunshine. "I've been thinking...if you could do anything besides teaching, anywhere in the world, what would that be?" She pointed to April like they used to when they were young. "Go."

April gazed out over the island. Not far away, the old Majestic Hotel with its red-and-white wooden cupolas rose from its seaside perch, its red roof contrasting with the bluest of skies. Last spring, her mother had led a community effort to block the owner's plan to modernize it. Ella Raines had fiercely argued against it at City Hall. She had prevailed, even though her tenacity had come at a cost to her health. Ella always pushed herself. This time, she had allowed her immune system to become rundown.

"This might sound wild," April began. "But that Victorian lady kindled my love of history. Remember the field trip we took there?"

"Do I ever. The manager let us climb the restricted stairway to the main cupola. The highest point of the hotel—four whole stories. It seemed to stretch to the heavens back then." Deb grinned. "You never answered me."

April blurted out the first thing that came to mind, "I would study the history of that hotel and Crown Island. We have such a unique past. It shouldn't be lost."

"Ghosts and all?"

"I don't think the Majestic is haunted," April said, despite Deb's skeptical look. "I found its history so intriguing. Film stars, presidents, royalty, and gangsters have stayed there. Until then, that was the oldest structure I'd ever seen. All those black-and-white photographs and stories of old movies shot there fascinated me."

"Obsessed is more like it." Deb laughed. "You were like Nancy Drew sleuthing all over the hotel. I was a little jealous because you wrote so many papers about it. You got A's on every one of them. If you want to write a book, why not one on the history of the hotel and the island?"

April leaned on her handlebars. "Wasn't someone working on that?"

"You're thinking of Ruth Miller. She collected a lot of material and spoke about the need for a preservation society, but sadly, she didn't live long enough to fulfill her mission."

"Oh, I didn't know. How sad for her. Still, the island needs a historical society." The idea intrigued April. As a member of a national historical association through her university work, she understood the significance of preservation and its impact on future generations.

"I could get behind a project like that," she said. "The Majestic Hotel has a wealth of stories, though there are many others about how this island developed and the indigenous people who lived here over the centuries. But the Majestic... that's the real jewel of the island."

"Maybe we'll meet the new owner soon." With a wink, Deb stood on her pedals, eager to go.

"Wait, someone finally bought it? Who?" She glanced at the hotel again, concerned about what would become of it under new ownership.

"Another investor. I haven't met him, but I will. The interiors of the Majestic need a redesign, and I want that job." Deb grinned and nodded toward the descent. "Come on, let's do this. You remember how, don't you?"

"Sure," April replied, forcing a grin as she gazed down the trail they had christened the Queen's Flight when they were kids. Legend had it a woman had fled from her husband down this hill, running so fast that she'd become airborne, rising to the clouds in her escape. It wasn't as steep as she'd recalled from childhood, but it was still unnerving.

"You have to clear your mind and keep your focus," Deb reminded her. "Don't do a Jimmy."

April cringed. She could still see little Jimmy Carlton, who had broken a leg when he'd lost control. They'd been about ten years old, tearing around the island with minimal supervision— swimming, surfing, biking.

Over the years, every time April had returned for a visit, her mother suggested they go for a bike ride along the strand. As the salt-laden wind whipped around her, April wished she'd taken more time to do that—and kept it up.

"Give me a minute."

Her heart pounding like a jackhammer, she drew another deep breath. As she recalled, the descent was magical, but only if you could empty your mind and imagine gliding across the terrain ahead, willing your wheels to find the unobstructed path. Over the years, the trail had hardened to a smooth surface, but rain still left dangerous pockmarks. She had no idea if kids still filled them in.

As children, this hillside, so regally named, had been their pinnacle of achievement, their badge of courage. It had also seemed much taller back then.

Amateur stuff, her oldest daughter would say. But then, May— or Maileah, as she now preferred—was an avid marathon runner and adventure seeker who also worked in technology. She functioned at a high level of intensity every day.

Not quite able to achieve the necessary frame of mind, April held up a hand. "I'm a little out of shape." Physically and emotionally. She used to work out a few years ago. But her life had changed so fast this summer she'd gotten emotional whiplash.

If that was a thing, as her students in World History 101 would say. First, it was Calvin's latest midlife crisis; next, her mother's hospitalization; then, a host of new family members in nearby Summer Beach. Not even her parents had been informed of April's family or ancestry when they adopted her. *Closed adoption* was all that Ella had been told.

All these incidents sent shock waves through April. However, the discovery of a new family was welcome, if not a little over-whelming. Unbeknownst to her, her daughter Junie had done a DNA test. Still, she'd been excited when Junie arranged a meeting with her cousin Ivy Bay and her family at the Seabreeze Inn. There, April presented the best version of herself, reluctant to share what was really happening in her life.

Although she loved digging into history, she didn't like sharing her own.

Having caught her breath, she lifted her chin toward her

friend. "It's hard to keep up with you."

Deb put a hand on her hip. "If you stay, I'll help get you in shape, professor."

April smirked back at her. "Calvin was the tenured professor. I was the lowly lecturer." That still rankled her.

"You raised the girls and did his laundry."

"And a lot more than that." No one knew, but she'd written most of his doctorate dissertation and almost every article he'd published after that. He'd been the university's rising star in the psychology department. She wondered how many women were the real force behind their husbands. Narrowing her eyes, she added to herself, "Look at how he thanked me."

Over the summer, April had reviewed her circumstances. Was it really love that still bound her to Calvin, or was it the uncertainty of being on her own? She'd spent most of her adult life with him. Even though he wasn't always considerate of her, would another man be any different?

Yet, as outrageous as his behavior had been, they had a history. To her, that counted for a lot. And now, he was on his way back to her.

Swiftly changing the subject, Deb pointed to the new water bottle she'd given April this morning. "You must be well hydrated, especially for the Queen's Flight. Drink."

"Yes, ma'am." As April swallowed a mouthful of cool water, she peered down the other side of the hill.

As a girl, this hilltop had seemed almost insurmountable. She recalled pedaling uphill, her skinny legs burning with exertion, determined to make it to the top, even when other friends hopped off their bikes to run beside her and Deb. To them, the burn was as satisfying as the flight down the other side and made that intense, windswept race even more gratifying.

Deb's face was pink with excitement. "Ready to fly?"

"I think so." Could she still do it? At her age, she hesitated whenever she thought of doing something physically demanding. The last time she'd gone skiing with Maileah, she'd kept to the bunny hills instead of the mogul-pocked expert slopes she'd once loved to tackle. Her daughter had left her at the base.

"On your right," came a deep voice behind her.

April turned to see a man in tight biking shorts and a

screaming yellow shirt whiz past her. He looked like he was training for the Tour de France. She nodded to him, but he stared straight ahead, intent on the path ahead. He careened down, seeming to find every bump on the trail and fighting his way over it.

That wasn't the way to do it, April suddenly remembered.

Lowering her sunglasses, Deb laughed. "Tourist."

"You think?"

"Nice muscles, but he didn't even twitch a finger toward us."

"You mean toward you." April laughed as she put her bottle away. Deb was what her mother called a real looker, even now.

As for the issue of acknowledgment, locals kept to a different code. A nod, a smile, a moment to talk about the high tide, the low tide, or what strange item had washed up on the shore last week. April understood.

Here, people never knew when they might have to call on a neighbor to help. Floods, fires, earthquakes—her parents had lived through a lot on this small island just north of San Diego.

April had left as soon as she could for the mainland, a mere fifteen minutes by ferry. But that had been far enough. Going to college in Los Angeles had been like living on another planet.

Deb pushed her sunglasses up on her nose, tilted her face to the sun, and drew a deep breath to get into the zone. "Let's fly. Meet you at the base, then we'll head to Cuppa Jo's."

Ahead of her, Deb glided over the path. Slowly, she released the handlebars, swept her arms to her sides, and lifted her palms skyward as her wheels skimmed the surface, seeming to find their way to the smoothest parts.

Closing her eyes, April recalled that feeling of meditative cruising. It had been easier back then. *It's mind over matter*, her mother always said. Like riding the moguls.

That attitude is probably what pulled her mother through.

Deb was right. April needed to get back into the rhythm of life. Now that her mother was better, she would return to Calvin, and they would go on as they always had. He would express his remorse, and she would forgive him.

One eye twitched at that thought.

Determined to follow Deb's lead, April pushed off down the hill.

2

*A*t the first bump on the path, April clenched her jaw and tightened her grip on the bars, bearing down. Deb would call that counterproductive, but she couldn't help it. Doing a Jimmy at this stage of life? She couldn't afford to break a hip.

Every muscle in her body was on high alert, and she seemed to attract every rock on the trail as she gained speed.

Frightening speed.

What was she doing?

Deb was waiting for her at the base, looking exhilarated. A younger version of her friend floated before her eyes.

But April couldn't release the handlebar. Instead, her hands became claws on the old grips, impossible to tear loose as the wind rushed over her, forcing tears from her eyes into her hairline.

This is crazy, she thought. *I'm a split second from a full-body cast.*

She could see Deb urging her on with lifted palms, though the stiff breeze swept her words out to sea. Despite every jolt and shudder of the old bike frame, April held fast. Seconds turned into eternity as she careened down the hill.

And in that space, the courageous little girl in her emerged and began to take charge, though a split second later, April screeched to a halt in the scrub-studded clearing at the base of the hill.

"Wow, look at you," Deb exclaimed, raising her hand for a high-five. "You made it."

It took April a few seconds to unhand the grips. Her legs were limp noodles and her jaw a vise, sore from clenching on the teeth-rattling ride down.

But she'd made it in one piece. More than that, she'd had a moment when she'd felt like she could conquer anything. That was encouraging. "At least I'm still upright."

"Yes, you are. Follow me to Cuppa Jo's. You deserve a mocha chocolate chip grande for your bravery." Deb started off on her bike.

April was still breathing hard, but she put a numb foot to the pedal and followed. The street was built on the incline, and Deb sailed across a crosswalk, waving at people she passed with little wiggles of her fingers. She seemed to know almost everyone on the island.

Deb had returned to Crown Island after college—and after her high school sweetheart married someone else in her absence. April had always admired Deb's courage in returning to the island and starting her interior design business. Preferring her freedom, she'd never married, though she'd had plenty of serious boyfriends.

April still felt wobbly on the bike, but she was trying to keep up with Deb. As she approached a stop sign, she glanced from one side to the other. No cars were coming toward her, so she swung wide, flying across the lane.

Just then, a Crown Island police cruise pulled along beside her.

The officer motioned for her to stop.

He couldn't mean her, could he?

April glanced in the other direction but didn't see any lawbreakers. Just the usual people strolling along the sidewalk or seated at cafes under brightly colored, hand-painted umbrellas. A guy with board shorts and a paint-splattered T-shirt led a string of dogs, and kids lined up at the ice cream vendor's cart. No criminals that she could see.

She turned back, and the officer repeated the gesture. April sighed as Deb pulled farther away. She eased to a stop by the curb and fumbled in her pocket. Her hands were still quivering from the ride.

After pulling behind her, the officer got out and walked toward her. He was young enough to be her son and had that good-looking, TV-extra look as if he'd just stepped off a set in a police officer's costume. Too pretty to be real.

Wishing her hand wasn't shaking, April whipped out her license and handed it to him. "Here. I'm April Raines."

The officer looked surprised before taking her license. "April Raines? Your parents had a sense of humor." He paused, his aviator lenses reflecting the sun. "You've probably heard that one before."

"Once or twice." She got off her bicycle and swept out the kickstand with her sneaker. "So, why did you stop me?" She peered at his name tag. "Officer Blumenthal."

The officer stroked his chin. "You failed to signal your turn."

One side of the officer's mouth quirked up again. April gaped at him. "You've got to be kidding. This is Crown Island. No one does that."

"Those who abide by the law do." He cast a glance at a man behind him. "You were also going awfully fast through that stop sign." One corner of his lip tugged upward. "People on Crown Island also observe those. You could hurt yourself at that speed."

April glared at him and waited.

The officer flipped open a pad and weighed her license in his hand. "Seattle, Washington. Is this your correct address?"

She sighed. Who gets a ticket on a bicycle? She knew it was possible, but she'd grown up here, riding the same bike on the same trail for years.

"I've been here on an extended visit. Actually, this is my hometown," she added, incredulous as he wrote her information on the form.

Calvin had been forwarding her mail, and he'd be furious at her for getting a ticket. That wasn't a good way for them to start over, but surely it wouldn't go on her driving record. It was a bike, for heaven's sake.

She exhaled, trying to lessen her annoyance.

While she waited, her mother's words swept through her. *The sea breeze will clear your mind.*

Maybe it had on that ride down the Queen's Flight. She held her head a little higher.

Her mother had always given her good advice. She couldn't imagine what she would ever do without her.

Slowly, an uncomfortable realization dawned on her. In the bright, unrelenting sunshine, she flipped through the mental pages of her past. Most mistakes she'd made in life were because she hadn't followed her mother's advice.

Like the riptide that had almost drowned her.

And the senior prom dress that really had been too tight.

Or Calvin.

The first time they'd broken up while they were dating, her mother had turned up a Carly Simon song on the radio and turned to her. *This is about Calvin*, she'd said.

The song? "You're So Vain."

Yet, April had been powerfully drawn to him, as sure as waves to the shore. She loved him—and a part of her always would—but she'd lost respect for him long ago.

"I'll need to run this license," Officer Blumenthal said, turning toward his patrol car.

April folded her arms and nodded.

As she waited, she chewed her lip in thought. As much as she wanted to go home, could she return this time? Before, her daughters hadn't known what she'd put up with in her marriage. But now, that illusion had been shattered.

Junie had said, *Mom, I'm worried about Dad. I think he might be having a midlife crisis.* This time, everyone knew. Even her daughters, to her mortification.

She pressed her fingers to her temples; the bone-chattering ride down the hill seemed to have shaken something loose in her mind.

With sudden clarity, scenes from her life shifted like pieces on a chessboard, begging for a new strategy. Where did she belong now? Certainly not at the university where she'd worked for the last ten years. April puffed out a little breath and straightened her shoulders. Pity was no substitute for respect. She still had some pride left.

Yet, she also had to earn a living, and she didn't relish tearing her family apart. She twisted her mouth to one side in contemplation. Life wasn't a textbook with the answers in the back.

Officer Blumenthal sauntered back to her. "If you decide to stay, you'll need to change that address."

Where would he get that idea? But she wasn't in the mood to elaborate. "I'm at my mother's home for now."

"Well, then. Welcome back to Crown Island." He motioned to a speed limit sign a couple of car lengths ahead of them. "As you can see, we still take it slow around here."

"Are you going to give me a ticket for that?"

Officer Blumenthal had the temerity to grin as if this was funny, instead of a costly inconvenience that would also drive up her insurance fee.

And today, of all days, when she could really use a break. "Can we wrap this up? Just give me the ticket."

The officer shook his head. "Sorry, can't do that."

"And why not? Since I'm an actual perp—or whatever you call people like me. Scofflaws, maybe."

"Scofflaw?" he repeated. One side of Officer Blumenthal's TV-perfect mouth quirked up again.

Even she cringed at the word that came out of nowhere in her mind. That's what she got for immersing herself in the past. She loved everything vintage—clothes, furniture, music.

More than anything, she loved researching historical mysteries, such as the enigma of Shakespeare's identity. Her money was on Mary Sidney Herbert, Countess of Pembroke and literary grand dame. But maybe she was projecting.

If only people didn't repeat the mistakes of the past. She gritted her teeth. That certainly went for her, too.

"We have a policy of sorts here on Crown Island. First offender scofflaws get a warning." He touched his forehead. "Consider yourself warned, Ms. Raines."

She gave him a curt nod. "I appreciate that."

"And give your mother my best." Officer Blumenthal turned and strode back to the patrol car.

April glared at him. He knew her mother, yet he still gave her grief?

She set her jaw and got back on her bike. As she rode to meet Deb, she reconsidered Calvin's visit. This morning, she'd promised herself she would not shed a tear when he arrived. She'd wept and heard it before. All she wanted was for them to simply get back on plan. This was just a day. Like any other.

Except that now, after the Queen's Flight, it wasn't. Once again, April recalled her mother's words. As the mist in her mind continued to clear, the world she'd once known slipped from its axis.

Or maybe it was regaining its balance.

By the time April pulled her bike outside of Cuppa Jo's, a retro diner with a beach view, she felt different. More confident. More like herself than she had in a very long time.

Decades, perhaps. But would this feeling last?

April parked her bike beside Deb's among the other bicycles and golf carts locals used to zip around the island. She glanced at the vintage clock on the red Cuppa Jo's neon sign. Calvin would be on the evening ferry in a few hours, and he expected the old, long-suffering April.

A gust of wind from the ocean blew through her, carrying with it a sudden premonition, warning her of a shift in all that had been. She shivered and opened the door to the diner.

3

"*I* can't listen to this anymore!" Junie hung up on her sister, threw her phone against the rumpled pillows on her bed, and screamed. May could be infuriating. This time, even more than usual.

Thank goodness her mother wasn't home. But she could hear her grandmother in the kitchen.

A muffled ring immediately erupted, and Junie snatched the phone. May was on video again, her perfectly blow-dried, strawberry-blond hair swinging around her shoulders as she strutted through an office complex in Seattle, complete with Roman columns and fountains. Her heels clicked on the hard surface.

"Now what?" Junie brushed straggly wisps of hair back toward her haphazard ponytail and straightened the collar of her husband's favorite blue cotton pajama top, which hung to her knees. It was the best she could do, though her sister still looked at her with contempt for her appearance.

"Hey, Maileah." A man's voice rang out, calling out to her sister with a name Junie didn't recall hearing. "Are we still on for drinks after work?"

"I'll see you there," her sister replied with an airy wave.

Junie waited until the man moved out of frame. "Did he call you May-*le-ah*? Is that your new name *du jour*?"

"Shh. You know it is." Her sister lowered her voice. "May is too plain for my profession, and I'd prefer not to be known as a weather forecast. May Raines-Smith. I sound like a weather-maker." She smirked. "It's okay for you and Mom. It's weird, but you'd think that after dealing with that, Mom would have chosen better names for us."

Junie had heard this before. "Except no one knows who you are from one week to the next."

"That's an exaggeration. I've been Maileah for a year. And this time, it's official. I filed a legal name change."

"Whatever, Maybelle." Her sister had been separating herself from the pack practically since birth. And their father only encouraged it. Choosing to ignore that, Junie asked, "Why did you call back?"

"To make sure you won't tell Mom what I said, okay?"

Junie twisted her lips to one side. "Don't worry. That's your job. I'm not doing your dirty work. Or Dad's."

"Just because I'm accepting this situation for what it is—"

"I get it," Junie snapped. "Your maturity is impressive. Is that what you want to hear? But whose side are you on?"

Junie pursed her perfectly outlined lips. "I can see both sides."

"Well, I can't."

"Don't be such a child."

Junie tamped down her anger. "You have the nerve to say that after what I've been through?" Although her sister was two years older, life had taken a greater toll on Junie.

"Look, I'm sorry." May—*Maileah*—actually flushed. "But I can't tell her."

"No, that would be our father's place."

"She'll find out sooner or later."

Junie couldn't bear that. Her mother had every reason to be angry and hurt over what their father had done, but she also wanted to reconcile and go home. Through her open window, she'd heard her mother and grandmother talking with Deb this morning.

"Maybe not," Junie insisted. "This can all blow over, just like before. And Mom didn't quit her job. She took a leave of absence."

Her sister heaved a sophisticated sigh. "That's called magical thinking, Sis. I heard even adult children dream of their parents getting back together."

"And they might. I heard her say Dad is flying in today. You know what that means. He wants her to fly back with him."

Junie couldn't believe her sister was accepting this separation as a *fait accompli*. She could hardly speak to her father anymore, not that he called very often.

"Junie. Listen to me."

Her sister's light green eyes bore into hers, even over a screen.

"It's true," Junie went on. "If Dad didn't want to see Mom, he wouldn't be making a trip here to see her. Crown Island isn't the easiest place to visit. Seattle is a fairly long flight, or two without a nonstop, then a shuttle or Uber car from the San Diego airport, or maybe Orange County, and finally, a ferry from Summer Beach to the island."

"I know how to get there."

"Do you? Because it's been a long time since you visited Nana. She was very sick this summer."

"Did you forget she was at the house last Christmas?"

"Of course not." Her sister was exasperating.

"You have to be prepared. That's all I'm saying. But don't let Mom know."

Junie clutched her phone. "It's not happening, I'm telling you." Her stomach clenched with anguish. If what her sister said was true—but no. She couldn't think that way. Anything was possible.

Junie *had* to believe that. Now that she couldn't create a family of her own, she clung to what she had. Nothing good could come from a splintered family.

As her sister opened the door to her office building, she whispered, "I have to go. Promise me?"

"Trust me, I won't breathe a word."

"And Junie?"

"What?"

"Get dressed." Her voice dropped a notch. "You'll feel better if you do."

"It doesn't make a difference, Maybelline."

"Maileah." She rolled her eyes, and with a flutter of her manicured nails, she clicked off.

Junie flopped onto the bed. The image in her mind of her father with another woman was almost more than she could bear. Her sister had never been married—or even in love, Junie suspected. She ran through men like mascara. Her sister couldn't comprehend how deep a bond could be between two people.

Junie ran a hand over her heart as her husband's face floated into her mind. He was never far from her thoughts, and she missed him with such intensity it brought a physical ache to her body.

She reached out a hand to the empty spot on the bed beside her. "You should be here," she said as she stroked the sheet, imagining the warmth of Mark's body there, as if he'd just gotten up to make coffee or catch a flight.

Like that flight to London.

The next day, without warning, her world collapsed. She could still hear the explanation the police offered. *He looked left, not right, before stepping into the crosswalk. Opposite to the flow of traffic he was accustomed to at home. Too many Americans make that mistake. If only the cab hadn't run the light.*

Mark had died instantly, she was told.

If Junie hadn't been sick, she would've gone with him. She might have looked in the right direction. She might have seen the cab.

Feeling the same guilt now as then, she stroked the sheet. Had she known she might never see him again, what would she have said or done differently? Did he really know how much she loved him? Those thoughts haunted her sleepless nights, and she could seldom alleviate the ache she felt to her bones.

When Junie had called her mother, she'd dropped everything to be with her and stayed by her side through every harrowing step. Her father had only called. Often enough, she supposed, grudgingly, but he'd remained at the university.

She never forgot that. Just last spring, he'd told her, *You're young. You'll find another husband.* She replied that if he really wanted to console her, he should have gone with her and her mom to London to claim Mark's body and bring him home for burial. But no, his students were more important. Junie curled her hands into tight fists. His empty platitudes meant little.

Besides, Junie doubted she could love another as she had

loved Mark. She curled onto her side, cradling her abdomen and thinking about the child they'd been trying to conceive.

She yearned for a piece of Mark, a reminder in a young child's face that she could cradle in her hands. Without Mark or his baby, Junie ached with a deep and profound loneliness for which she had few words.

As a widow—how she hated that word!—she understood the potential loss her mother was facing in a way that her sister could not. The breakdown of her parents' marriage was the death of a relationship, even if it wasn't perfect by most standards.

A tap sounded at the door. "Hi, honey. Are you okay in there?"

"I'm alright, Nana." Junie sniffed and wiped hot tears from her eyes.

"Who were you yelling at, dear?"

Junie got up and opened the door. "May. Excuse me, she's now calling herself *Maileah*."

Her grandmother nodded. "You once changed your name."

"What was I, two years old?"

"Three, as I recall." Ella smiled and touched the doorjamb. "How about breakfast? Your mother went for a bike ride with Deb."

"I heard." Junie was worried about her grandmother, even though she was regaining color in her face. "But let me make something for you. Mark taught me how to prepare the best Eggs Benedict. And it's not that hard."

"I'd love that." A smile bloomed on Ella's face. "I shouldn't have such rich foods, but just once won't hurt." She held out her hand.

Junie grasped it like a lifeline. Tucking her arm through her grandmother's, they made their way into the cozy blue-and-white kitchen where they often talked. Junie touched her head to her grandmother's. "I love you, Nana."

"I love you, too, sweetheart." Ella paused. "Want to talk about it?"

"*Maileah* called me a child."

"She only says that to make herself feel superior. Probably because she's not getting the sort of love you had with Mark. A love like that makes you feel confident, on top of the world." Ella's voice gained strength as she spoke.

Junie nodded. "I always felt like there was nothing Mark and I couldn't accomplish together." She hadn't considered that about her sister.

Ella eased onto a cushioned bench at the rustic kitchen table. "I'm glad you experienced such a great love. Your Mark was a lot like my Augustus. Smart and talented, with the biggest heart of any man I'd ever known."

"That's exactly right. You always understand how I feel." Junie drew in her lip. She wished her mother could say that, too.

Ella plucked a few basil leaves from a potted plant on the table. More herbs lined the window over the sink, tucked into pottery pots that April had made. Chives, oregano, dill. "These will be good as a garnish. Let me know if you need any help."

"You're fine where you are. Just relax." Junie brought eggs and butter from the refrigerator. Being with her grandmother always made her happy. Now she felt useful, too.

Ella cleared her throat. "Your father called this morning."

"I heard." Junie slid a pair of English muffins into a toaster oven and placed a pot of water on the stovetop. "He's coming, right?"

"Yes. I'm sure he's missed you."

"I doubt that. When I was living at home, all he talked about was my getting a job and moving out."

"Your father only wants you to be happy. While it's fortunate that Mark left you well-situated financially, having a purpose in life is healthy. Have you thought of what you'd like to do?"

"Mark was the computer genius. The only experience I had was in a shop." Junie shrugged off the idea. "Dad is more concerned with what he wants, not his family."

Her grandmother frowned and plucked a few more basil leaves as she listened.

"Mark made me happier than I'd ever been, but Dad could never accept him because he hadn't gone to college. But Mark was brilliant. He'd been coding since he was ten years old. He'd traveled the world and knew more about people and cultures than any of the fraternity guys I had dated." She eased eggs into the simmering water with a spoon. Next, she sliced a chunk of butter into a saucepan to make hollandaise—just as Mark had taught her.

"I was tremendously fond of him," Ella said. "And he would want to see you creating a new life."

A new life. Junie thought about that. She had met him at a party in Seattle the day she graduated from college. From that night on, they'd been inseparable. When he saw her collection of shoes for every sport and heard how hard it was to find exactly what she wanted, he had an idea to sell specialized sports shoes online. She was all in. Her father had been pushing her to follow him into academia, but that was the last thing she wanted.

Junie had worked at a retail shop during her summer breaks, so she helped him design the online store and select merchandise to appeal to their generation. He coded the entire site. Within months, they were successful.

"Even after the business took off, Dad still couldn't accept Mark. He refused to contribute anything toward the wedding—did you know that? I didn't care. By then, we were making enough. All we wanted was to start a family."

Sniffing, Junie realized she'd forgotten about the toasted English muffins. She scooted them onto plates just in time. Next, she topped them with smoked salmon and sliced avocado, California style.

"You had the most magical ceremony I'd ever seen," Ella said. "Whose idea was it to marry in the mountains?"

"Both of ours."

Junie paused to combine the egg yolks and lemon juice with a little Dijon mustard, salt, and pepper. A whirl of an immersion blender made quick work of it.

"We were hiking and found that beautiful little inn with the most incredible views. As soon as we saw it, we knew we'd found the place we wanted to marry."

"What a sweet story," Ella said.

Junie pressed a hand to her chest. Just thinking about that weekend flooded her with the same overwhelming love she'd felt for Mark that day.

Ella rose to set the table with utensils and cloth napkins. "I'm sure if your father could do it over again, he would have welcomed Mark into the family. Sometimes men do things they regret."

As Junie slid the poached eggs onto the layered muffins, she bit her lip. Did her grandmother have any idea what her father had been up to with the Russian woman? The butter sizzled, and Junie removed it from the heat. "But Dad has been…"

"I know all about what he's been up to," Ella said firmly. "So does your mother."

"I'm angry at Dad, but I miss him, too." More than anything, she yearned for the family life she'd known as a child—before she learned of grown-up faults. She combined the butter with other ingredients as she spoke. "I miss having a father who cares about me—and his family. Do you think he's capable of that again?"

Ella touched a hand to her brow. "I honestly don't know, sweetheart."

"Do you think there's anything I can do to help fix this?"

Her grandmother looked doubtful. "I don't know, but try to spend time with him while he's here. He's always been difficult, but he's getting older. Shocking as it is, some men mature much later than women. There's still hope."

Junie poured the velvety sauce over the poached eggs and placed the plates on the table. "And for Mom?"

Her grandmother smiled. "Your mother is a smart woman. She'll do what she has to do."

"You didn't answer my question."

"Oh, but I did." Her grandmother took her hand. "This looks and smells utterly delicious. Let's enjoy this sumptuous feast and talk about our plans on the island."

"We're having lunch with the Bay family tomorrow, remember?"

Last month as her mother's birthday approached, Junie discovered a DNA match. *Shelly Bay Kline.* Attempting to ease her mother's worry, she pursued the match and visited Shelly at the Seabreeze Inn in nearby Summer Beach.

"You and your mother must do that, but I should rest. I wear out so quickly now."

"I wish you could join us."

Ella rubbed Junie's hand. "Enjoy getting to know this new branch of your family. I'll spend more time with them when I'm stronger." She took a bite of the Eggs Benedict. "This is marvelous, truly the best I've had. Thank you, sweetheart. Nourishment like this will speed me to full recovery."

Junie appreciated the compliment. "I love it when we hang out, Nana. And I love cooking for you."

The Bay family lived nearby in Summer Beach, a small town just a ferry ride away on the mainland. Junie had arranged a meeting on her mother's birthday, and they'd met most of the family at once during a reunion.

Junie thought of something. "Does it bother you that we're having lunch with the Bay family?"

"Not at all. Good heavens, I'm not going to live forever."

"I wish you would."

Ella smiled in that way she had. An all-knowing, slightly mysterious, Mona-Lisa-of-grandmother smiles. "One life isn't enough. That's why you must live the very best life you can. And I can think of nothing better than you, your mother, and your sister being surrounded by a large, loving family after I'm gone. The Bays are good people."

Junie and April had visited them in Summer Beach, and the Bays came here to meet Ella. The mother and matriarch, Carlotta Reina Bay, thanked Ella for adopting April. She assured her that her sister Pilar would have wanted it that way, which brought a smile to Ella's face.

"But you're not gone yet." Junie smiled. "You're not feeling even a little jealousy?"

"Not a smidgeon. Who'll be at lunch?"

"Carlotta, Mom's new aunt. My great aunt, I guess. And her daughters, Ivy and Shelly. I'm really enjoying getting to know my new cousins." Shelly had just had a baby, and Ivy had lost her husband, too, although she'd recently remarried.

Junie was still adjusting to the big, boisterous family. But it was fascinating to see the physical resemblance between them all.

"I think it's wonderful that you discovered the connection, my dear." Ella sighed softly. "Your mother was such a gift to us. After she learned of her adoption, she had a thousand questions about her birth mother and her heritage, which I knew was normal. I wish I could have given her the answers she needed. I'm glad you could provide them."

"I was curious, too," Junie said.

But it was more than that. While her own family fractured, maybe Junie had been subconsciously looking for a replacement, the way some friends formed bonds with others they called family, even though they weren't related. Like her mother and her friend Deb, who referred to each other as sister. Junie wished she could be as close to May.

Maileah. Maybe she should start by trying to honor her sister's wishes.

As Junie took a bite of her egg dish, memories of long weekend brunches with Mark sprang to mind. She closed her eyes, reliving the feeling.

"Mark's recipe is delicious," Ella said as if reading her mind. "He would be proud of you."

"I like to think so, too." Junie smiled at her grandmother. "Between my issues with Maileah and Dad dividing us, maybe I needed this new family connection as much as Mom."

Her grandmother smiled at Junie's use of her sister's new name and clasped her hand with surprising strength. "But you don't want to lose your father or sister."

"No," Junie said softly. "Although I'm not sure how to stop that from happening." A lot would depend on what her father had to say when he arrived.

4

*W*ith her legs aching from the Queen's Flight ride, April walked into Cuppa Jo's vintage diner and saw Deb sitting at the red Formica counter.

Deb looked relieved. "What happened? I was about to go look for you. Are you okay?"

April smirked and eased onto a red vinyl-covered stool. "I nearly got a ticket."

"On a bicycle? For what?"

"Not signaling a turn. Do you know Officer Blumenthal?"

Deb grinned. "That's Blue. He was probably looking out for you. Or checking you out."

"Hardly. I'm old enough to be his mother."

"Blue likes to know who's new in town. You haven't been out much."

"Well, he knew Mama, too." But then, Ella had been a nurse in the emergency room, so that wasn't surprising, now that she thought about it.

"Everyone loves your mother."

April realized that. Ella Raines had lived here all her life. After nursing school, she returned to the island with her new husband, a surgeon. Together, she and Dr. Augustus Raines spearheaded the effort to build a small hospital on the island so people wouldn't have to take a ferry to the mainland for every broken bone or case of appendicitis. Unfortunately, her father died of a heart attack when April was barely a teenager. Her mother carried on, though she never remarried.

April touched her friend's shoulder. "Even though I was pretty clunky on the path, I want to thank you for pushing me out there."

"Whether you realize it or not, you're a lot like your mother," Deb said as she signaled the young woman behind the bar.

"If I were more like her, I would have tossed out Calvin when I was still young enough to start a family with another man."

Deb looked at her in amazement. "Sounds like that ride did some good. Still, don't be so hard on yourself. Your daughters were born before he showed his true colors." She took April's hand. "Whatever your decision, I'm here for you. You're my chosen sister, aren't you?"

"And I'm yours," April replied, as she always did. She didn't have any siblings, while Deb had only brothers.

A young woman, thirty-ish with short, curly dark hair and a gray sweatshirt, leaned across the counter to top off Deb's coffee. "Hey, April. One for you, too?"

"I'm here for the mocha chip grande I was promised."

"Sure." Jo laughed. "Deb told me she led you down the Queen's Flight."

"It was terrifying but incredible. I still feel wobbly." April unzipped her hoodie. A couple of men in the diner looked their way, but their gazes were drawn to Deb, not her. "I'm a little old for that."

Deb threw her a look. "Where did that comment come from?"

"I'm not as young as I used to be." She watched Jo combining the ingredients for her sweet, icy reward.

"Hold it right there—we're the same age." Deb added softly, "I see we've got work to do on you. Before you leave, promise? Surely Calvin will give you a few days before he steals you away." She made a face.

"I'm not you," April said, raising her voice over the sound of Jo's blender. "I'm being realistic."

"So am I. And I won't take no for an answer."

"The last time I let you do that, I ended up with orange hair."

"Today, that would be fashionable."

"Well, it wasn't back then."

Deb arched an eyebrow. "Maybe I need this just as much as you do."

A wistful note in her friend's voice caught April's attention. "Is it Jeffrey?"

Lifting her chin, Deb nodded. "Next, as they say. You should bring Junie, too."

"I don't know if she's ready."

"Funny. That's what she says about you. What is this, some sort of mutual excuse you've agreed on with your daughter?"

Maybe it was, April granted. "We'll do it. But first, I want to take in a couple of the bikes for a complete overhaul. Junie can take Mom out when she's feeling better."

"You have to see Adrian," Deb said. "He's running his dad's bike shop now. And his son Sailor is working there, too. When he's not out surfing, that is. The kid's a natural. He's been competing around the world."

"I'll do that." It was interesting to see everyone she'd known again.

Jo returned with the iced coffee. "Here you go."

"Thanks." April stuck a thick paper straw into the slushy. The cool jolt of caffeine was just what she needed. She caught Deb's eye and grinned. "That ride was worth it, after all."

Deb smiled back. "So, will you reconsider staying?"

"I'll hear what Calvin has to say." She didn't have to spell it out.

"It will be good for Junie to stay."

"Mama still needs help, and they can help each other. Besides, her dad would pressure her to find work. To 'get out there,' as he says. But grief doesn't have a timetable."

Deb nodded. "She's better off here."

April could imagine her next line: *And so are you.* But to Deb's credit, she didn't say it. She didn't have to.

Last spring, April had urged Calvin to go with her to family counseling so they could help support Junie and work on their marriage. That was before Olga, as far as she knew. Yet, he'd refused.

"If Calvin stays a few days, that will be good for Junie. They need to spend time together and settle their differences." She paused. "Could you introduce Junie to a few nice people here on the island? It would be good for her to make friends."

Deb arched an eyebrow. "Like a grown-up playdate? I'll see what I can do."

April had to laugh. "Not like that. Casually. You know what I mean."

"I imagine she'll gravitate toward her own kind. People usually do."

One of the most difficult challenges April had as a mother was watching Junie suffer the death of her husband and being powerless to alleviate her pain. She was desperate to see her daughter create a new life for herself. If only she could bear the burden of Junie's anguish for her.

Worse, Calvin had never approved of her husband, Mark, so his condolences were hollow.

Junie was devastated, hurt, and angry with her father over that. April had never forgiven him either. She couldn't imagine how he justified not supporting his daughter at the darkest time of her life. Whenever April brought it up, Calvin said she was being melodramatic.

After Mark's death, Junie sold their online shoe store to a competitor. Between that, Mark's life insurance, and the settlement from the cab company, Junie didn't have to work. At least there was that blessing.

Nevertheless, Calvin argued that Junie should return to work to feel worthwhile. April agreed that Junie needed to find a new purpose, but she didn't like the pressure Calvin put on her.

Junie was mourning more than her husband.

She and Mark had been trying to start a family. Although Junie had recovered from the worst of it, she still needed support. She tried spending time with Maileah, but her older sister liked to party. Junie wasn't up to going out every night, and Maileah tired of staying home.

April wished her daughters could be as close as they once had been. Just two years apart in age, they'd gone to different colleges and drifted apart. When Junie married, and Maileah's fiancé severed their engagement the weekend of Junie's wedding, Maileah seemed to hold Junie responsible. April wasn't sure what had happened.

Jo topped off Deb's coffee. "How about breakfast? The California omelets are looking good today. We have perfectly ripe avocados."

"Just my usual green smoothie for me," Deb replied.

April was tempted, but her stomach was still queasy from the intense ride. Maybe it was time to start eating healthier anyway. "I'll have a small smoothie to go."

Deb grinned. "Oh, so now you have someplace to go?"

April smiled at the mild dig. "I have a meeting with a landscaper today. He's giving me a quote on the yard."

Her mother loved gardening and used to care for the yard, but it was too much for her now. It had been neglected, and April thought a fresh look might lift Ella's spirits, too.

"You didn't ask me for a referral?"

"I knew you were busy." One of Deb's specialties as an interior designer was creating turn-key residences for part-time owners, with everything from indoor and outdoor furnishings to forks and towels. She often referred gardeners, housekeepers, and property managers as well. "I saw him at that big white house on the corner. Maybe you know him. His name is Derek."

"Oh yes, I've heard of him. He usually does large jobs."

Unlike the original bungalows that lined Beach View Lane, the newer, blindingly white house on the corner had been built on two large lots where neighbors had walked their dogs when April was young. The front of the huge home faced Beach View Lane on one side, though it was so large that it wrapped around to the other street where it had full-on ocean views. The home would have been attractive, except for the plain stucco wall surrounding it.

No one knew the owner except that he lived somewhere back east. Chicago, or maybe it was New York. Her mother had met him once a few years ago, and he told her he was in real estate. The house was usually rented during the high tourist season in the summer, though it hadn't been this year. The owner remained an enigma.

"Two smoothies," Jo said, sliding cups across the counter. April took a sip and went on. "Last week, this landscaper, Derek, took me on a tour of that big house's rear gardens to show me what he can do on a smaller lot. The drought-resistant landscaping looks lush but requires very little water. Derek planted succulents that were quite pretty—ones I'd never seen before. He's providing an estimate today."

"Good luck with that," Deb said. "You'll have to tell me all about it. And let me know if you want a second opinion."

"Sure will." April hugged her and left. Feeling energized by the combination of caffeine and green vegetables, April got back onto her bike. She tucked her drink into an old cupholder on the frame and started toward the beach.

Crown Island had changed little since April had grown up here. The shoreline looked the same, though many beachfront homes had changed hands. The original cottages sported new room additions, fresh coats of paint, high-efficiency windows, and air-conditioners that hummed all summer.

April loved cycling along the ocean and wished she'd done it more often. She passed homes in a dizzying array of sunset colors, from vivid purple to dusty blue and warm yellow. She loved growing up on Crown Island, especially on Beach View Lane. While not directly on the beach, the home still had the advertised view and was only a short walk away.

Even though her mother was still regaining her strength and her cough was lessening, Ella enjoyed having a full house. April was sleeping in her old room on the twin bed she'd had forty years ago. Her mother had transformed it into a daybed and used it for her grandchildren. Her high school knickknacks were gone; otherwise, the room had the same furnishings.

April had given Junie the beautifully decorated guest room. Her daughter had been staying with April and Calvin until her mother, known as Nana to her daughters, became ill. When April returned, Junie had come with her. Given Junie's situation, she would probably be here longer, and April wanted her to feel comfortable.

Cycling along the shore to the sound of crashing waves, April thought about her daughters. Although Junie was slowly healing from Mark's death, she was still at a crossroads. Her eldest daughter Maileah worked in technology marketing in Seattle. She had always been closer to her father. Sometimes April wondered if Maileah was still jealous that Junie was born. As a two-year-old, she'd thrown a fit.

But no, that was a silly thought. They were both grown women, though they differed in style and temperament. Still, it seemed like something was amiss between them, especially this summer.

Just then, her phone buzzed in her pocket. She recognized the tone. Calvin. She pulled over and stared at the phone.

Change of plans. As soon as I arrive, we need to talk. Without Junie or your mother. Meet me at the ferry, at 6 pm.

April sucked in a breath. That sure sounded different from his warm call this morning. *What does that mean?* she tapped. Her finger hovered over the tiny send icon. Inexplicably, her chest tightened. Thinking better of it, she erased the message, even though the little message dots on the other end would give her away.

April, I know you're there. Answer me.

She could imagine his irritation. If he wanted her back, establishing new communication rules was up to her.

Super busy. See you at the ferry, darling! She turned off the phone, pocketed it, and shoved off on the bike again. She didn't have time to argue, nor did she want to ruin a beautiful day. After all these years, Calvin hadn't learned how to start a conversation that didn't sound like a confrontation—unless he wanted something.

And after years of her coddling him and dealing with his outbursts, she'd learned she couldn't change him.

April heaved a sigh. Regrettably, other women had tried, too.

If only she and Calvin could return to happier days. He'd been a good father when the girls were young, although Maileah had been the clear favorite. Junie was a colicky baby, and her cries exasperated him.

Since their daughters left, April had been trying to recapture those days, surprising him with weekend getaways, his favorite meals, and tickets to music venues he liked. She was planning for their retirement and all the trips he talked of taking. Just the two of them at first, to rekindle their marriage. And then, with the girls. Later, with their husbands and children. Her grandchildren.

April lifted her face to the sea, imagining the life they could have—if only Calvin would let himself. Hadn't they earned it?

There she was, projecting again. But she was sure they could have that life if they worked at it.

Deep inside, a speck of intuition gnawed at her. She blinked and shook her head.

April continued cycling along the ocean-front street until Beach View Lane came into view. As she passed the large, stark white home on the corner, she recalled the succulents that bloomed with beautiful pink flowers Derek had shown her. She didn't know what that plant was called, but her mother had a spot on her property where it would be perfect. Snipping a piece to show Ella and the landscaper wouldn't hurt.

After easing her bike to the curb, April hopped off, shuddering at the white, nondescript wall. Even a serene beach mural would be better than a blank canvas that looked unfinished.

The house had been vacant for months, so she slipped inside the gate Derek had used and strolled toward the backyard. Inside, the wall was as plain as it was on the outside. The only view left was from the upper level.

"If this were mine, I wouldn't have ruined the view with an ugly wall," April said to herself. She reached down and plucked a piece of the succulent she wanted. And another one.

Above her, a voice boomed against the sound of the ocean. "Since you're trespassing, your opinion doesn't really matter."

April whirled around, her heart thudding with shock. A man stood on the balcony, which was lined with clear plexiglass. "Who are you?"

"That's what I'd like to know," he replied.

"The owner—"

"That would be me," he interrupted.

So, this was the mysterious owner. Even though she was far past the age of blushing, April's face warmed. The Adonis who towered above her clutched a towel around his hips as if he'd just stepped from the shower. His chest was bare, revealing an athletic physique, and his thick, salt-and-pepper hair was still wet. Her heart quickened. She'd never seen a man like this on her little street.

"Who are you?" he called out in a gruff voice.

"I live in the rosy pink house down the street."

"No, you don't," he said as he tucked in one edge of the towel. "That's the nurse's home. She lives alone."

"It's my mother's," she corrected him, matching his rude tone. "And how dare you question me like I'm some kind of criminal?"

"You're on my property. Uninvited." He crossed his arms over his chest.

Incensed, she snapped, "I have to go. Sorry I interrupted your—whatever."

"Look, I don't like people nosing around." He held out his arms. "For obvious reasons."

"Won't happen again." She started to leave. He might be a neighbor, but he seemed a loathsome one.

Before she got very far, he gestured toward her. "Hey, what's that in your hand?"

She hesitated, staring at the incriminating evidence. "It's just some sort of succulents."

"You're stealing plants?" Hitching up his towel, he stepped closer.

"I wanted to show these to my landscaper."

He furrowed his brow. "You've been here before?"

"Relax. It's just a couple of tiny pieces." Still embarrassed at being caught, April tossed them onto the ground. "There. Keep them." She was through arguing.

With him, with Calvin, with all men like them. Officer Blumenthal included. She was far too old for it.

April rushed through the gate and fumbled onto the bike, snagging her shorts on the cracked seat as she slid on in haste.

Just then, the landscaper's truck came into view, and she waved at Derek, as if in validation in case that old grump was still watching her from above. She sneaked a look over her shoulder.

He was.

That was all she needed. An obnoxious neighbor flashing her from the balcony. What a colossal jerk. Even if he did look good with wet hair and a towel. He was just the sort that would be proud of that.

Vain.

That's exactly what he was. Now she could spot men like that.

To own a house on the beach that he seldom visited and didn't care if it was rented, he must be worth a fortune. It was probably his second, third, or fourth home. Yet he had treated her like a thief for picking tiny pieces of succulents that would need trimming anyway.

April tilted her chin, reclaiming the confidence she'd gained on the Queen's Flight. She was a well-regarded history teacher. An intelligent woman and a good mother. And she would not be treated like a child for taking snips of vegetation. Or trespassing on what was usually a vacant property. He should be glad the neighbors were watching his home.

No, the man had no couth, no understanding, no manners.

April tilted her chin, casting her egregious neighbor from her mind. She had plenty to think about without him.

Such as, what was on Calvin's mind now?

5

*R*yan watched the intruder race from his property and pedal off on her ancient bicycle to make sure she left. He tucked the edge of the bath towel around his waist.

"What an attitude," he muttered.

Still, something about that woman was mildly appealing. It was her eyes, he realized. From when he was a boy, he'd been fascinated with deep green eyes like hers. He shrugged it off. He couldn't risk getting involved. What kind of a person steals plants, anyway?

Ryan ran a hand over his wet hair and shook the water from it before stepping back inside. Still, he watched through the glass. The woman made her way toward a vintage pink bungalow down the block.

One of the quirky things he enjoyed about Crown Island was that most of the locals painted their houses in all colors of the rainbow, not unlike the tasteful Victorian homes in San Francisco people referred to as the Painted Ladies. However, a chaotic, casual island approach reigned here, more akin to the colorful cliffsides of Valparaíso on the coast of Chile.

The woman parked the old bike in the driveway and went inside.

Ryan pushed a hand through his hair in consternation. He didn't relish living so close to her.

Then, to his surprise, a truck pulled in front of her house, and his landscaper stepped out. He would talk to Derek about that woman later, not that he cared to know more about her. He'd met the energetic older woman, a nurse, who lived in that house once, and she'd seemed pleasant enough. But he didn't care to meet his neighbors. He had no time and no interest.

He wasn't on Crown Island to make friends outside work. A property manager cared for this house, and when Ryan visited, it was only a place to sleep.

He finished getting ready, waiting for the call he hoped would come. Sure enough, on the hour, the phone rang. He recognized his attorney's office number but kept to his usual formality. "Ryan Kingston here."

"It's me. I've confirmed that Larry is gone, so you're free to go to the hotel now."

Margie had kept her promise to call as soon as Larry Winston vacated the hotel. Ryan's former business partner took up residence just to infuriate him. Since Ryan had a restraining order against Larry, he could not enter the hotel until he was out.

Ryan didn't want to risk running into Larry in town, so he stayed off the island. But last night, he'd taken the ferry to Crown Island to be ready for Margie's call.

"Thanks, Margie. On my way now."

"Enjoy your new project. It sure cost you."

His advisors thought he'd overpaid for the property, but he had a vision. Not everything was about money, he told himself, though it had been years since he'd acted any other way.

Ryan picked up his keys and a bespoke camel-colored sports-coat—his version of relaxed business wear. "I appreciate you staying on top of this for me. I owe you."

"You'll get my bill." Margie chuckled. "Do you have anything special planned for your birthday?"

"I have a project to oversee. That's plenty." As much as he liked Margie, he didn't share his personal life.

While he'd never been married, this partnership breakup from Larry was as bad as any divorce, he imagined. The sound of his parents bickering over money still rang in his ears from childhood. It didn't matter how much or how little some people had.

If he had to marry anyone, Margie would be ideal. She was whip-smart, attractive in a polished way, diplomatic when needed, and had a sharp tongue when it wasn't. She was quite a bit younger than he was, but most of the women he saw casually were.

Not that he was concerned about this birthday, which would put him a year's worth of breath from fifty. He was mentally and physically in his prime, and he could outmaneuver most any competitor.

A relationship with Margie would be nice until she wanted more, like marriage and children. Younger women usually did. That wasn't in his game plan. Not that he dated much anymore. He was too busy, especially with the Majestic Hotel now. Besides, most women couldn't relate to his upbringing. He'd learned not to discuss that.

Standing in front of the mirror in the contemporary white living room Ryan found too plain for his taste, he slipped on the tailored linen-and-silk blend jacket and adjusted his starched shirt cuffs. Ironically, he nearly matched the living room, except for his brightly patterned socks.

Ryan was ready. He was prepared to do whatever it took to restore the Majestic Hotel, his most treasured acquisition, to its former glory.

He locked the house and eased his rental car from the garage. If he stayed longer, he might buy a car, but he'd found nondescript rentals usually served him better. In building the investment partnership, he traveled nonstop. His bases were hotel rooms in Los Angeles, New York, and Miami. Because of how he'd been brought up, he was comfortable with that. As a boy, he'd practically grown up in the hotel business.

And the fact that he owned a home here? It was complicated, and he didn't share private details with many people.

After driving the short distance to the Majestic, he pulled to one side of a vintage port-cochère and stepped from his car, pausing to take in the grand Victorian-era hotel he knew so well. The structure had been framed with the finest Douglas fir. California redwood, once thought impervious to termites, had been applied to the exterior, which was painted in regal red and pure white in striking contrast to the sparkling blue waves beyond.

Nodding toward the valet staff, Ryan started up the wide front steps, which creaked under his foot step. The entrance seemed weary, as if the hotel were trying to put on a smile despite its advanced age and arthritis.

Still, satisfaction surged through him, and he felt as if he was coming home, with all the emotion that entailed.

Unexpectedly, his chest constricted from the suffocating feelings he usually kept locked away. He blinked against memories that swept over him with surprising force. Clearing his throat, he quickly composed himself.

All eyes followed Ryan. Perhaps the staff recognized him. While necessary to attract investors, publicity was his least favorite part of what he did. He felt like an actor playing a role.

Ryan would have a series of meetings to speak to all employees. No telling what his ex-partner had said about him, though he could imagine. Larry had been the senior partner in their partnership, a parsimonious billionaire who hated dealing with people. In fact, Larry abhorred most people.

He paused by the massive wooden doors that stood open to the sea breezes off the Pacific Ocean. Next to the doorway hung a polished bronze plaque that gleamed in the sunshine. *The Majestic Hotel, 1889.* He touched it with reverence.

"Good morning, sir."

Ryan nodded again to the bell captain who dared to approach him. With a name tag that read *Ethan*, the younger man looked smart in his hotel uniform, even if it was a little frayed at the lapel.

"Hello, Ethan. Looks like someone takes care to polish this plaque."

Ethan puffed out his chest with pride. "Every morning, sir." Gesturing to the plaque, he explained, "The Majestic opened the same year as the famous Hotel Del Coronado farther south near San Diego."

Ryan lifted a corner of his mouth. "If I'm not mistaken, the Reid brothers served as architects on both projects, didn't they?"

Ethan's eyes lit with passion. "They were Canadians, like my folks, and built one of the top architectural firms in San Francisco. The Fairmont Hotel on Nob Hill is another hotel they designed."

Along with the Cliff House and Call/Spreckels buildings, Ryan silently added to himself. "Their designs certainly stand as a testament to their talent."

"We're quite proud of the Majestic Hotel," Ethan said. "Will you be staying with us long, sir?"

"I certainly plan on it. Thank you for sharing that information." Ryan also made a mental note to order a new uniform for Ethan. First impressions mattered.

Renovating the beachside resort weighed heavily on Ryan's mind, but he was more than ready for the challenge. In Southern California, where reinvention was heralded and cultures fused in food, fashion, and art, the beloved Majestic remained.

His former partner had planned to strip her of her Victorian elements, deriding them as passé. Ryan fought Larry to retain the hotel's character, though it was the island community that defeated him. Still, Ryan's passion for the Majestic cost him in the partnership dissolution. It wasn't his best financial decision, but in his heart, he knew he'd made the right choice for Crown Island.

He stepped across the threshold, sizing up the hotel. Clearly, the Majestic had been languishing for years. Now it was his job to bring the former reigning queen of hotels, as travel magazines of yesteryear had gushed, into the new century.

Nevertheless, upon entering the lobby that soared three stories, Ryan was again impressed by its grandeur. The rotunda was a masterpiece, with its ceiling finished in white oak, cedar, and hemlock. At one time, architectural students often visited the Majestic. He wondered if they still did. Restoring the hotel would cost a fortune, but Ryan was committed to raising enough funds to do it right. That was critical to filling rooms again.

And if he didn't?

To him, bankruptcy was not an option.

Lifting his chin, Ryan strode past the front reception desk of mahogany, nodding toward the receptionists who were busy taking care of guests. Silently, he corrected himself. Guest Experience Specialists was the title his former partner had devised in lieu of granting raises. *They'll feel more important*, Larry insisted, arguing that they couldn't afford modest raises, even as the money he withdrew from the partnership continued to spiral. Although Larry was notoriously cheap, his yacht wasn't.

For years, Ryan and Larry had done well buying distressed property, but the purchase of this hotel had always been personal to Ryan. Few knew why, but Larry did. Ryan spilled his story over martinis one night, and Larry used that information to his advantage in their bitter negotiations. Even so, his ex-partner didn't know the whole story.

Finally, Ryan was free of him, and the staff would have their raises. Keeping morale high was crucial this year. Now he could begin his work in earnest.

A stately man in a smart, bright coral jacket strode toward him, his face wreathed in a smile. "Welcome back. It's a pleasure —and a relief—to see you again."

"Likewise, Whitley." Ryan embraced his general manager, who'd been with the hotel for forty years and had once helped him with homework while his parents were busy.

John Whitley had risen through the ranks from the catering department, where he began as a teenager. Now, his temples were dusted with silver. He dressed with taste and elegance, had a dry wit, and treated everyone with respect.

Ryan clapped him on the back, genuinely glad to see him. Whitley's attitude and professionalism had infuriated Larry, who took perverse pleasure in belittling staff and making demands. As long as Ryan kept Larry away from the properties they acquired, he was tolerable, but he and Whitley had major disagreements.

"I see you've taken good care of the Majestic. All things considered," he added with a note of understanding.

"It's my life's work. So glad you're back, Ryan." At once, Whitley's face shaded, and he dipped his head. "Pardon me, sir. I should call you Mr. Kingston now."

"Come on, now. I'm still Ryan to you." How could he be anything else to a man who'd been like an uncle to him? "This is a new era. Let's be more casual now." He tapped Whitley's lapel. "I see you're still wearing your technicolor jackets."

"Makes me easy to find in a crowd."

"And you match the neighborhood."

Whitley smiled with pride. "I admit I draw inspiration from

our surroundings. Though we still have our standards at the Majestic."

"Relaxed standards, as I recall." Ryan glanced around.

The Majestic was like a favorite aunt's gracious summer house. Across the lobby, guests with children and beach toys in tow were heading to the beach, which was still sunny and warm on this September day.

From relaxing at the spa to cycling on the beach, the Majestic offered a menu of options. In the evening, a couple might relax at dinner on the moonlit terrace while their children had supper in the kid's beach club. Or the family could dine together in the casual cafe.

Whitley waved a hand. "What do you think of our grand lady?"

"All things considered, you've done a fine job." Ryan immediately saw areas for improvement, though he meant no disrespect to Whitley.

Snapping his fingers, Ryan added, "Let's start making changes today. Would you order a new uniform for Ethan and have the grounds staff fill the entryway with a blaze of flowers."

Whitley smiled. "Right away."

"Take me on a tour, Whitley. I'd like to see the state of affairs here."

Walking beside the man he'd long admired, Ryan crossed the high-ceilinged lobby. The wooden parquet floors creaked beneath a thick wool rug—a handwoven Persian rug that Larry had tried to sell. That alone was worth a fortune.

In one corner, a gilded-cage elevator rested with a red velvet rope blocking its entrance.

"The old elevator still looks good. Is it operable?"

"It's no longer safe," Whitley replied. "Just a curiosity now, though Stafford dusts it every morning."

At the mention of the former elevator operator, Ryan asked, "How is Stafford?"

"Doing well for his age, happy to say. He spends his days at the beach cafe at table number one, regaling visitors with stories of bygone years. Our return guests love to see him."

"Good to know."

Whitley smiled as they neared the boutique corridor. "He appreciates what you did for him."

"It was only right."

When Ryan gave Stafford a room for life upon his retirement, Larry exploded. *We're not running a charity hotel.*

But Ryan refused to turn out Stafford. The man had lived and worked at the hotel for seventy years and knew everything about it. For years, guests had come to watch Stafford turn on the Christmas lights on the soaring pine tree outside.

The Majestic was like a quaint old aunt that people loved to reminisce about. But to friends, they recommended posh new inns or short-term Airbnb rentals. Ryan had to change that—and fast.

Many employees depended on him and the hotel's continued operation, including Stafford and Whitley. While Ryan was prepared to spend whatever it took to restore the Majestic, his cash runway was not endless. Occupancy was the holy grail.

The sooner, the better.

Guests bustled past while Ryan stopped at the entry to the boutique corridor. A line of shops sold beach wear, souvenirs, and gifts. An old-fashioned ice cream parlor anchored the end and opened to the beach. Except for the hotel gift shop, the boutique windows were well-decorated, though the hallway needed repainting. Old, enlarged photos from the hotel's glory days lined the walls.

"The gift shop needs remerchandising," Ryan said, strolling by the shops, most of which were leased.

Whitley nodded. "It's on my list."

"And I want to keep all these vintage photos. They were beautifully framed." Pausing by one photo, Ryan leaned in and allowed himself a smile. There she was. The first girl he'd ever had a crush on, though he'd been too shy to talk to her. She was a few years older, and he'd watched her in awe at the hotel. Surprisingly, his heart still quickened at the sight of her.

Ryan moved on, shifting back to the task at hand. "I'd like to meet every person who works here. Would you set up staff meetings?"

Whitley nodded in approval. "They'll be pleased. What else can I do?"

"Help me plan a VIP reception right away, and let's make a spectacular impression. I want to have people talking about the renovation as if it's the best thing that's happened to Crown Island in years."

"That's not an overstatement," Whitley said. "Local shops depend on tourist traffic. With our occupancy levels down, it hurts the economy."

Ryan was aware of the economic impact. "I'll make an official announcement and bring in a publicist to broadcast the event. We're turning this ship around, and I want every travel professional around the world to know about the new Majestic."

"Bold plans," Whitley said, smiling with renewed confidence.

Ryan started back toward the stairs to the management office. "Before I get situated, is there anything I should know?"

Whitley hesitated. "We have a problem with Room 418 again. Hasn't happened in years."

Four-eighteen. Memories surged through his mind. The staff had always been skittish about that room. "Is she...back?"

Whitley looked from one side to another. "Who can say?"

"I trust you've moved the guests and closed the room." Ryan paused. "Let's have a look. I need to see the guest rooms anyway."

They took the stairs to the fourth floor. Ryan touched the wooden railing, worn smooth over the years. Rooms opened onto broad walkways that overlooked a garden lush with tropical plants. In a clearing, white folding chairs were set up for a wedding.

The corridors and stairs had been built wide enough for women to pass in ballgowns without mussing their attire. Fresh sea air wafted through the wide hallway, and they continued to the far end. Without light, the enclosed end of the hallway was dim.

Whitley paused and looked up at the light fixture. "I'll have that looked at today. Must be a bad light bulb or a circuit breaker."

"It happens." Ryan stopped at room 418 and drew a deep breath, recalling the first time he'd ever entered this room.

After Whitley opened the door, he stepped back and gestured

for Ryan to enter before him. "Have a look. I'll call maintenance on that light."

Ryan entered the room and breathed in the sweet, musty aroma of aged wood and furniture polish. Except for occasional updates of new carpet and upholstery, the room looked as it had when he was a boy.

In his mind's eye, he envisioned how the room would look after the renovation. He was no interior designer, but he knew what he liked in hotels. Every room would need updated bathrooms, furnishings, and additional electrical outlets for phones and gadgets.

The guests appeared to have made a hasty exit. The room seemed cool but not overly so. He turned on the lights, and the electrical current seemed steady. The drapes stood still at the windows. The mirrors were clear and fog-free.

Nothing seemed amiss. Still, something had rattled the guests.

It was worth a try.

Ryan jammed his hands into his pockets and rocked on his feet. "It's been a long time." He waited, half-expecting an answer.

Many old hotels had unexplained occurrences. The Sagamore, the Langham, the Parker Inn, the Don CeSar. The Hollywood Roosevelt claimed sightings of Marilyn Monroe gazing into a mirror and Montgomery Cliff rehearsing lines or practicing his trumpet skills. The Stanley in Colorado, where the original owners still played billiards and the Steinway, inspired a Stephen King novel, *The Shining*. Even the nearby Hotel Del Coronado had its share of spirits.

No, the Majestic wasn't unique. People often died in hotel rooms by natural causes, suicide, or something darker. The Majestic was no different. Its history spanned more than a hundred years, so its stories and oddities had grown.

After a long moment, Ryan turned off the lights and stepped out, closing the door behind him. Accounts of strange happenings in this room were published online, and he wouldn't be surprised if the guests had known about that. Perhaps they scared themselves into thinking they'd experienced something.

Whitley made his way back to Ryan. "See anything?"

"Everything looked fine."

Whitley looked down. A thin strip of light shone from under the door. "I'll turn off the lights, and then we'll be on our way."

"But I…"

"Yes?"

Ryan turned. Sure enough, the lights were on. He coughed into his hand. "I don't want to keep you from anything."

After opening the door again, Whitley flicked off the lights and closed the door. "Nothing is more important than making sure you have everything you need."

As they walked away, Ryan couldn't help glancing back. A light shone beneath the door again. He suppressed a smile.

Like him, the lady in four-eighteen was back in residence at the Majestic. Or maybe she'd stopped by to welcome him.

Stories abounded about who she might be.

Ryan had heard one version about a woman from a deposed European royal family whose country was under siege. According to legend, Princess Noelle fled to the Majestic to meet her lover. They'd stayed in a suite on this floor for a blissful week until she left, planning to return. Supposedly she had left something behind, so noted in a letter that was oddly never mailed. *As I depart, I shall leave my most precious possession…* Some thought she was murdered before she could mail the letter or leave. Others thought she had returned, only to yield to a sense of hopelessness.

Over the years, there had been much speculation about her final letter. Would-be fortune hunters assumed it was her inherited stash of jewelry or gold from the country's coffers. But Ryan wasn't so sure.

Larry had been intrigued with the story, too, even going so far as to order the dismantling of the suite where the couple had stayed on the fourth floor. Larry found nothing, but Ryan wasn't surprised. For whatever reason, the lady had always been in four-eighteen. Or maybe that had been her maid's room.

Whether this lady had anything to do with the other story, Ryan didn't know. But she seemed to be a benevolent spirit. To him, at least. He chuckled to himself. His grandmother had once insisted on staying in this room.

Suddenly, the fine hairs on Ryan's neck bristled as a cold

breeze swept across the hallway. He rubbed his neck and turned to Whitley. "Did you feel that?"

"Feel what, sir?"

Ryan started to explain, but a guest stepped out into the hallway in front of them. "Never mind."

This was yet another item Ryan would have to deal with. He couldn't afford negative publicity.

6

*S*eated at the small vanity in her bedroom, April peered into the mirror and applied a sheen of mauve lipstick. She brushed back her hair and took extra care perfecting soft waves to frame her face and shoulders.

To welcome Calvin at the ferry, she chose her white pearl stud earrings, his first anniversary gift to her. They'd had a tumultuous year. She had to make this reunion special.

After assessing her look, April turned to her daughter. "What do you think?"

"You look gorgeous. Dad should be impressed." Junie pushed off the bed, where she'd been watching her mother dress. "Need some help with that necklace?"

"Thanks. The clasp is so small." April swept her hair to one side.

This was the precious gold heart that had belonged to Pilar, her birth mother. It reminded her that she'd had two special women looking after her in this life. One before her birth, and one after.

For this special day, April had chosen one of her favorite vintage dresses, a soft green linen, 1950s-style. Very Grace Kelly. Paired with low-heeled sandals, the understated outfit was perfect for a casual dinner near the ferry.

It had been years since she and Calvin had dined at one of

the chic beach restaurants like the Ferry Cafe. Surely, he would be hungry. If not, maybe they'd have a glass of wine there, or even at the Majestic, her favorite romantic spot on the beach for sunsets.

"Nana says too much is never enough." Junie picked up a green Bakelite bracelet from the vanity. "Give me your wrist, and I'll put this on, too. There." Junie peered over her mother's shoulder at her reflection and smiled. "You look awfully nice. Good luck with Dad."

"I'm sorry, but your father wants to speak to me about something in private. After that, I'll see if he'll come to the house, or maybe you can join us for dinner. The Ferry Cafe would be nice for all of us. I don't imagine your grandmother would want to go, but would you be ready, just in case?"

Junie folded her arms as a hurt look washed across her face. "I don't need to see him. It's not like he cares about me."

"Honey, he's your father. You have different opinions, but he loves you." April was accustomed to being the mediator in the family. She and Calvin might have their difficulties, too, but she wanted her daughters to have a good relationship with him. However, he hadn't made it easy on Junie.

April loved having her daughter home, but Calvin wanted his privacy. A man did, she supposed. April realized Junie needed to reboot her life at some point, and she was confident that her daughter would when the time was right.

"How's the dress?" April smoothed the linen, which would soon be a losing battle.

"Too good for him."

"Junie, dear. Try not to feel such animosity toward him." She slid on the plain gold wedding band she hadn't worn this summer. She could feel her daughter's eyes on her as she did. "What will you and Nana do while I'm gone?"

Junie shrugged. "Popcorn and an old movie. Nana wants to watch *Some like it Hot*. Do you know it?"

"Sure do. It's a madcap comedy with good actors. Marilyn Monroe, Tony Curtis, Jack Lemmon."

Junie shrugged. "Except for Marilyn Monroe, I have no idea who those other people are. They must have been popular when you were young."

"That movie is from 1959, before I was born. It was filmed at the Hotel Del Coronado. Quite a few old movies were filmed on Crown Island, too." She paused and pressed a finger to her chin. "That's the sort of thing a historical society might have tracked. Or the studio."

April had been mulling over the idea of starting a historical society, but once she returned to teaching in Seattle, it would be challenging to keep it going. And Calvin would only say it was beneath her position at the university. Still, it would be fun, even if she could only manage it from Seattle and when she visited her mother here.

She picked up her purse. "You should ask your grandmother about the story. She might have been an extra in the film. You could watch for her."

Junie's eyes lit. "Is that really true?"

"Ask her." She hugged Junie. "I'll call you, sweetheart. You might like to say hello to your father, at least."

Junie let out a little puff of air in disgust. "Then maybe I'll surprise him."

April leaned against the wooden railing near the dock, watching the ferry approach. Around her, people stood waiting, too. Some were day tourists with sunburned shoulders. Others, like her, were waiting for friends and loved ones to return. A few kids were tossing balls to a Labrador retriever. Laughter filled the air.

A light breeze ruffled her hair, and April swept her waves over her shoulder, feeling a little like Grace Kelly with her chic linen dress. She'd be just as cool and poised, too, she decided.

Nothing else had worked.

April gripped the sturdy wooden railing, worn smooth over the years. She knew what she was dealing with. Life wasn't perfect, and it wasn't always pretty—for her and other women she knew. They made the best of what life had served up and carried on, being there for their children, parents, and husbands. Stretched between it all like a length of elastic.

Sometimes they snapped—mentally or physically—under stress. She sure had. But when they did, the lucky ones had friends who helped them fashion something serviceable from the tattered fabric of their dreams.

April had such a group of friends at the university in Seattle. But even they hadn't been able to shield her from the whispers and looks of other faculty and staff. At the thought of returning with Calvin, she squared her shoulders. She was stronger now. Judging from Calvin's impassioned call this morning, his affair with Olga was over. April would be the magnanimous one, forgiving him and getting on with their lives.

And this will be the last time.

The thought shot into her mind with such certainty it surprised her. Yet, at that moment, she knew there was no other course for her. She'd given him all the chances she had to offer.

This time was a stretch.

As the breeze picked up, a young woman next to her in a thin bikini cover-up shivered, and her boyfriend put his arms around her and drew her close. As they traded a sweet kiss, they reminded her of how she'd once been with Calvin.

She had been so excited to bring Calvin home to meet her mother on Crown Island. They'd stepped off this ferry, but she was so nervous they'd stopped for root beer floats and sat outside watching the waves. When they'd gotten their courage up, they'd walked to her house, and she'd introduced him to her mother, who hadn't known April was bringing him home. She wondered if Calvin would remember that.

The cherry red ferry was close enough now that she could see her husband. Calvin was tall and broad-shouldered and still looked like the weightlifter he had been in college. He wore casual chino trousers and a white shirt with the cuffs turned back. His brown hair looked a little longish as the wind whipped it from his forehead. Even scowling into the salty breeze, he still had the charisma and movie-star looks that had initially attracted her and still made younger women swoon.

Men of any age looked rugged with a frown, she thought. Even the lines on his face were flattering. That simply wasn't fair. Rising on her toes in anticipation, she waved at him.

Calvin hesitated as if he wasn't sure who she was, then lifted his chin toward her.

"Off to an underwhelming start," she said to herself. But she was up to the challenge—for her family's sake.

As she watched the ferry approach, she twisted her wedding band. How odd it felt after not wearing it all summer. It didn't seem to fit right anymore.

The ferry pulled alongside the dock, and Calvin stepped off.

Moving along with the small crowd, April strode toward him on the sand-strewn path.

"Hi, honey." She leaned forward to hug him with a kiss on the cheek, but he shifted, and she was left grasping at air as people swept around them. Recovering quickly, she straightened.

"Sorry," he said tersely. He leaned in for an awkward hug.

Laughing it off, April said, "We're both a little clumsy—out of our old groove, I guess. Why don't we start over?" She smoothed her hand along his surprisingly taut forearm as she spoke. Had he been working out?

"Listen, about that..."

"I sure enjoyed your call this morning. That was such a nice treat." She lowered her voice. "And I've been thinking about you."

"Let's talk." Calvin looked around. "Where can we sit?"

He seemed a little harried, but then he'd been traveling and in meetings all day. "If you're hungry, there's the Ferry Cafe. You liked their linguine with clams." She glanced at the cafe, where a line of people waited at the take-out window, which was painted like a ticket booth. The exterior was splashed with cherry red paint like the ferry. Others were waiting for a table. Calvin wouldn't do that. "Or we could go the Majestic and watch the sunset."

"Wait." Calvin caught her hand. With a sweeping gaze, Calvin took in her outfit. "Maybe you misunderstood my last message. I grabbed a salad at the airport. Watching what I eat these days." He patted a trim stomach.

"I can tell. You look good, Cal." That was an honest compliment—he had trimmed down. "You've had a long day. How about a glass of wine or one of your whiskeys? We can walk to another cafe."

Calvin rubbed his neck. "I need to make this quick so I can catch the last flight tonight."

It was then that April realized he didn't have any luggage, or even the briefcase or backpack with a change of clothes he often carried for quick trips.

"We haven't seen each other in months. I had hoped you'd stay longer."

Calvin glanced down at his now dusty shoes. "I had another call that came in right after we spoke."

She couldn't keep the disappointment from her voice. "If you bought a change of clothes, you could stay a few days to see Junie, and I can go back with you."

Still, Calvin didn't move. "You told her I was coming?"

"Why wouldn't I? She's your daughter."

"This is between us, and I'd prefer to keep the girls out of it."

"And just how do you think we'll manage that? We're a family, Calvin."

He didn't answer.

Something serious was going on; April could feel it. She tried again, cajoling him as she used to do. "What happened between this morning when you told me you didn't want to lose my love—and now? I want that husband back."

Calvin scrubbed his face with his hands. "That man... I'm afraid he's gone, April."

In one fell swoop, he'd ripped her breath away. She felt as if she were careening on a rollercoaster—and the track had dropped out from under her. "Are you ill?"

He held his arms wide. "Look at me. Do I look sick?" Calvin thrust out a hand, shooing off the idea as if it were the craziest question he'd ever heard.

She recognized that gesture from his classroom when a student gave an incorrect answer. Others would squirm until he called on another victim. She would not be treated like that. Steeling herself, she asked, "Then what is it?"

"I have a...situation."

April hugged her arms across her midsection. The area had cleared, and they were nearly alone except for the crowd at the Ferry Cafe and a few tourists watching the ferry cross the water. This wasn't how she had imagined the evening unfolding.

"Sounds like I'm going to need that drink now." She started toward the other cafe.

Calvin took her arm. "Let's get this over with. It won't take long."

"Not like our marriage, you mean."

"Okay, I deserved that. But you need to understand the situation."

"Oh, really? I understood it quite well a few months ago."

"It was over with Olga, I swear to you. But then she called this morning…"

"Olga is pregnant."

Calvin's lips parted. "How did you know?"

"I'm a historian, and this is an old, old tale."

If April had listened to that nagging feeling, she wouldn't have dressed up for this. The wind whipped her hair, and she turned into it, welcoming the stinging, windswept salt spray.

"I told her she needed to do something about it."

"Of course you did." How had she managed to stay married to such a jerk?

"But she refused."

April wanted to scream and slap his face.

Before she could do either, Calvin began to explain matter-of-fact mannerly, as if he were in front of a classroom imparting the obvious.

"Naturally, Olga doesn't want to raise the child alone, yet she doesn't want to give it away. Therefore, we have two solutions. One is for us to adopt the child. Olga says it's a boy, and I always imagined I would have a son to carry on my name."

"As if your name is so rare, Professor Smith."

"You don't have to be facetious about it."

This was even beyond Calvin's usual self-centeredness. With a hand on her hip, April glared at him. "Surely I didn't hear you ask me to raise a child you fathered during an illicit affair. And well into my happy golden years at that."

"It's one idea of how we might work this out." Calvin rotated his shoulder, squirming at her words. "You're adopted, so you should understand how much this child needs your guidance."

April pressed a hand to her eyes. He was good; she'd grant him that. Calvin knew how to appeal to her desire to be loved and needed by serving her family. But this time, they'd been separated long enough for her to yank down that curtain of delusion.

She whisked her hand away. "If this were a one-off time, and I wanted to be a candidate for sainthood, then I might consider that. But I would only be continuing this cycle of enablement. I've made excuses for your abuse, covered for you, and protected you from consequences. Why? For love—misplaced love, that is."

Calvin started talking over her, but she refused to yield to him this time. "Maybe it was to convince myself I had control over our marriage, though I never did. And to shore up my feelings of inadequacy, which I didn't want to face. You knew, and you took advantage of that." She sliced the air with a hand. "Not anymore."

Calvin sneered at her summary of their marriage. "You sound like you've been sitting in on my class."

"I wrote the book, and I finally looked in the mirror. What did you expect?"

"Obviously, I'm left with little choice."

"Except to change your behavior."

He ignored that, instead returning to his infuriating, logical professor tone. "Olga says if she has to raise the boy, he'll need more than a part-time father. They will need me. Since the girls are grown, I'm not needed here anymore. We've had our time."

She would not give him the satisfaction nor excuse him so easily. Pacing the pathway, she tapped her fingers.

"And what about all those planned trips, the RV you liked, the grandchildren we talked about?" Without waiting for a reply, she continued. "I suppose I'll grow old by myself and take solo cruises."

"April, don't be this way."

She whirled around. "And just how would you have me be? Shall I send you off with pressed clothes and a box lunch into the arms of a woman our daughter's age?"

"She's a year older than May."

April arched an eyebrow. "That much?"

As the wind picked up and swept his hair back, she spied fresh hair plugs at his hairline and an unnatural tightness along his jaw. Faint scars lined his ears.

This was a man grasping at youth at any cost.

Quickly, Calvin brushed his hair down over his forehead.

"Olga and I have a child to consider. You have to understand that."

April pressed a finger to her throbbing temple. Why did he keep insisting on her understanding? She wouldn't waste her brainpower anymore. That was his need to be absolved of his transgression as if he was acting as any reasonable person would.

He was gaslighting her. "Do you think she'll understand when the grandchildren visit you?"

Calvin twisted his mouth to one side. "Little chance of that at the rate our daughters are going."

April advanced on him and jabbed him in the chest with a finger. "If Junie's husband hadn't died, Olga would be dating a grandfather. Maybe that would've changed the way she thought of you."

Calvin stepped back and shifted on his feet. "Age is just a number."

"Until it isn't." She'd struck a blow to his vanity, and now she was going all in. "Tell me, does she like the same music you do? Or does she flip your favorite oldies station?" When his face reddened, she knew she'd hit a nerve.

Let him squirm, she thought. He truly deserves every bit of this and more. But she wasn't through yet.

"You're nothing but a middle-aged man grasping at his youth through a younger woman. One whose rose-colored glasses haven't yet slipped from her nose to see the real you. Or maybe Olga is smarter than you thought. She knows what's in it for her. A quick marriage, the opportunity to stay in the country, and access to health insurance and financial support. Now, you're the enabler."

Calvin's face contorted with sudden rage. "I didn't come here to listen to this. I thought you would be reasonable."

"Looks like you were wrong."

The truth dawned on her as she twisted the ill-fitting ring on her finger. "All those years ago, my mother was right."

"What are you talking about?"

"That day after we had root beer floats and you met my mother, she said you weren't good enough for me."

Calvin's face darkened. "Root beer floats? What the hell are you talking about?"

"It's not important. But Olga's writing skills are. She'll have to keep you published."

Suddenly, Calvin puckered in his lower lip, his supreme self-assurance evaporating like mist on the warm sand. "That doesn't have to change. In fact, I have a paper—"

"No." What a lovely word that was. Why hadn't she used it more often?

He stuffed his hands into his pockets. "Olga can't write as you do. I would pay you."

"Your ghostwriter just quit. And you'll be paying me plenty."

The scowl returned to his face, but it wasn't even remotely attractive this time. "If you're talking about the house, I need it for Olga and my son."

"No." April stood straighter.

"You could stay there when you visit May."

"Honestly, you amaze me." April was through holding back. "You're a pompous old fool with the absurd notion that the world revolves around you and your ego. Your idea of teaching is performing for an adoring audience. Judging from your hair plugs and facelift, you're scared to death of aging. You might lose the adoration of women now younger than your daughters. And as for your position, Professor—we both know how you earned it. What a waste of intelligence."

"No one knows that, and you can't prove it."

She advanced, pointing a finger at him. "You forgot how organized I am about my work. Remember all that scanning and uploading to the cloud I did for security? But don't worry, I'm not usually vindictive. However, this is where I get off the circus ride."

She tugged off her ring and threw it at him.

Calvin winced as the gold band bounced off his chest and landed on the sandy path. "You'll tell May about this, won't you?"

"Her name is Maileah now. And she's your daughter, too."

April threw her shoulders back and strode away like a queen. She would not let him see the damage he'd done to her. From this moment on, her life was her own, and her service to her lying, conniving, narcissistic husband was over.

This time, Calvin had made her decision very easy.

April started toward her car. While she'd managed to rein in her emotions, the toll he'd exacted on her over the years had become costlier.

As she crossed to the parking area, an unbidden physiological reaction seized her chest. She blinked rapidly, her eyes blurring with the hot, pent-up tears of repressed anger.

How dare he toss away their family with such a cavalier attitude, expecting her to convey their separation to their daughters? She would, but not because he asked her to.

April wiped her face with the back of her hand. Her carefully applied makeup was likely ruined. How was she going to tell Junie? As her panic rose, she counted the paces to her car, desperate to make it home. Still, she lifted her chin higher.

Her breath was coming in short raspy sounds. But she would not break down now. She would not give Calvin the satisfaction. Part of her had known it might come to this, even as she tried to salvage their family and future together.

Twenty paces more. Her knees wobbled, and she touched a palm tree lightly for support before continuing. Ten more.

Suddenly, it was as if a cloud had passed over the sun, and her vision grew dark and sparkly. Her nervous system was not cooperating with her will. She fumbled for her car keys. Could she make it?

7

*J*unie was mortified by what she'd seen. Seeing her mother wavering, she sprang from a mosaic park bench and sprinted toward her. When she reached her, she swept her arm around her, and her mother nearly collapsed against her.

"Mom, I'm here. Oh, my gosh, I saw what happened." Junie wanted to scream at her father, but her mother needed her now.

"We have to get out of here." Pressing a hand to her stomach, April added, "You should drive."

"Okay. Just breathe. Deep breaths, like you used to tell me. I've got you."

Junie grabbed the keys as they tumbled from her mother's hand. She unlocked the passenger side and helped her mother in. She'd come over in Nana's golf cart, but she could leave it.

April leaned her head against the headrest and closed her eyes.

If Junie was angry and disappointed in her father before, she was utterly livid now. She couldn't believe what her father had done to them. A sickening feeling rose in her throat. Swallowing hard against it, she hurried around the car.

From the corner of her eye, Junie spotted a man standing where her parents had argued. He bent down. *The ring.* Well, he could have it. Her mother would never wear that again, and her father had walked away from it.

Unbelievable.

Junie got into the car, shoved the gear shift into reverse, and backed out of the space. She turned toward the house.

April put a limp hand on her shoulder. "I'm sorry about that. I tried to keep our family together for you, sweetheart. But I couldn't do it alone.

"I know, Mom." Junie gritted her teeth. "If it makes you feel any better, I was proud of you for standing up to him."

As Junie followed the beachfront street back to her grandmother's house, she fought back angry tears of her own.

She thought of all her mother had done for her, especially after Mark died. That her selfish, egotistical father could do this to her mother was beyond her comprehension. It was wrong on so many levels.

"Almost home. Are you still taking deep breaths?" Junie worried her mother was having a panic attack.

April drew in a long, ragged breath and exhaled. "I'm so glad you were there."

"Nana shamed me into going to see Dad." Junie threw a look at her mother, feeling a little guilty for eavesdropping. But she'd only been waiting for the right moment…which never came.

Junie swallowed hard. "I thought I'd let you guys talk, then surprise you. I was sitting on a bench on the other side of the bougainvillea and could hear most of what he said. I know you want me to mend my relationship with Dad, but there's no way. He's dead to me now."

Her mother reached a hand to her shoulder. "I'm sorry you had to hear that."

Junie shook her head. "It was horrible, but I'm kind of glad I saw it. Especially now." She wished Maileah could have been there, too, because she wouldn't believe their father's cruelty.

How could her sister possibly take their father's side after what he'd done? Junie dreaded telling her mother that part of it. She didn't know if she could—that would be like twisting the knife of betrayal even deeper in her wounded heart.

Still, she was proud of her mother for sticking up for herself. *Finally.* Having been married, Junie knew what it was to compromise—they both did—but nothing on the level her mother had endured.

How could her father be so cold to her mother, who'd devoted her life to him and the family? And why were family relationships so complicated? Especially when you needed them the most.

Junie drove on, anxious to get her mother home.

Realizing what her father truly was made Junie doubly grateful for Mark. While they'd had their differences, those were minor compared to what her mother had suffered. No one was perfect, but Mark was pretty darn close.

Junie pressed a hand to her heart. If only he hadn't gone and died on her. Now, here she was, desperately wanting a family of her own before it was too late, but no one could compare to Mark. Not that she even wanted to look.

April sighed and pressed a hand to her forehead. "Are we close?"

"Almost." To one side of the street, the ocean rushed toward the beach. Beach View Lane was straight ahead, just past the stop sign.

Junie glanced around. No one was coming. She paused at the stop sign, then rolled through it.

However, after she turned onto Beach View Lane, a flashing light appeared in her rearview mirror. It was the police.

"Where the heck did he come from?" Junie pulled to the side in front of her grandmother's home and rolled down her window.

April turned around in her seat. When she saw the officer walking toward their car, she huffed. "Not again."

Junie stretched for her purse. She'd thrown it in the back seat before her mother sat down.

"That's the same officer who stopped me on my bicycle."

"For what?"

"I'll tell you later."

Junie wiggled her fingers toward her purse, which had fallen on the floor. She turned in her seat and half climbed into the back between the seats to grab it. Only now, she was off balance and wedged in between the seats.

She was stuck.

"Excuse me, ma'am." The officer paused. "Ma'am?"

April patted Junie's rear end. "Hi, Officer Blumenthal. This is my daughter, Junie. What's the problem this time?"

"There's a stop sign."

"You must think we're a family of scofflaws," April said. "But not Junie. She's the good one."

Junie kicked her legs, banging her ankle on the steering wheel. This was beyond ridiculous. "Mom, I can't get out. I'm really stuck."

"Officer, could you give my daughter a hand?"

"Are you okay, ma'am?"

"Not really." April sniffed. "My husband just told me his girl-friend is pregnant, so we're finished. If Junie hadn't followed me to the ferry, I don't know that I could have made it home. Which is right here."

Blood was rushing to Junie's face, and she squirmed between the seats, knocking her knee against the gear shift. "Ouch! Hey, I still need help here."

The back door to the car opened, and Junie could make out a pair of sturdy legs clad in uniform-blue. Two strong arms reach for her.

"Try to relax."

"As if," Junie muttered.

While she didn't know how the officer managed to extricate her, he'd somehow lifted her from between the seats. A few moments later, back in the driver's seat and purse in hand, she pushed her hair from her face, which felt blazing red-hot. "You didn't have to do that, but thanks."

"It's a pleasure to serve. License and registration, please."

April leaned across her. "You're not going to give my daughter a ticket, are you?"

"Ms. Raines—"

"Mom, please." Junie fished in her purse and handed over her license.

Just then, the front door banged, and her grandmother crossed the yard, sizing up the situation.

"Blue, it's good to see you," Ella said, smiling as if the officer were paying a social visit. "You've met my daughter and grand-daughter, I see. Won't you come in for a glass of lemonade?"

"Ms. Raines, ma'am. Good to see you."

Junie peered up at him. The officer's demeanor changed when Nana came out. He drew a hand over his mouth, but not before Junie saw him concealing a grin. "Why does my grandmother call you Blue?"

"Most folks on Crown Island do." He tapped his name tag. "It's Blumenthal."

There was something about the way he smiled at her grandmother. They were friends, Junie surmised. She peered up at him. "I would usually stop—I'm super careful. But my mom isn't doing very well. I'm worried about her, and I want Nana to look at her."

"I'll help her into the house." Officer Blumenthal went around to the passenger side and opened the door. "Ma'am, lean on me. I've got you."

His words struck Junie. *Mark used to say that.* She slid out of the car. Despite her pinched side, sore shin, and what would surely turn into bruises, she hobbled after them as quickly as she could.

Ella held the door while the officer helped her mother inside, and Junie followed.

"Oh, Mama, you were right," April began. Her expression shattered, and she leaned into her mother's arms.

"No need to talk. From the look of you, I have a good idea what happened." Ella pressed her lips together and shook her head. "That scoundrel. Never thought he was good enough for you."

Junie turned to the police officer. "I'm sorry you stumbled into a mess here. And I should have been paying attention, Officer Blumenthal."

"You got your mother home safely. That's what counts." He handed Junie's license and vehicle registration back to her. "I won't need these anymore. I should be on my way."

Ella brightened. "Won't you stay a spell, Blue?"

Blue checked his watch. "It's time for me to run off the skateboarders from the steps of City Hall. They need to be home for supper anyway."

"You do that," Ella replied. "Better than seeing them in the emergency room with broken arms. That's a steep incline on those steps. But they take them like champs, I'll grant them that. Until they don't, that is."

"I'll see you out," Junie said, even though the living room was only a few steps from the front door. She was grateful that he'd helped her mother inside.

Blue touched the brim of his hat, lingering by the door. "Are you staying with us long on the island?"

Junie darted a look at her mother. "Looks like it. I think it's a good place to land." She turned back to Blue.

"Then I hope to see you again. Just not when you're breaking the law."

"I'll try not to." Junie opened the door for Blue, and he stepped outside. She watched him get into his car, and he nodded to her as he drove away. She lifted her hand to him. Even the police officers on Crown Island were good-looking. When he was gone, she turned back to her mother and grandmother.

April drew her hands over her face. "Mama, I hope you don't mind if Junie and I stay on for a while."

"Why, that's the best news I've heard in a long time."

Junie sat down beside her mother and grinned. "Now we're both couch surfing."

April put her arm around Junie and pulled her close. "I never thought I'd sell the home in Seattle where we raised you girls. I know you have a connection with it, but I can't bear the thought of that Russian woman in my bathtub."

Or her bed, Junie silently added. She couldn't imagine visiting her father and seeing another woman in her mother's kitchen.

"I don't blame you one bit, Mom. But it's just a house." Junie looked up at her grandmother. "This is home."

For how long, she had no idea. Crown Island and her extended Bay family were growing on her.

8

"*S*omeone to see you, sir," Whitley said, tapping on the door to Ryan's office.

Ryan looked up from the massive antique desk that now held the modern accouterments of a laptop, mobile phone, and large screen for meetings, as well as an old set of architectural plans. He couldn't help smiling at his general manager's banana-yellow choice of jacket. "What did I tell you about keeping it casual around here?"

"Old habits," Whitley replied. "Deb Whitaker is here. She says she has an appointment with you."

"Tell her I have ten minutes, then buzz me."

Ryan rolled up the blueprint plans. The old hotel had so many problems, and each of them was at the red alert level. The new chef at the restaurant was threatening to quit because of the poor-quality seafood and produce supplier Ryan's old partner had engaged to hide money.

Since arriving at the hotel, Ryan had discovered that Larry had cut costs to draw out money undetected. He'd created fictitious businesses and had routed funds to himself without raising suspicion on the monthly financial statements.

The Majestic was in a larger mess than Ryan had thought. But one thing was certain. If he couldn't increase occupancy within the year after the renovation, he might lose everything he had, including his credibility, borrowing power, and career. He'd worked his way up the ladder but didn't relish doing it again.

"Don't forget to see Giana, our new chef," Whitley said. "She's issued an ultimatum and wants to see you personally."

"We can't lose another chef. Cancel all shoddy suppliers and ask Giana which ones she wants to use. I'll talk to her as well."

Whitley acknowledged him with a sharp nod. "I also had special food deliveries brought in this morning to placate her."

"You're a good man, Whitley." Ryan walked around to the front of the desk and leaned against it. Although the desk was suitable for working on projects, having a grand desk meant to intimidate others was not his style. "Show her in, please."

Deborah Whitaker. Of course, he knew of the family. Everyone on Crown Island did. Old man Whitaker still owned a great deal of commercial real estate, which he assumed was how Deb got her start as a designer.

Deb's designs might be interesting. With Crown Island's reputation as an artist colony, he had no idea what to expect. Some of her father's buildings were undoubtedly painted in a rainbow of colors. They might even feature murals, a trend here on the island, but not what visitors wanted at the Majestic.

Ryan would need a skilled interior designer on the project, and it wouldn't hurt to have a well-connected local if she shared his vision and could handle this. He had to admire her ambition. She was the first to call on him at the hotel.

A tall, athletic blond appeared in the doorway.

"Hello, I'm Deb Whitaker."

He stood, mildly surprised. She wore monochromatic shades of creamy white—silk blouse, fitted jacket, and twill trousers. A hint of a sophisticated perfume and a blazing smile of confidence matched the outfit. She carried an ivory leather portfolio. At least she looked the part.

"Please, have a seat. I don't have much time today, as you might imagine." Ryan quickly dispensed with the pleasantries.

Deb remained standing, facing him at his level.

"I'll be brief," she said. "To compete in the luxury vacation market, the Majestic Hotel needs a complete renovation. I'm local, I know what your clientele wants, and I'm ready to work with you."

She was direct; he liked that. Deb didn't even try to charm him as many women would.

She put her portfolio on his desk and opened it, pointing to a collection of images. "Something like this. Comfortable, upscale, beach luxury. Artistic accents. The Hamptons meets Barcelona in Southern California. True luxury without the fuss."

Ryan glanced at the photos. A hotel lobby, a gallery, an inn. Classic luxury with unexpected, artistic touches. "Are these projects you've designed and executed? Or photos you grabbed from the internet?"

"It's all my work." Deb regarded him cooly. "This is a small island, and I have a reputation around here. You will, too."

"I had to be sure."

One side of her mouth lifted. "My father is a builder. He vets his tradespeople, too."

Ryan folded his arms and watched her flip through projects. Not bad, but he wondered if a major, international designer might be better for publicity.

"Nice," he said in a noncommittal voice.

"I know the hotel well, and I can work up a bid for you." Deb eyed the rolled-up blueprint. "Mind if I have a look?"

Ryan stood and rolled out the old plans. "This is only part of the hotel. The lobby, library, card room, tearoom, and so on. A few outbuildings."

"The lobby is a masterpiece." Deb gestured to several small rooms on the plans. "Do you plan to repurpose these old rooms?"

"Of course, but I mean to retain the Majestic's original architectural features. This hotel is a treasure trove of history and craftsmanship." He tapped the library on the plans. "No one but a professional well versed in restoration will touch the wood paneling in there. That stays." It would cost him dearly, too, but he knew his clientele.

Deb raised her brow. "It should. That's stunning, but you can also repurpose the library. Make it available for high-end wine tastings or corporate retreat planning—for a fee."

"Not bad." He liked how she thought, but on-time execution was what he needed. "Go on."

"As for style, retain your finest antiques and add modern

touches. A color palette of marine blue, pearly gray, and cool white with high-end beach and artistic accents will create a relaxed, inviting atmosphere." Deb tapped the blueprint. "What about that structure?"

"The old dance hall. It's been closed for years." The hotel had numerous free-standing buildings and cabanas dotted around the property and connected by pathways.

Deb barely lifted an eyebrow, but Ryan caught it and realized he'd slipped. He wasn't ready to broadcast his former affiliation with the Majestic. Quickly, he outlined other plans.

Deb listened intently. "Have you approached the city about this? Your partner's modernization plan failed to pass because our community feels strongly about the Majestic. It's not just a resort. It's where we celebrate the memorable events in our lives."

Ryan nodded. He understood this far more than she realized. "Ex-partner. And I never endorsed it. I plan to restore decorative elements stripped away over time."

Deb looked quizzical. "How would you know that?"

"Research. The Majestic has long been a favorite of photographers." Ryan smoothed over that and finished sharing his vision and requirements.

"You'll need building permits for all that."

"Naturally. Shouldn't take long on Crown Island."

"You'd be amazed." Deb looked up from the plans. "But you could speed up the process."

Ryan was certainly not surprised. He'd worked in many major cities around the world. While he didn't condone paying fees to pave the approval runway, he recognized that was a cost of business. Still, he hadn't expected it on Crown Island.

Ryan crossed his arms. "Pouring millions into the city's major tourist destination should count for a lot. I shouldn't have to increase my approval budget."

"What I meant was—"

Whitley buzzed through on the intercom. "Excuse me, your next appointment is on the line."

"I'll be right with them." Ryan tapped the phone. "I'm not lining your friends' pockets at City Hall, Ms. Whitaker." He needed her to spread that around.

"That's not what I meant," Deb said quickly. "Look at these unused rooms. If the community had access to them—"

"If you have a design proposal, I'll consider it along with others," he said evenly. "As for how I run this hotel, that's my business. Good day."

Whitley appeared at the door on cue. "This way, Ms. Whitaker."

Ryan watched Deb fasten her portfolio and hasten to leave. He was always dismayed to discover unethical practices. In some countries, it was how business was done. But not here. And he was determined to play by his rules.

His parents and their strict morals were to thank for that.

He watched Deb walk out. She was an attractive woman, but she wasn't his type—or rather, he wasn't hers. He'd consider her proposal and let her down gracefully if she wasn't up to a job of this size. Still, she was a Whitaker, and he might need her on his side.

Whitley appeared at his door again. "Shall I add her to the VIP reception list?"

"Please. And her father as well." Ryan checked the time. "Excuse me; I have a lunch meeting."

"With the chef, of course. I'll make sure you have a table as well."

"I'll meet briefly with Giana, but I'll dine off-site." He paused. Whitley was the only one he could tell. "I'll be at my folk's house."

Whitley's face brightened. "Do give them my best. How are they? In good health, I hope."

Ryan nodded. "And stubborn as ever."

"I'll let reception know you're in a meeting."

"I appreciate that," Ryan said, retrieving his jacket from the old-fashioned coat hook. "I'll stop by the kitchen on my way out."

*a*pril stepped from the car under the port-cochère at the Majestic and gazed up at the hotel that held so many memories for her. Her shower luncheon and wedding, her parent's anniversary, fireworks and ice cream on the beach, and the lighting of the outdoor Christmas tree. Over the years, she'd visited countless times.

"Welcome to the Majestic," an attendant said while another held the passenger door for Junie. "Are you staying with us?"

"We're here for lunch," April replied.

"You chose a beautiful day for it," he said.

It *was* a perfect day. April looked up at the grand hotel entryway filled with flowers. Those looked like a new addition, she thought, determined to appreciate everything good in her life.

This morning, it was all April could do to pull herself together after last night's fiasco with Calvin. Still, she would not let that memory spoil a lunch date she'd been looking forward to. Or any other part of her life.

Not anymore.

April left her car with the attendant. She and Junie could have walked the fifteen minutes to the hotel, but April wanted to dress up for this luncheon with her newly discovered family. She had offered to meet them in Summer Beach, but Carlotta and her daughters wanted to visit her this time.

As April caught a glimpse of herself in a gleaming window, she smiled. Today, she wore a wrap dress in emerald green that brought out the color of her eyes. It was one Deb had urged her to buy at a local resale boutique, insisting that she needed something fresh and stylish in her closet. April had resisted at first, but now she was glad she'd bought it. It was amazing what a new outfit could do for you.

She'd also worn her gold heart necklace. In her small straw purse, she'd tucked a delicate, white linen handkerchief embroidered with the initials PR. Pilar Reina—her birth mother and Carlotta's sister.

Just then, she was surprised to see her friend emerge from the hotel carrying her leather portfolio.

"Well, look at you," Deb said, greeting her and Junie. "Love the dress." She whispered, "Are you okay?"

"Never better, as it turns out," April replied, intent on having a good day. She'd cried to Deb on the phone last night. "And you look like you just stepped out of *Vogue*. What are you doing here?"

"I didn't mention it last night." Deb patted her portfolio. "But I decided to take my shot. I just met with the new owner, Ryan Kingston, and promised to work up a design proposal for him." She lowered her voice. "He's pretty easy on the eyes, too."

"You work fast."

Deb shook her head. "He's not my type, but I wanted to be first with a design proposal. There will be plenty of others. Are you having lunch here?"

"With the Bays from Summer Beach. Want to join us?"

"Thanks, but I have another meeting. The view is still spectacular, but be careful what you order," she added softly. "The food isn't what it used to be. I'd stay clear of the oysters. Hopefully, Kingston will bring back a quality menu. He seems fairly tough."

"I'll keep that in mind," April said with a little wave. She turned back to her daughter.

"I haven't been here in forever," Junie said. "When was the last time you ate here?"

"Last spring, your Nana and I had dinner on the beach veranda. This is her favorite place on the island for lunch, and she knows practically everyone here. I hope she can join us next time."

Junie caught her hand and squeezed it. "Mom, if I forget to tell you, I think you're amazing. You're my inspiration."

"Thanks for that, sweetheart." They'd had a rough night after Calvin dropped his bombshell. She'd hardly slept, and she was weary, but she refused to let him destroy the rest of her life.

They stepped into the lobby, and April saw the manager talking to a man with his back turned. A guest, she imagined. He had an air of confidence that wealth brought. From his starched shirt and impeccably tailored jacket to his polished shoes and sleek black hair, he looked like he'd just arrived from a cosmopolitan city. She tilted her head. Maybe New York or London, she surmised.

Not at all like her beefy husband with the floppy hairstyle he still had from college. She shook her head, dispelling the memory.

That was over.

The man strode away, and Whitley turned to her. "Good afternoon. It's nice to see you here again. I've heard your mother is doing well. Do give Miss Ella my regards."

April smiled and touched his hand in gratitude. "Thank you, Whitley. And what a lovely jacket. I've always loved that color."

"I call it banana-yellow." Whitley's eyes twinkled. "Makes it easy for guests and staff to spot me."

April smiled. "You're not one to blend into the woodwork. I'll tell my mother she's missed here."

"Indeed, she is," he replied, his voice implying great respect and admiration.

And may even something more. Friendship, April surmised.

Ella Raines knew many people on the island. April's father had been a surgeon here, and her mother worked at the same hospital as a nurse. They were well known around town for charitable works for people who needed medical care.

April used to wish she'd had the inclination and aptitude for healthcare. Yet, all through school, history had fascinated her. In fact, what Deb said the other day was correct; April's love for history began at this old hotel.

April introduced Junie, adding, "My daughter is staying with me at my mother's home, so we hope to visit more often."

Whitley bowed his head to Junie. "It will be a pleasure. I remember when your grandmother brought you here as a young lady."

"It was always my favorite place," Junie said.

Recalling what Deb had told her, April commented, "I heard the hotel has been sold."

"Mr. Kingston is the new owner."

The name meant nothing to her. "He's not local, is he?"

Whitley hesitated. "Mr. Kingston has spent time on the island, but he's very private."

Junie glanced around. "With the kind of money it took to buy this place, I guess he would be."

"I hope he doesn't change it much," April added. "This is an important part of the island's history."

With pride evident on his face, Whitley stood taller. "Indeed. We've hosted several presidents in our finest suites. Important world decisions have been made within these walls."

"And a few movies were filmed here, too," April added.

Junie piped up, "I just saw one with Marilyn Monroe filmed at the Hotel Del Coronado. And my grandmother was an extra."

"Miss Ella is the real star." Whitley put a hand over his heart.

April smiled as Junie told him about the film. They'd stayed in and watched it last night as her mother had planned. April needed something to take her mind off Calvin. Not that it did, but it helped. That and a couple of glasses of wine Ella had poured after she'd checked April's vital signs and determined she simply needed to relax.

That had helped, too. April loved old films. A few years ago, she had served as a historical consultant on a Hollywood film shot in Seattle, but that had been a fluke. Perhaps she could do that again, along with a historical society. Because without Calvin or her teaching position, she'd have to act fast to make a living.

Last night, Junie had promised to support her if needed, but April wouldn't take money from her children. Maybe someday, if she were elderly and unable to work, but she was far too young for that now. She needed to create an income and be a role model for her daughters.

Because their father certainly wasn't.

From the corner of her eye, April noticed the guest Whitley had been talking to when they arrived. He was still turned away, but he was attractive from that angle. That is, she was impressed with the way he carried himself.

Or could that be the new owner? Not that it mattered to her, but she was curious.

Before April could mention that, her newly discovered aunt, Carlotta Reina Bay, sailed through the entryway. Her dark, silver-threaded hair fell to her shoulders, and silver-and-turquoise bracelets gleamed on her arms.

"My dearest April, *mi sobrina.*"

"Aunt Carlotta, you look radiant." Although she was older, she was quite fit and stylish. She wore a vivid turquoise dress that swirled around her toned calves. Counting herself lucky, April hugged her in greeting.

Following Carlotta were her daughters, Ivy and Shelly. Shelly carried her baby in a cloth carrier fashioned around her midsection. Ivy wore white jeans with a lacy floral blouse and a mint-green denim jacket. Shelly wore a billowy beach dress, her hair in a casual half updo. They were the cousins April would have loved to have grown up with, but none of them had known of each other's existence until Junie and Shelly connected through a DNA match.

Carlotta's older sister had been pregnant at the time of her death. She was an unmarried teenager, and in those days, adoption was the only socially acceptable solution among their upper class. Although the auto accident was fatal to Pilar, her unborn child was miraculously saved, and the adoption continued as planned.

As far as anyone could ascertain, Carlotta and Pilar's parents never knew April had survived. And April's parents had not been told any of this. Ella was as surprised as April to learn of the Bay family and the connections between them.

April was still amazed at the family's physical resemblance to her. Ivy was a little younger than April, and Shelly was close in age to Junie and Maileah. Ivy had the same deep green eyes and brown hair that April and Junie had, while Shelly more closely resembled Maileah with her lean frame and light chestnut hair.

"Since we're so close, we have to get together more often," Ivy said, clasping April's hands. "You're welcome at the Seabreeze Inn anytime."

"It's really close by ferry." Shelly bumped fists with April and Junie over little Daisy, who cooed with excitement and waved her tiny hands. "Winter is slower at the inn, so if we have rooms open, you two are welcome to escape."

"We'd love to entertain you here, too," April said. "I'm afraid we don't have as much space as the inn, but we have a lovely guest room." Junie could always stay in her room.

As they walked to the terrace cafe overlooking the ocean, April noticed that the man waiting for Whitley was still turned away. The way he held his head seemed familiar, but April couldn't place him. What she could see of him—dark, thick hair and broad shoulders—was oddly compelling.

She turned to Carlotta. "Are you sure you and Sterling can't stay a little longer?"

"We've already extended our stay. My other daughter—you remember Honey, I'm sure—and her husband just left to return to Sydney. We'll meet them there and make sure the boat is ready for the next leg of our journey."

Ivy and Shelly shared a wistful smile, and April knew they would miss their parents. April would, too, even though they had just met. Carlotta and her husband, Sterling, were fascinating and such an inspiration. Sailing around the world at their age— at any age, really—was an amazing accomplishment.

April and her party wound through the old hotel and gardens until they came to the terrace cafe. They were steps from the beach with a broad view of the sea. Although summer was officially over, September was often the warmest month on Crown Island. Children played in the surf, and couples strolled along the water's edge. All around them, guests relaxed under colorful umbrellas with cool drinks in hand, talking and laughing.

"We've reserved our best table for you," a server said as they were seated. Their table was at the edge of the terrace, where they could watch other guests strolling by and children playing on the beach.

"What's good here?" Shelly asked when a server brought menus.

"At lunch, we're known for our salads and burgers," the young woman replied.

She did not mention the seafood, April noted. "And the oysters?"

"We're out of them," the woman said quickly. "But the rest of the seafood looks very good now. We received a fresh delivery this morning."

"We used to come here for prime rib," Carlotta said. "That's Sterling's favorite. But I love the shrimp Louie salad and clam chowder. In fact, if you have the chowder today, that's what I'll have."

"Good choice," the waitress said, nodding her approval. She gave them a few minutes to decide, and when she returned, they ordered.

A moment later, another server arrived with a trayful of colorful drinks. "Today we're serving something new," he said as he placed one in front of each of them.

"Excuse me, but we didn't order these," April said.

"These are compliments of the house, ma'am. This is a non-alcoholic smoothie made with fresh strawberries and lime. Would you like to try it?"

"Sounds delicious, thank you." April took a sip. "It's heavenly."

The server held up another icy glass. "And this one is a mango slushy with chile lime."

Shelly leaned forward. "What's the green one?"

"Honeydew, cucumber, and kale."

"You can put that right here," Shelly said, grinning.

The young man passed out the drinks. "Now that we're under new ownership, our menu will change. This is a preview, compliments of Mr. Kingston."

Carlotta smiled, pleased with the mango drink. "Is the new owner on site today?"

The young man inclined his head. "He's right over there, talking to the bartender."

April turned around. Behind her was the man who'd been talking to Whitley.

Glancing in that direction, Carlotta said, "Would you ask him to come by the table when he can? I'd like to introduce him to another local hotelier."

Ivy laughed. "An inn isn't exactly a hotel, Mom."

"Of course, it is. You should know each other. Tell him the proprietor of the Seabreeze Inn is here. A smaller establishment, but Ivy and Shelly are happy to send their frequent overflow of guests to the Majestic. And vice versa."

"Yes, ma'am." The young man hurried away.

Shelly laughed, and little Daisy joined in. "Mom, you sure know how to spin it. I hope he hurries because I need to feed Daisy before the food arrives."

"Our server is talking to him now," Ivy said. "Oh, here he comes."

"Wow, is he hot," Shelly said. "I mean, for an older guy."

"Shh," Ivy whispered. "And he's not old. He's probably not even fifty."

"Like I said."

Junie grinned and nudged her mother. "They sound like us."

"They sure do," April said, and they all laughed. "Now I have to see him." But before she could turn around, he arrived at their table and stood behind April.

"Ladies, I hope you're enjoying your day." His deep voice seemed edged with the saltiness of the sea. "I'm Ryan Kingston. I understand the proprietor of the Seabreeze Inn is here?"

At the sound of his voice, April sucked in a breath in mid-gulp, choking on a chunk of fruit in her drink. *It couldn't be him, could it?* Her rude neighbor from the balcony. She began to cough.

"Mom, are you okay?" Beside her, Junie looked concerned.

While Carlotta introduced Ivy and Shelly, April stole a look at the man behind her. Immediately, she regretted it. She tried to draw another breath but could only cough.

"Mom?"

Shaking her head, April pointed to her throat. "Stuck," she croaked, with the last bit of breath in her airway.

Junie clapped her on the back, but now April couldn't

breathe at all. She shook her head, trying to turn away from the man.

Alarmed, Junie said, "She needs some water or something."

April shook her head again. She was feeling light-headed and began to panic. She knew what to do, but did anyone else?

A server rushed a glass of water to them, and Ryan leaned over to check on her.

Try as she might, April could neither drink nor expel whatever had lodged in her throat. Or even breathe.

"She needs help," Ryan said to Junie. "Please move aside." With a swift motion, he pulled April from her chair. He wrapped his arms around her from the back, positioned his hands under her diaphragm, and gave her a sharp abdominal thrust to expel air from her lungs.

Once, twice, three times.

Finally, the force expelled a partly mangled piece of strawberry from April's airway that landed on the sandy beach in front of them. She collapsed in the chair, weak and mortified, and leaned against Ryan's solid frame.

He placed his arm protectively across her shoulders. "Can you breathe?"

"Sort of," she managed to say, nestled in the crook of his muscular arm.

The warmth of his body radiated into hers. April might have enjoyed it if she hadn't just been near death. After all, he was in fantastic shape for his age—not that she had let her eyes linger too long the day they'd met. Her face blazed, as much from the thought as from the exertion and embarrassment.

Tension drained from his body, and he rubbed her arm. "I'm relieved you're okay. What's your name?" Gently, Ryan pushed her hair from her face.

She couldn't escape. "April," she replied, raising her eyes to his, which were impossibly blue under a slash of dark eyebrows.

At once, he frowned, and then his lips parted. "I know you."

Wincing, she whispered, "I'm your plant thief." Her throat burned with the effort.

"So you are." Ryan drew his hand over his jaw in surprise. "Looks like you'll live to steal again."

April couldn't tell if he was kidding or not. She glanced

around, feeling self-conscious. Everyone in the terrace cafe was looking at them.

When Ryan stood up, guests around them applauded with relief.

Her daughter reached out a hand to him. "Thank you for knowing what to do," Junie said. "You saved my mom's life."

Ryan shrugged it off with modesty. "Many people are trained. I just happened to be here. If you'll excuse me, I'll make sure the fresh strawberries are well pureed."

April glanced around the table. Her new kin smiled with relief.

"It's fortunate that Mr. Kingston knew the Heimlich maneuver," Carlotta said, pressing a hand to her chest with relief. "*Dios mio*, if he hadn't been here, we might have lost you."

"And so soon after finding you," Shelly added, trying to quiet Daisy, who'd started crying with concern when April was choking. "What a bummer that would've been."

Ivy poked her. "My sister meant what a tragedy it would have been. Shelly, don't you have to feed Daisy?"

"Tragedy, bummer—it's all the same. But I'm really glad you're okay, April." With her quirky, lopsided grin, Shelly cradled Daisy. "I'll get up as soon as she's settled down a little."

April's breath was beginning to return to normal. She drank some water to soothe her throat.

Carlotta leaned forward with interest, her silver bracelets jangling on her wrists. "What was that about a plant thief?"

April's cheeks burned again. "As it turns out, Ryan Kingston is my neighbor, although I'd never seen him there. I thought his house was vacant—it had been all summer—so I borrowed some tiny pieces of succulents to show my mother and a landscaper."

"And he caught you at it?" Carlotta asked, clearly intrigued.

April nodded, hating to confess, but she had little choice. This was the sort of mess one of her students would get themselves into, not her. Not at her age or with her experience.

Sipping her water, she gathered her thoughts. "He heard me. I suppose I interrupted his shower."

"Oh, my." A smile danced on Carlotta's lips. "Well, you could certainly do worse."

"That didn't come out exactly right," April said, feeling the heat rise in her chest. "Actually, my husband and I are…"

She couldn't bring herself to say the D word out loud, but that was the next step for her. She'd have to engage an attorney and begin the process. This time, there would be no going back.

The table fell silent as if no one knew how to respond. April didn't dare turn around again, yet, Junie was right. If Ryan hadn't been here and known what to do, it might have ended badly for her.

And solved Calvin's problem. She grimaced at the morbid thought.

Carlotta's gaze flicked to April's bare ring finger. "We wouldn't want to intrude on your private life."

"But we're family," Shelly said, jiggling Daisy, who now had a smile on her sweet face. "And you know what that means. So, what's really going on with that? I haven't seen you wear a wedding ring before."

She hadn't worn her etched gold band all summer because she'd been furious with Calvin. And now, she'd flung it at him, and who knew where it had landed? Surely, he picked it up.

"We've decided to part ways."

April glanced at her hand. The news was public now, and a fresh ache seized her. She never thought she would ever be divorced. That was something that happened to other women, not her. Still, this was her new reality, and she was determined to get on with it. No more wasting time or energy over Calvin. She lifted her chin. "I'll tell you all about it sometime, but it's for the best."

Swiftly, Ivy chimed in, "We're here for you if you ever need to talk."

"What happened?" Shelly asked.

"Excuse me?" Ivy turned to Shelly with a pointed look. "Just look at how hungry Daisy is. If you don't feed her right now, you'll regret it."

"Oh, all right." Shelly rose and headed toward the ladies' room, her full cotton skirt swishing as she threaded through the fashionable beach crowd.

"I'm sorry." Ivy reached for April's hand. "I know this must be a difficult time, but don't let Shelly bother you. She's our wild child and often speaks before thinking."

"Our family has its wild child, too." Junie raised her brow and sipped loudly on her fruit smoothie for emphasis.

Under the table, April nudged Junie's knee. "Shelly is like my other daughter, Maileah. They say what's on their mind. I hope you'll all get to meet her soon."

As a newcomer to the family, April wanted to leave the Bays with a good impression.

Ivy reached out to April. "Do you think you'll stay on Crown Island?"

"I plan to," April replied. "I'm a historian, but I can't return to my teaching position in Seattle. I've arranged to meet my mother's accountant and attorney about setting up a historical society here. I'd like to work with the local tourist bureau and schools."

Just saying those words lifted April's spirits, and from the corner of her eye, she could see Junie beaming at her.

"You'll find your way," Ivy said. "I went through a similar situation when I was starting the inn. What's that old saying? Sometimes we're born entrepreneurs—"

"And sometimes entrepreneurship is thrust upon us," Carlotta finished. "We're here if you need us."

"I appreciate that." Changing the subject, April added, "Speaking of history, we have so many stories to share. I'd love to hear more about your family."

Carlotta rested her chin in her hand with a faraway look in her eyes. "At one time, my sisters and I were inseparable. Would you like to hear more about Pilar?"

"I'd love that," April replied, relieved that Carlotta sensed that. She still had many questions about her birth mother, but she also wanted to become better acquainted with her aunt before she left.

More than anything, April simply wanted to enjoy her new DNA-blended family today before her real work began. This was the beginning of her new life here, and it would be months before Carlotta returned. She was determined to make the most of her time with family and friends these next few months.

April realized this precious time with Junie might prove fleeting, too. Even though she didn't think of herself as old, she was old enough to know that nothing lasted forever. Much as she hated to admit it, she might not have survived lunch if Ryan hadn't been here.

While April turned her attention to Carlotta, she also resolved to see Ryan again and thank him properly. If he'd allow her on his property again, that is.

10

*J*unie had enjoyed lunch with her new cousins, although she'd been worried about her mother. Thank goodness Ryan Kingston knew what to do. Her mother was still stricken from yesterday's encounter. Junie hadn't spoken with her father, nor did she expect to hear from him. He was such a coward.

After lunch, the group dispersed, with Ivy, Shelly, and Carlotta leaving to catch the return ferry to Summer Beach.

"Are you ready to go home?" Junie asked her mother as they left the cafe.

"Actually, being out takes my mind off many things," April replied. "How about we look at some of the hotel shops here?"

"We could take a surprise back to Nana."

"She'd like that," April said.

Junie paused. "I don't think I've been shopping since before Mark passed away."

"You always enjoyed it."

"Except now, ordering whatever I need online is so easy. And I don't need much."

"It's not always about what we need, but what lifts our spirits. Even small items that make us smile or have meaning to us. And you know how I love shopping for gifts."

"No one does Christmas like you, Mom."

"We'll make some new traditions this year," April said.

Junie admired her mother's confidence in the face of the pending divorce that would affect her and Maileah, too. If her mother could face the future with optimism, she should, too. "That will be fun. Nana will love having us here."

"One of my favorite memories from childhood was coming here to see that towering pine tree here at the Majestic. Every year, we would all dress up for the occasion. The hotel's lobby elevator operator would flip the switch on the lights, illuminating the entire tree, and everyone would cheer. I can still taste the rich, creamy hot chocolate they would serve. It was topped with mounds of real whipped cream."

That sounded wonderful to Junie. "I wonder if they still do that."

"We'll find out."

As Junie strolled through the Majestic Hotel with her mother toward the boutiques, they admired vividly colored art glass and paintings of Crown Island. Likely from local artists, she mused. The hotel had a distinct personality, where beach living met traditional luxury. It was unlike other cookie-cutter hotels that looked alike, regardless of location.

"I'm beginning to understand your appreciation of history," Junie said. She peered at several old photos on the wall from the early days of the hotel and Crown Island. "This hotel is a real gem, isn't it?"

April agreed. "We should cherish it. In an era of mass production and homogenization, true craftsmanship should be treasured and preserved when possible. We'll never see another hotel built like this one. It was unusual, even for its time."

Junie paused by a pair of antique sideboards flanking the long hallway. "These are incredible. Do you know anything about them?"

"These are English Hepplewhite," her mother said, running her fingers along the smooth patina." "This is probably mahogany with burlwood inlays. I hope the new owner doesn't replace these with something modern. They're quite valuable. From about the turn of the century, I imagine."

"The last century, you mean."

"Likely around nineteen-hundred," April said. "Or possibly

before then, depending on whether it's an old reproduction or one of the earlier Hepplewhite pieces. Either way, it's beautiful. This hotel has such a fascinating history. So many lovely old photos, too."

She paused by one on the wall and leaned in. "Junie, come look at this. I found something that will make you laugh."

"What is it? I see a bunch of kids."

"It's from my grammar school field trip to the Majestic. We cobbled together period outfits for the trip." April chuckled at the memory. "My mother sewed matching long cotton dresses for Deb and me. There we are," she said, pointing to the two of them in front. "My dress was green gingham, and Deb's was blue. The photo has faded, but they looked like something out of *Little House on the Prairie*."

June laughed. "Oh, how cute you look, Mom."

"We had so much fun. It was on that trip that I became enamored with history and the hotel. I've never forgotten that. It still seems like yesterday." April paused. "Time goes so fast, don't you think?"

"Not for me," Junie replied. "Sometimes days seem endless."

Lately, though, she had become a little restless. Her mother went out more than she did, and once her grandmother was feeling better, there would be no stopping her. Ella was devoted to her yoga practice to build her strength. Some days, she had more stamina than Junie.

How long could she spend thinking about Mark? Wishing she'd told him how much she loved him before he left for London instead of the quick breakfast and send-off she'd given him. That reel had run so many times in her head that she'd memorized every movement, every word they'd exchanged. She could have —*should* have—done better.

But that was in the past. She could dwell on it or embrace the life she had left. Intellectually, she knew that. Yet, taking those initial steps was more challenging than it seemed. Few could understand that. She turned back to her mother.

"Between last night and today at lunch, how are you holding up, Mom?" Junie asked. She admired how her mother had rallied for lunch today after yesterday's disaster.

"I'm still in shock that your father and I finally came to this crossroads, but I can't say I haven't seen it coming for a long time, honey. When I got up this morning, it felt like a release. At least I know what the future won't be now."

"I know what that's like," Junie said. "I have no idea what I'll be doing this time next year. But your historical society idea sounds cool. Have you been planning that?"

"It's been on my mind," April replied. "There's a need I think I can fill. You'll find your way when the time is right."

"I sure hope so. Still, I'm so angry at Dad. I can't believe he's done this to you. And all of us." She slapped her cheek and moaned. "Oh, my gosh, this means I will have a little brother. And probably a stepmother my age. Unbelievable. What's wrong with Dad? You have always been there for him."

April heaved a weary sigh. "I don't know, Junie. I thought your father and I had plans about what we would do after he retired. I suppose I was the only one planning."

"Now you're making new plans," Junie said, sliding her arm through her mother's. She wished she could have done something, but her mother was right. Their marriage was doomed due to her father's philandering.

Junie counted herself lucky that Mark had been faithful to her.

She shook off those thoughts, determined to enjoy this day with her mother. They hadn't been out much this summer, but that had been because of Junie. She wanted to start making up for it.

In the shopping corridor, they passed a children's clothing shop—Beachwear for Kids—and Junie paused outside, admiring the small outfits in a rainbow of colors. Tiny surfing shorts, mermaid swimsuits, miniature sandals.

"I've always liked this store," Junie said. "I had planned to shop here when we started our family."

"You're still young," April said.

"Not as young as I was. I'm thirty-two and starting over."

"Starting over at any age is difficult, especially when unexpected."

"And now you're going to say I should play the hand I'm dealt, right?" When April offered a small, guilty smile, Junie said, "I've heard every platitude in the last two years, Mom. I know I need to get out there again. It's just not as easy as it sounds."

"You came to lunch today. And you're the one who connected us to the Bay family. I think you're on your way."

"It's easier to do things for other people than for yourself."

"It's a good time to change that," her mother said. "We should schedule massages and pamper ourselves a little. We could come to the spa here."

"I'd like that," Junie said, surprised at herself. "My therapist told me to take baby steps. That made me feel infantile. But I'm beginning to see her point." Still, putting herself back out there was daunting.

She'd sold the online shop because she couldn't handle the technology like Mark did, and shoes and accessories had suddenly seemed pointless. Sleep eluded her, and she had difficulty making even minor decisions. If she hadn't sold the company, it would've lost its value because she wasn't managing it well.

"I could see you with a shop like this," April said, motioning to the next boutique. "Or that one, The Body Boutique."

"That looks like a nice one. Let's see what they have."

Looking over her shoulder, April hesitated. "Why don't you look around without me? I should find Ryan Kingston and thank him properly. It's better to do that now."

Junie watched her mother go. She seemed preoccupied with her task, which wasn't like her. Maybe she simply needed time to herself. Junie would probably feel the same way if she'd just had a brush with death.

*a*fter leaving Junie, April made her way to the lobby, hoping to find Whitley, but she didn't see him anywhere. She wanted to thank Ryan Kingston before she lost her nerve.

They might not have started off well with her traipsing through his yard disparaging his home. But if he hadn't taken such swift action at lunch…well, she hated to think about what the outcome might have been.

She approached the front registration desk. "Hello, I was wondering if I might speak to Ryan Kingston."

The young male receptionist gave her a cordial smile. "Do you have an appointment with Mr. Kingston?"

"No, but I just saw him at the restaurant. I won't take much of his time."

"I'll try to reach him. Your name?"

"April Raines, thank you."

While waiting, she saw him exit the side of the hotel near the front porte-cochère. "There he is."

The clerk looked up. "I'll call him for you."

Before April could say anything, the energetic young receptionist had bounded toward the entry and signaled the bell captain, who gestured to Ryan.

He turned around.

April stepped outside under the wide port-cochère lined with a profusion of white daisies, red geranium, and glossy green ferns that were just being set out in lovely white planters.

She lifted her hand to Ryan, and he started toward her. She watched him approach, his long stride filled with confidence. She wondered what it would be like to be as sure of your position in the world as he was. To be a man of stature born into a world of privilege. They really had nothing in common. Nevertheless, she must thank him. She was raised with manners, if not great wealth.

As Ryan neared, her heart quickened. He was undeniably handsome, but more than that, he had an intriguing aura about him, as if he didn't care what others thought. He was bent on a mission, whatever that was.

He stopped in front of her, his dark eyebrows drawn together in concern. "Is there something else I can do for you?"

April introduced herself. "I know we didn't meet under the best circumstances," she began, concerned that her voice was still hoarse. Facing him nearly took her breath away, so she paused. Her chest and throat were still sore from her ordeal.

Waiting for her to go on, a shadow of a smile crossed his face. "It's not every day I step out of my shower to find a plant thief in my yard."

"I won't do that again." Heat rose in her cheeks, but she had to go on. She'd come this far, and it was awkward enough with him living on Beach View Lane, a stone's throw from her bedroom window.

She looked up at him, stricken by eyes that seemed to bore into her soul. "Thank you for acting so quickly back there. When I think of what might have happened, especially with my daughter there…" She shook her head. "Life has been hard enough for Junie."

Ryan reached out and brushed her hand, sending shivers through her. She recalled the feeling of his arm around her.

"I'm sorry to hear that. Is Junie…alright?"

"Her husband passed away two years ago."

Ryan furrowed his brow. "She's very young."

"Yes, she is. It was unexpected."

"You care more for her than yourself."

He said it as a statement of fact, not a question. This wasn't how she'd envisioned the conversation going. April nodded and cleared her throat. "I wanted to thank you properly, so you know how much I appreciate what you did."

Ryan took her hand and held it in his, staring at it as if he were at a loss for words. With a swift motion, he brought her hand to his lips, kissing the air just above her skin so that she could feel the warmth of his breath.

"Only doing my duty," Ryan said. "I must go now. But may I check on you, April?"

She wasn't sure what he meant by that. But she liked how her name sounded in his rich baritone voice.

Sensing her hesitation, he quickly added, "As a neighbor." With a slight lift of his mouth, he continued, "Since we're so close."

"So close, yes," she intoned, mesmerized by his gaze.

He turned, and April watched him stride toward his car, never looking back at her. She covered the back of her hand with her fingers, drawing them lightly over the spot still tingling from his nearness.

She turned back toward the entry, not wanting him to see her gazing after him like a puppy who'd just received a treat. His effect on her was so surprising, and she couldn't understand why. Maybe her emotions were simply raw—from Calvin, from her close call at lunch—but the attraction she felt was nothing like she'd known, even for her husband.

Excruciatingly aware of her foolish reaction—he must be used to women falling for him—she walked into the lobby.

Ryan Kingston was nothing like her husband, but he was out of her league. Not that she should be interested. Even though she and her husband had been separated, and she couldn't remember the last time they'd shared a bed, their marriage was still legal.

Her emotions were raw right now. That was all.

The receptionist looked up. "You spoke to Mr. Kingston?"

"Yes, thank you." April drew on every bit of her resolve to maintain her dignity. She was far too old to have this sort of reaction toward a man, especially a man so far removed from her station in life. He could have any woman he wanted, and he would never understand all she'd been through.

"Is there anything I can help you with, ma'am?"

"You've been very kind, thank you. I must find my daughter."
She turned and hurried away.

It wasn't until she reached the shopping corridor that she realized she was shaking. No doubt a delayed physiological reaction, her mother would say. But whether it was from her brush with death or her encounter with Ryan Kingston, she couldn't say.

April pulled her shoulders back, refusing to give in to either of those feelings. She had far more important issues to deal with. And she needed to find Junie right away.

12

*J*unie strolled into the spa store and browsed through the assortment. Being around a familiar retail environment was calming.

She recalled how much she enjoyed helping people find what they wanted or needed, whether online or in a store. Merchandising and creating an atmosphere with eye-catching displays were fun for her, too. She missed that, but she still didn't know what she wanted to do.

Having the money to do as she pleased wasn't much motivation to get out of bed. At least, not for her. She'd always been driven by accomplishment.

A country-chic French display of Provençal body lotions attracted her. She wanted to surprise her grandmother with a little gift. Junie hoped she'd be strong enough to get out soon. She selected a fresh, lemon verbena-scented lotion she thought her grandmother would like.

Junie sized up the inventory. While attractive, she noticed the store carried plenty of national brands but nothing that was a unique reflection of the Majestic Hotel or Crown Island. That piqued her curiosity, and she sensed an opportunity for someone.

A friendly young woman about her age approached her with a bright smile. "Hi, may I help you with something today?"

"Do you have any local or hotel-branded merchandise?"

The woman nodded down the corridor. "I don't have anything like that, but the hotel gift shop has a few T-shirts. People ask for that sort of thing a lot, but it doesn't go with my assortment."

"Thanks. I love the shop, by the way. It is yours?" Junie had heard the woman speaking to other customers about items she seemed passionate about.

"It is. I started this shop several years ago. It's fun because I get to travel for buying trips."

Junie held up the lotion she wanted. "France, right?"

The woman laughed. "I love shopping there for my customers. I'll ring that up for you."

Junie made her way toward the other store. As she entered the gift shop, she was immediately struck by the vintage mouldings and hardwood floors. A chandelier sparkled overhead, and the bright, airy room with an ocean view was filled with an ordinary assortment of candy, magazines, cheap beach toys, and T-shirts, which dulled the impression.

Immediately, Junie's experienced eye for retail swept over the space, reimagining it. She sensed a need for exclusive, upscale merchandise. Guests at the Majestic would probably prefer higher-end chocolates and hardcover books, but it was more than that. She imagined luxurious Majestic Hotel robes, high-quality monogrammed polo shirts, and thick hoodies for cool evenings. Maybe exclusive artwork by local artists, like the art glass sculptures and intricate mosaics that were popular on the island. And unusual items for children, like wooden toys.

Turning slowly, taking it all in, her mind wandered across a range of possibilities. If this were her shop, she'd stock candles with ethereal beach scents to fill the air and bring people in. Like Cinnabon did at shopping malls. And then, at Christmas, she would—

Just then, a commotion erupted near the register between the sales clerk, who looked like he'd rather be surfing, and a harried customer, who clearly wasn't getting the help she needed. She held a folded T-shirt in a shopworn plastic bag.

"I'm not wild about these, but they'll do. I need it in a small."

He tapped a text on his mobile phone. "I don't think we have that one in a small either."

"You don't think?" The woman inclined her head. "How about checking in the back?"

Acting greatly inconvenienced, he looked up from his phone. "I already looked for the blue one you wanted."

"Could you look for other colors? Pink or yellow, or whatever you have. I could use six, two each for my girls. That should last us through tomorrow."

"Look, I'm new, and I don't know where to find anything back there," the young man said, jerking his head toward what Junie surmised was a storeroom. "You should try another shop."

"My girls are probably tearing up the room right now, and these can work. If you'd just check." She nodded toward a tattered sign that read, *Ask for Additional Sizes*.

"Everything is probably out, okay? If it's not there, I ain't got no magic wand, lady."

The woman narrowed her eyes. "Where's your manager?"

"Give me a break, will you?" He heaved a sigh.

Junie turned to the other woman. "I could look for you. That is, if you don't *mind*," she added to the young man. "I used to work in retail, and I'm sure I can figure it out."

The clerk turned back to his phone. "Have at it."

As Junie dipped through the curtain dividing the shop from the storeroom, she heard the woman's voice rising in anger as she berated the clerk. With good reason, Junie thought. She was doing her best to defuse the situation and help the woman, who was now completely frustrated. The situation was escalating quickly.

Scanning the shelves, Junie spied the shirts the woman was looking for stuffed haphazardly near the bottom. Plenty in all sizes, she thought, reaching for several colors in small, which should have been on the sales floor—including the blue ones.

Next to the shelves was an open carton of T-shirts that looked cuter. She added them to her armload and whisked from the storeroom, ready to hand off the merchandise and find her mother. The gift shop was a disaster.

But when Junie emerged, she saw Whitley, the hotel manager they'd met on the way in.

"Go straight to human resources," he was saying to the young clerk. "That's not how we serve guests."

Junie ducked past him and made her way to the woman. "I'm sorry about all that," she said softly. "I found these in the back for you."

"Thank you," the woman said. "Now I feel terrible. Our luggage didn't make it, and I need a change of clothes for my daughters. They're such a mess; they got into a food fight at the airport. But I think I just got that kid fired."

"He clearly didn't want to be here."

The woman's face brightened. "Do you work here?"

"No, but I figured I could help." Junie glanced over her shoulder at Whitley. "I'd better go. I hope your luggage makes it. Have fun on Crown Island. Most people here are pretty helpful." She headed for the entryway.

Whitley's deep voice stopped her. "Would you wait a moment, miss? I would like to speak to you."

Junie slunk back inside. She was surely in trouble now. Whitley took the woman's room number and put the charge on her room.

After the woman left, Junie looked up at Whitley. "I'm sorry I went nosing around back there."

"I'm glad you did." Whitley looked at her with a mixture of surprise and gratitude. "We can't afford to alienate our guests, and she'd had a rough day of travel already." Recognition flashed across his face. "We met earlier. You're the Raines granddaughter. Junie, right?"

"One of them, yes, sir."

"And how was your lunch today?"

"Very good. I've always liked this hotel. My grandmother has brought me here since I was a little girl. It feels like home. I guess that's why I stepped in to help that woman."

Whitley nodded thoughtfully. "I could use someone like you to run the gift shop."

"Well, someone like me is available right now," Junie said, making a joke. Or was it? Instead of thinking about it, she blurted out, "I'm sure I could do it."

Before she lost her nerve, Junie told him about her retail experience. As she spoke, the idea of running the gift shop became more appealing.

Whitley extended a hand. "The human resource department

is on the second floor to the left. Stop by there and tell them I sent you to fill out the paperwork." As he shook her hand, he added, "This is record time for filling an open position. Welcome aboard."

Junie emerged from the gift shop feeling exhilarated by the challenge. She saw her mother looking into other stores for her.

"Mom, over here." Junie waved and started toward her, hardly able to contain her enthusiasm.

"My goodness, what happened to you?" April asked, taking her hands.

"I just got a job." She was giddy with excitement.

"Why, that's wonderful. Here?"

Junie nodded and told her the story as they continued through the hotel. "I know it's only a hotel gift shop, but I'm happy about it. The Majestic feels like home, and I have all sorts of ideas for the inventory already."

"Like what?"

Junie ticked off her thoughts on her fingers. "First, I would mark down most everything to get rid of it and donate what won't sell. Next, I'd create a new, higher-quality merchandise assortment. The visual merchandising would be fun. I'll bet I could work with the special events department, too. I see a lot of business opportunities here."

When Junie saw the expression of joy on her mother's face, she laughed at herself. "Do I sound like I've been in hibernation?"

"They'll appreciate your enthusiasm." April swept her arm around Junie's shoulder. "And I'm so relieved to see you happy about something again."

Junie drew in a corner of her lip and sighed. "Dad would probably say it's beneath my skill level. And Maileah would definitely say it's beneath my pay grade." As these thoughts occurred to her, they were like pinpricks deflating her enthusiasm. "What do you think, Mom? Is this too much of a baby step? Am I silly for doing this?"

"Not at all, and who cares what they think? Or anyone else, for that matter. If it makes you happy, that's all that counts. I'm proud of you for taking this step, which is more significant than you think. I'll wait while you go to human resources."

At her mother's encouragement, a warm flush of happiness filled her again. "Did you find Ryan Kingston?"

"I did." She smiled. "We might even see him around the neighborhood."

Junie laughed. "I can't believe you scaled that wall around the house to steal plants, Mom. You didn't tell me that part."

"I did not scale a wall," her mother said, sounding horrified. "I went in through an open gate. The landscaper showed me around the property earlier. And you know as well as I do that place has been vacant all summer."

"I hadn't noticed, but it's not anymore." Junie grinned but then thought about the application she had to fill out. Although she was thrilled to return to work, she was still nervous. "Would you come with me upstairs?"

Her mother instantly understood. "Let's go," she said, taking Junie's hand.

Feeling a little embarrassed, Junie tucked her hair behind an ear. "This is pathetic, isn't it? My mom taking me to fill out a job application. I don't think you did that when I was sixteen."

"You're pretty gutsy. You've always landed your jobs all by yourself."

As they approached a door marked Human Resources, Junie drew a breath. It was time to change her life, even in a small way. It had been a long time since she'd jumped into the ocean of life, and she hoped she remembered how to swim.

$\mathcal{R}$yan strode from the port-cochère toward his rental car, his thoughts centered on the woman he'd rescued. He was relieved that he'd been there. A death at the hotel in the first week would not have been an auspicious beginning.

And of all people, it had to be his plant thief. *April.* Ironically, that fit. He couldn't help grinning. She'd had some nerve to show her face at his hotel.

But then, she wouldn't have made the connection, he realized.

He chuckled at the irony of it. Of all the women, he couldn't stop thinking about a shameless plant thief. Not many women stood up to him as she had, even though she'd been trespassing and clearly in the wrong. Her blazing green eyes, filled with outrage, had intrigued him.

Unlike Deb Whitaker, April was more his type. Holding her in his arms today—even for a moment—had stirred a long-forgotten feeling in him. His heart hammered as he recalled the look of gratitude in her eyes. Even then, she'd been more concerned about her daughter.

April was genuine. That's what was different about her. And she wasn't trying to impress him.

He sensed there was more to her. Right now, her life seemed complicated, and he certainly didn't need that. He recalled the conversation he'd accidentally overheard while waiting for take-out at the Ferry Cafe. That guy, presumably her husband and soon-to-be ex—if she had any sense, which it seemed she did—was a real piece of work. Educated yet arrogant, he had clearly taken his wife for granted.

What a jerk.

A woman like April was one to be cherished. The way she expressed her appreciation—she had class and manners. She cared deeply about her daughter, her mother, and her friends. During his career, he'd learned to quickly read people. What he sensed in the depth of her startling green eyes was a woman who had values and knew her worth.

Ryan slid into the car and rested his hands on the steering wheel. In the rearview mirror, he watched her walk back into the hotel. He recalled how her slender hand felt in his and the sweet scent of her skin as he brushed his lips so close. The feeling of her body collapsing against his in the restaurant was almost too much for him. He longed to wrap her in his arms and taste her kiss.

Yet he barely knew April. He searched his mind, recalling everything he could about her, challenging himself to find fault to diminish the feelings erupting in him. He had to get her off his mind so he could focus on the job at hand. His future, the Majestic.

The hotel was a jealous lover, stealing every hour he had. His livelihood and reputation depended on his success with the Victorian lady.

Nothing would derail him from that.

As April fell from sight, an idea occurred to him. If he could spend a little time with her, he would likely find something about her that annoyed him. No woman was perfect. Once he did, she would be out of his system.

One more conversation should do it.

Ryan couldn't risk a distracting relationship. He nodded in satisfaction. He knew himself. He would get April off his mind as quickly as possible.

After leaving the Majestic, Ryan drove his rental car to the other side of the island, where the well-heeled guests of the Majestic would seldom venture. He passed work trucks lining the street, rambunctious kids flying past on skateboards, and colorful cottages jammed on small lots. Windows were flung open to capture the ocean breezes, and clothes dried in the sun on clotheslines.

Ryan knew every inch of this neighborhood and many of the older people who still lived here. As he slowed the car, he raised a hand from the steering wheel in greeting. Women chatted on porches, and a few older men gathered for a card game under a shade tree, cold beers lined up on the wooden table. Two kids were painstakingly painting a mural on a wooden fence. They all turned as he passed.

News of his visit would zing the neighborhood before he left, even though he had a decidedly non-flashy rental car.

On one corner stood a neat house splashed in a bright, cheerful shade of turquoise with white trim and a red door. *Just like in the old country,* his father had said. Although that house had been a stiff wind away from falling and barely had plumbing enough for the extended family. Still, the color scheme fit right into the island's brightly colored neighborhoods.

Ryan parked in the neatly paved driveway and got out. Bright turquoise hand-glazed pots filled with tropical flowers lined one side of the driveway.

Palm trees swayed overhead, and the sweet scent of roses filled the air. To one side of the yard stood a line of fruit trees: lemon, orange, and a towering avocado tree. On the other side was a well-tended vegetable garden that was the pride of Mary Kingston Finley.

The door flew open as he approached, and a stout, red-faced man stood in the doorway, his face wreathed in a smile. "Well, if it isn't me prodigal son, returnin' at last. Thought you'd forgotten about us. Happy birthday, son."

Ryan wrapped his arms around his father. "I've missed you, Dad. Good to see you."

"Finally got your hotel. I'm happy for you, son. Come on in. Mum is in the kitchen preparing a special feast for you. Is Whitley still working there?"

"He sends his best. Still wearing his crazy colored jackets, too." Ryan stepped inside after his father, noticing a limp in his stride. "The Majestic hasn't changed much since you retired, except that it needs even more work to bring it into the present century."

"You're up for it, to be sure. I did my time there, keeping every blessed light fixture and doorknob in good repair."

"Indeed, you did." His father had worked in the janitorial department, and his mother had been in housekeeping. As a boy, Ryan had torn around the basement and service areas of the hotel. The Majestic had been his home—much more than the drafty rental house his parents could barely afford.

On a side table, Ryan spotted red roses in twin vases wrapped with green ribbon. "You're still doing that?"

"A promise is a promise, even to oneself. She's retired, but the other nurses are delighted, so I keep on brightening their day. I'm thankful for you every day, son."

Ryan's birth had been difficult, and he'd barely survived his first year. In gratitude, his father had delivered a single red rose, all he could afford, to the nurse who delivered Ryan. Since then, every year on Ryan's birthday he brought his wife roses and took others to the local hospital where the nurse worked.

Ryan often wondered if his father's sentimental act was appreciated or understood.

The scent of corned beef spices wafted through the air. A woman's voice floated from the kitchen. "Patrick, is that our birthday boy?"

"In the flesh, he is."

As Ryan paused in the entry, a red Irish terrier jumped up and wagged her tail in greeting. "Well, hello, Molly. How's my girl?"

With the dog by his side, Ryan made his way through the comfortable cottage. It was small but furnished the way his parents had wanted. His mother had chosen the bright floral sofa with embroidered pillows, leather recliners, and lace curtains. Knickknacks with the Irish phrase *Erin go Bragh* that people had given his father over the years were displayed on a bookshelf with well-worn books. His parents loved the house, and it had pleased him to buy and furnish it for them. They'd more than earned it.

On the other hand, buying the large house on Beach View Lane for them when he'd closed his first big investment deal had been his folly. He surprised them with the two-story contemporary home. Although they were grateful, his father took him aside. *We don't belong on this side of the island, son.*

Instantly, Ryan realized his error. The next day, he bought the neat bungalow in the neighborhood where many of their work friends from the hotel lived.

His parents appreciated their modest home far more than the hulking white house on Beach View Lane. *We're not comfortable putting on airs,* as his mother put it.

Ryan greeted her now in her cozy, well-organized kitchen. Her hair had more strands of white than the last time he'd visited. But as his father often said, she would always be a beautiful English rose to him, even though a life of labor had left her with stooped shoulders and aching joints.

"How are you feeling, Mum?"

"A little stiff in the morning, but working in the garden keeps me strong." She held him by the shoulders. "You're looking thin. I'll have to send some of this food home with you."

"Mum, I don't—" Ryan stopped. Maybe he didn't need it, but he couldn't turn it down. "I don't think I've had a good meal since I was here last."

"Aw, now you're having me on."

"You make the best corned beef and potatoes this side of Ireland."

His mother smiled and kissed his cheek. "I've been making it long enough now for your father. Speaking of which… Patrick, we'll need salad from the garden. Would you be a love?"

His father kissed his mother's smooth cheek. "For you, the world."

Ryan loved seeing how sweetly they still treated each other. "I'll set the table for you, Mum."

Molly trotted after him into the dining room. Ryan removed his jacket and folded it over the arm of a chair. As he did, he glanced at the framed photos that lined the top of a polished buffet.

His parents had met in New York, working at a hotel while they were young. Together, they arrived at the Majestic shortly after they married. Patrick Finley came from Ireland as a teenager, and Mary Kingston, whose family had been in service in England, was born in New York. Although they'd hoped for a larger family, he was their only son, and they had just one daughter.

From the polished buffet that held a whiff of orange oil, he took fine plates he'd bought for them. He brought out neatly ironed cloth napkins and set the table as his mother had taught him as a boy.

When Ryan was twelve, his life changed. A fellow countryman from Ireland who had done well for himself was a regular guest at the hotel and befriended his father. After playing chess with Ryan and hearing how well he performed in school, the man took his parents aside. He'd never had children, and he told them he could arrange for Ryan to attend a private boarding school on scholarship.

Ryan peered at the old photo of his high school graduation that his parents cherished.

At the time, Ryan hadn't wanted to leave for school, but his parents insisted, saying it was an opportunity he couldn't pass up. To his immigrant father, such an education was an otherwise unattainable dream.

His father registered him as Ryan Kingston, using his mother's maiden name, after having suffered discrimination when he'd arrived in New York. Many people looked down on the poor Irish then, as they did every new wave of impoverished immigrants. Patrick Finley was determined to give his son every advantage in their new country, even if it meant suppressing half of his son's heritage.

Today, no one outside of this mixed, working-class neighborhood knew Ryan Finley, son of an Irish immigrant and janitor. To the rest of the world, he was Ryan Kingston, known for his astute investments and Ivy League connections.

Only once had he introduced a woman he'd dated to his parents. *Elizabeth Whitney Livingston.* A woman with more pedigree than a thoroughbred racehorse. That had gone about as well as the first house he'd bought his parents.

He'd asked Elizabeth to marry him, but when he told her about his background, she was horrified. That was the weekend he was to be honored in New York, and they'd planned to introduce their parents. However, she told him she could never introduce *the help* to her parents as their prospective in-laws. Couldn't he understand that?

Like a cold shower, he most certainly did. To this day, Elizabeth would never admit they'd been that serious.

But that wasn't even the worst of it.

He shrugged it off. The only thing he regretted was not giving his parents grandchildren. Now, it was too late for that. He would not be an elderly father with a trophy wife young enough to be his daughter on his arm. A caricature of the wealthy investor, he was not. He could have company when he wanted, but he was selective and careful. He managed his private life with discretion.

That's how he would be with April. But he was bound to find something about her that irritated him long before they reached that stage. Maybe just two conversations.

Besides, his younger sister had provided the grandchildren their parents wanted. Pippa had little interest in academics, but she excelled as a mother and volunteered in a solidly middle-class community. Ryan couldn't be prouder of her.

"Now that's a fine, vine-ripened tomato for you," his father said, walking into the dining room with a succulent, late-harvest tomato. "Smell that, will you? It's got the aroma of the sun, sea, and warm minerals of the earth. This is a luxury that many folks don't even know about. The pale tomatoes at the grocery store can't compare with this genuine beauty."

"Magnificent." His father was right. No wonder the chef was irate.

As they sat down to a lunch of salad, corned beef, and boiled potatoes, his mother didn't waste any time. "So, have you met anyone?"

"I meet a lot of people," Ryan replied.

Mary laced her hands. "You know what I mean. Anyone special?"

"Unless you want to count a shameless plant thief I caught trespassing on my property, no." Ryan stroked his chin. From the moment he'd met her, she'd disturbed him.

Mary stared thoughtfully at him. "She enjoys gardening? We would have a lot to talk about."

Ryan shifted uncomfortably under his mother's gaze. He

should act fast. Except, what if April became serious? He didn't relish the idea of hurting her.

His father let out a laugh. "Your mother hasn't given up hope for you."

"At my age?" Ryan raised his brow, thankful for his father's intervention. "That ship left port years ago, Mum. Besides, Pippa has enough children for both of us." His younger sister had two girls and two boys across high school and college.

"If only she and Richard would visit more often," Patrick said. "Their children are all going in opposite directions."

Mary sighed. "What a pity. A fine, good-looking man like you without a wife or family. Why, you could have settled on Crown Island now."

Ryan reached under the table to scratch the dog's ruff. "That's why I gave you Molly. You're the surrogate grandchild, aren't you, sweetheart?"

Molly barked her agreement, and they all laughed.

Once when he was young, staying on the island had been his dream. He remembered his first love. Plenty of kids went to the Majestic with their parents, but this girl was different. As she wandered through the hotel, it was as if she saw its magic, too. He didn't know her name; he only watched her from afar.

A memory tickled the edges of his mind, and he frowned.

Although he wouldn't admit it to his mother, he missed having companionship, but Crown Island was too small.

Other than the Majestic and his parents, Crown Island had little to offer him. Years ago, the wealthy townsfolk had shunned him and his family, and he wanted no part of them—other than to take their money at the hotel.

Yet, there were things on his list he had vowed to do. Just to satisfy that small boy in him.

As he cleared the table for his parents, he tossed out the idea. "I'm planning several events at the Majestic. First, a VIP reception to meet community leaders. And once the renovation on the Majestic is complete, I'll have a grand reopening. I'd like for you to attend one or both." He wanted to do this for his parents, and he was confident that none of the townspeople would remember him.

His mother and father exchanged looks.

"You move in very different circles," his father said, pressing his lips into a line.

"Mum? I know you'd like to dress up and have a dance with me."

"You know I would." Mary clasped Patrick's hand. "But not without your father."

"Why would you want us there now?" Patrick asked.

"That wasn't my doing before, Dad." Ryan knew what he was referring to. Immediately, a wave of shame and guilt washed over him.

At a previous society event, when Elizabeth's parents learned that Patrick and Mary were attending and they were expected to sit together, they'd done something unforgivable. Elizabeth's father had called Patrick and offered to send them on a vacation in lieu of attending the event.

Ryan's father was shamed and insulted. Patrick declined every invitation afterward. *We don't want to hurt your chances in life,* his father told him.

But now, Ryan wanted to make it up to them in their town. "Things are different now," he insisted. "Would you think about it?"

Patrick shook his head. "Why? To spend a fortune on fancy garb to sit in the back with the help? You know it would be uncomfortable for all of us."

"I became what you dreamed of, Dad. What you wanted for me."

"We're terribly proud of you," Mary said. "Isn't that enough without parading your parents around? Newspapers would be sure to write about this, and your father and I don't want that sort of attention. That's for you, not us."

Ryan understood, but a part of him wished they could be like other families. He had a foot in two distinctly different social classes.

Mary brightened as if that were settled. "Now, let's have your birthday cake."

"I'll get that for you, love." Patrick placed a hand on her shoulder and rose.

"Mum, you shouldn't have."

"Nonsense. We love to celebrate your birthday. It's certainly a day I'll never forget. You were our miracle baby."

"And it was a miracle your mother survived," Patrick added. He carried a double-layer carrot cake, Ryan's favorite.

He was touched and honored. "You never forget what I like."

"It's the least we can do for you." His mother's eyes glittered with happiness. "And the carrots are straight from the garden."

"Then it will be doubly delicious." Ryan kissed his mother's cheek. "Thank you, Mum. I love you. You mean the world to me. And Dad." He hugged his father. For all his success, no one understood him like his family.

Before he left, he tried to wash the dishes for his mother, but she shooed him out of the kitchen.

"That's my job, and it's your birthday. But come back later when you can stay longer. We know the importance of what you're doing at the hotel, but we still miss you."

"Don't forget your jacket, son." Patrick picked up Ryan's jacket and passed it to him.

A ping sounded as something bounced on the hardwood floor.

Patrick bent over. "Well, what have we here?" He held up an etched gold band. "Looks too small for you."

Mary sucked in a breath. "I thought you weren't seeing anyone."

Ryan shook his head. "Don't get your hopes up. That's just something I found on the beach. I'll be returning that to the owner."

Or not, he thought to himself. He had no idea why he'd picked it up, especially after what he'd witnessed. Instinct, perhaps. Yet, returning it would be awkward and potentially even harmful.

Ryan took the ring from his father, shoved it into his pocket, and started back to the hotel.

14

*A*pril opened the door to the city offices and looked around. With its wooden beams, hardwood floors, and large windows opening onto tropical gardens, the building looked like it was designed in a similar style to the Majestic, although the hotel was in a class by itself.

As long as Junie was returning to work, April decided it was time for her to take the plunge as well. She had no time to lose now.

She stepped up to the front desk. "Hello, I'd like to apply for a business license."

"I'll be happy to process that request," the woman behind the counter said. "What kind of business are you planning to operate?"

"A historical society for Crown Island. A nonprofit organization."

"Why, you don't say?" A smile grew on the woman's face. "You must be the one carrying on the torch of history for Ruth Miller. News travels fast here."

"I understand Mrs. Miller had an avid interest in preservation. Did you know her?"

The woman nodded. "She was a peach, just the kindest person you'd ever want to know. Her children should have her old papers unless they've thrown them out."

"I'll contact them right away." The thought of losing precious documents was disturbing to April. She wished she'd known Ruth Miller better. What a loss to the community.

"I'm Hazel." The woman took a piece of paper and scribbled a name and phone number. "You tell them I sent you. Now, back to your application." She began to type on the computer keyboard. "Business name?"

"The Crown Island Historical Society."

Hazel twisted her mouth to one side. "Not very original, but it gets the point across. Place of business?"

"I'll work out of my home for now." April gave her the address.

"I know that address. That's Nurse Raines, right?"

"Ella is my mother."

"Well, you tell her hello from Hazel." She tapped her fingers as if searching for a thought. "You could probably take the space that Ruth made sure was earmarked for the historical society."

April hadn't heard anything about this. "There was a physical location?"

"It's on Orange Avenue next to the library. Backs up to the Majestic. Ruth meant to organize and open the society there, but her health was declining."

"I'm sorry to hear that."

"You can confirm the use with the mayor. She or Ruth's children should have the key. The place is a mess, from what I understand. It's been boarded up for years, and it needs work. Used to be an old dance hall for smaller parties than those in the large ballroom. Ruth told me people held square-dancing nights, *quinceañeras*, and wild Prohibition parties." Hazel chuckled. "Times have sure changed, haven't they?"

"But I want to make sure they're not forgotten. I'll look into the location. Thanks."

If what Hazel said was true, this was an unusual turn of events. April would investigate; that's what she did, after all. Her heart quickened with excitement. This was the opportunity she needed to change her life.

Her idea was taking shape, and she could hardly wait.

On the way back to the house, April took a detour by the address Hazel had mentioned. Sure enough, on the corner of

Orange Avenue by the Majestic was what looked like a vacant building.

She cycled around the back, and just as Hazel described, the other side of the building opened onto the Majestic property. Originally, it might have been one of the service buildings, she thought. And then converted to a dance hall. She recalled seeing old photos of the hotel surrounded by other small structures, their uses long since updated.

A shiver of excitement coursed through her. "Thank you, Mrs. Miller," she murmured to herself. If she could raise the money to transform this property, the location would be ideal for what she had planned.

"ARE YOU READY TO GO?" Deb called out as she banged on the screen door.

"Be right there." As April tied her old sneakers, she recalled how Deb used to bang on her door years ago.

April glanced at herself in the mirror. Her old jeans and slightly wrinkled polo shirt were comfortable, and she'd become accustomed to them. She had packed few clothes in the suitcase she'd brought from Seattle because she thought it would be a short visit. But her mother needed attention, and the separation from her husband lengthened.

Here, she had a few good dresses, and that was enough. In Seattle, she had a closet full of comfortable, dark clothing for teaching, too-small dresses she'd worn when she was younger, and more raincoats and rainboots than she would ever need on Crown Island.

April opened the screen door. "Wow, look at you." Deb wore a hot pink tank top with a short skirt. Not everyone could pull off that look, but with her highlighted hair and toned body, Deb could. She looked a decade younger than she was.

Deb arched an eyebrow at April's outfit. "And just look at you."

"No one cares what I wear around here. Can you ride a bike in that short skirt?"

"These are skorts," Deb said, flipping up the short, ruffled skirt to reveal shorts underneath. "Skirt meets shorts. The mullet version of fashion—feminine on top and playful under—"

April burst out laughing while Deb's face turned red. "You did not just say that."

"Guess I have to lose that analogy," Deb said. "Anyway, I love these for running around town."

"You've got the legs for them. But then, you always did."

"Hey, don't discount yourself. Isn't that what you tell your girls?"

That was true. "But it's easier for you. You're tall and lean, and I was always the shortie."

"We all have to accept what we can't change. You're the brainy one."

"So are you. What were you just saying about discounting ourselves? I couldn't read a set of plans or quote a design job if I had to. And I wish I had your nerve."

"You did in school. You'll catch up fast now that you're not yoked to old what's-his-name."

They laughed together, just as they had long ago. Although April had friends in Seattle, Deb was like a treasured sister. They could tease each other, have the occasional disagreement, and hold each other to their promises and goals. They could be their own wacky selves with each other.

Deb struck a pose with one hand on her hip and the other behind her head. "You think I don't work at this rockin' body? Come to the club and work out with me. You don't have to play golf or tennis to use the clubhouse facilities. And you never know who you might meet there."

"Seriously? It's a little early for that."

"Sweetheart, Calvin has already started another family."

Ouch. "I see your point. But that's not all there is to life."

Deb laughed again. "No, just the fun part. Come on, you deserve a little breakup hanky-panky."

"I'm not even going there," April said, grinning. Even though it had been a long time, she was still married. As if that made a difference to Calvin, but it did to her. She had to make that call to her attorney friend in Seattle.

"Come on. Let's go get those bikes." April slung her arm around Deb's shoulders, and the two friends began walking toward the village. On the island, nothing was too far away, as long as you weren't in a hurry to get there.

They turned onto the main street, Orange Avenue, which really was lined with orange trees. Deb slowed by a boutique, Beach Babes, with sunny yellow awnings and a beach mural painted on one side of the corner building.

"My friend Babe owns this place," Deb said. "We should go in."

"I can't think of anything I need."

Deb glanced down. "Aren't those your old aerobic shoes?"

"Sure. What's wrong with that? They're comfortable."

"Shades of Jane Fonda." Deb made a face.

"What? No, she was way before my time." When Deb arched an eyebrow, April sighed. "Okay, maybe they are the ones I left at Mama's house a few years ago. They're practically vintage now. And besides, I love vintage clothes. They have such history."

"Oh, honey. There's a difference between vintage and just plain tired. Those are long past retirement age, and they're making you look like that, too."

"What's wrong with being a young retiree?"

"Age doesn't matter," Deb said. "What matters is how you look at yourself. Your self-esteem."

April opened her mouth in surprise. "And what are you saying?"

"That you sometimes look like life hasn't been fair, and I mean that in the kindest way. It hasn't been, but we're going to start changing that."

"I've already started," April said, grinning.

"Let's start with some new sneakers." Deb pointed to a pair in the shop window. "How about those white ones with the sparkly stars? They scream fun."

April hesitated before she laughed at herself. "Why not? What would I do without you?"

"Have a lot less fun. We should take Junie shopping, too."

"She's been wearing Mark's pajamas, but she jumped into the deep end and got a job yesterday."

Deb pumped her fists. "That's amazing! Where?"

"At the Majestic. She'll be managing the gift shop, and she's thrilled. Scared, but I know she'll manage."

Deb pressed a hand on April's arm. "Good for her. I can't imagine what it must have been like to be widowed at such an early age."

"None of her friends truly understand," April said, nodding. "She was awfully young to have life come at her like that. Most of her friends drifted away a couple of months after the funeral. They turned out to be just acquaintances."

"Does she know anyone here?"

"Not really. There were some kids she used to play with when she visited here years ago, but I think they've moved. She'll meet plenty of people at the gift shop. Maybe I can pick up something for her here."

"Let me do that." Deb grinned as she walked into the shop. "The honorary aunt can get away with more. Today is your turn to be pampered."

"Hey, Deb," called out a younger woman in trim jeans and the perfect white T-shirt. Even her hair, done in rich mahogany beach waves, was casually perfect. "I've got some new goodies that are screaming your name."

"We're here for April this time." Deb introduced her to Babe and plucked the sparkly pair of shoes from the window. "She wants to try on these."

"A hot trend right now." After measuring her foot, Babe disappeared into the back.

The shop phone rang, and they could hear Babe answer it. "Beach Babes—you know you want it. How can I help you?"

Deb gestured toward a display of a vivid yellow flared skirt with a matching floral top. She lifted the short skirt. "See, skorts. They're everywhere again, like comets that keep zipping around every thousand years or so. Just try this on. For me, please?" She whipped out April's size from the rack and nodded toward the dressing room.

"Okay, but you'll see. I'll look ridiculous." April took the clothes and slid the curtain shut.

After pulling off her old jeans and shirt, she shimmied into the lightweight top and skorts. Turning, she peered at herself in the mirror.

"So? Let me see." Deb pushed back the curtain. "Oh, la, la."

"I'm a history teacher, for Pete's sake. I can't go running around like this."

"You're not one here, so why not? We're on an island." Deb waved a hand for emphasis. Don't they feel great? You can even get in and out of an SUV without flashing the world."

"Comfortable. And kind of cute." The outfit felt better than her restrictive jeans, and it was flattering, covering the right amount of upper thigh—admittedly not her best feature anymore. She'd work on that, she decided. The sleeves were slim and ended just above her elbow. "Boat necklines always looked good on me," she ventured.

"Happy birthday," Deb said. "It's yours."

"But it's not—"

"Call it an early one. You deserve it, and I won't let you say no. Junie is next on my list."

When April stepped out, Babe clapped her hands. "That's fabulous on you. You just took off ten years. Amazing."

"Not too young for me?"

"Everyone dresses like that on Crown Island."

How could she have forgotten? Suddenly, she loved the idea of trying on a new persona. "Okay. May I wear this out?"

"You'd better," Deb said. "Can I be honest? I cringed when I saw what you had on."

Babe held out the box. "Now try the shoes."

While Deb scooped up an outfit for Junie, April slipped her feet into the cushiest sneakers she'd ever tried on. "These feel like they have little pillows inside. Wow, these are so comfortable."

"See? Style doesn't have to be painful anymore, not like those stilettos we once wore all the time." Deb winked. "Now, I only wear them to parties and find a stool to perch on. But hey, they look great. Like jewelry for your feet."

Babe laughed at that. "Deb likes my glittery heels."

"It's been a long time since I've been to anything but the faculty holiday party." As soon as the words were out of her mouth, April regretted them.

Deb touched her shoulder. "Hey, gorgeous. Why the sudden frown?"

"I suspect Calvin met Olga at the last party we went to."

April sniffed. "Come to think of it, I was wearing very sensible shoes."

Deb nodded knowingly. She twirled her around to a mirror. "Look at you now. Flirty yet comfy. Fresh. Playful. The new you. Who says we can't have it all?"

Babe nodded with enthusiasm.

April wasn't sure she was ready for flirty and fresh, even if the outfit was cute. "But I'm still a historian."

"I don't know what that means. Do you usually wear hoop skirts and corsets?" Deb threw up her hands. "And if you say that one more time, I'll throttle you. I don't care if you're the president of a billion-dollar company. Dress however you want when you're not at work. Who's going to care on the island?"

April smiled at her new image in the mirror. "No one but me."

"And maybe some handsome guy who'd treat you the way you deserve. Or no one at all. Your choice, this time." Peering over her shoulder, Deb said softly, "You can be anyone you want to be here. Old what's-his-name is in the past. Why not give it a go?"

All at once, the possibility of remaking herself seemed incredibly appealing. "Won't Junie be surprised?"

Deb laughed. "I'll bring her here," she added, winking at Babe. "And add this outfit to my bill for Junie. It's perfect for working in the gift shop."

Babe rang up Deb and turned to April. "I'll cut the tags and put your things in a bag for you."

April glanced at her rumpled clothes in the fitting room. "I don't really need them. Is there still a shelter here?"

"They'd be happy to get them. Well, probably not the shoes. Shall I toss those?"

"Please," April said in unison with Deb. Laughing, the two women hugged each other.

As they strolled along Orange Avenue, April felt lighter than she had in years. In the next block, she opened the door to Regal Bikes, where she and Deb had dropped off her bike and another she'd found in her mother's garage.

The owner looked up in surprise and let out a whistle. "Wow, is that you, April?"

"Hi, Adrian." She pinched a fold in her skirt. "Deb talked me into this."

"She didn't need much encouragement," Deb added, leaning against a glass counter.

Adrian grinned. "You look amazing. But then, you haven't changed much since high school."

"Now I know you're kidding." Still, April enjoyed hearing that. It had been a long time since she'd had a compliment. "Your message said the bikes were ready."

"Right here." Adrian gestured toward two gleaming vintage bikes. "My son took care of these."

"Sailor, right?" Deb asked.

"That's the one. He brought home another surfing trophy from Hawaii last week." Adrian smiled with pride. "Sailor runs the bike concession at the Majestic when he's in town."

"It's amazing what a coat of paint and new tires will do." As April inspected the bikes, she remembered Adrian, who'd worked here as a teenager when her father had surprised her with a shiny bicycle under the Christmas tree one year.

Only now, Adrian was the one with the gray ponytail, just like his father, April recalled. He even looked like him now. Did they all grow to look like their parents? Adrian was only a few years older than she was, but to an eight-year-old, a gangly teen working in the store with his father had seemed very grown-up.

Adrian called to the back. "Sailor, April Raines is here for those bikes."

From the back, a younger version of Adrian emerged, and April grinned. Sailor had the same easy-going countenance, though his short ponytail was bleached blond. He had the fit body of a strong ocean swimmer. "Nice to meet you, Sailor."

"You have a couple of vintage beauties here," the younger man replied.

"There are more in the garage I'd like repaired, too." She needed a third one for her mother. They could all ride together when Ella was a little stronger. Or maybe Maileah, if she ever came to visit.

Deb bumped fists Sailor. "So how are you and Layla doing?"

The young man made a face. "We broke up. Layla couldn't handle the other women on the beach. I told her they were just spectators, but she's always been jealous, even though I don't give her any reason. I can't deal with that. So, she took off to Florida with some guy she just met." He shrugged.

"Poor Sailor," Deb said. "Love is tough. You need some new friends." She snapped her fingers. "Hey, you should meet Junie, April's daughter."

"Yeah, maybe." Sailor blushed. "I'll be right back with your bikes."

"Don't embarrass the guy," April said, smiling.

A few seconds later, Sailor wheeled out the bikes. One had a fresh coat of bubble-gum pink, and the other was sparkly turquoise. "Back then, these babies were made to last."

"Hope that goes for us, too." Deb admired the shimmery pink one. "Wow, Patty is looking good."

"That's Peppermint Patty to you," April said, checking out the bike.

Adrian chuckled. "Where do I know that name?"

"It's from the Peanuts comic strip," April replied. "My dad used to call me that. I had the same mousy brown hair and freckles. Fortunately, I was a better student than Peppermint Patty, who was in the D-Hall of Fame." A memory popped into her mind. "We were all Peanuts fans back then. You dressed up as Charlie Brown one year for Halloween."

"You remember that? I'd forgotten." Adrian shook his head. "I only remember the rock star costumes. That dream didn't quite come true, though I still jam around town."

"He's at Cuppa Jo's on Friday nights," Deb said. "You have to come with me sometime."

"There's a lot I'm starting to remember." April bent to inspect the new tires. And much she wished she could forget. April ran her hand along the new seat. Or was it a saddle? She'd forgotten that, too. She inspected the turquoise one.

"Do you ladies want to take these for a spin to see if they're alright?"

"I trust you," April replied. "I want to surprise Junie with this one today. I'll bring another one in soon."

"You're teaching history, I heard." April must have looked surprised because Adrian quickly added, "Your mother told me a while back. Are you planning to go back to teaching?"

"It's what I do," she said automatically. Or was it? She'd been married, too. And that was likely over. At least she could still call herself a mother, not that her girls needed her anymore. That is, they thought they didn't.

If only she could be more like her older friend, the supremely confident Ginger Delavie in nearby Summer Beach. Math whiz, code breaker, world traveler once married to a diplomat. Ginger had taught math for a few years in Summer Beach, and April had volunteered to tutor children in her class. Ginger had inspired her to teach, although she had been mildly disappointed that April had chosen history over math. April still enjoyed visiting her.

Or maybe she could be more like her new cousin Ivy Bay. Or her Aunt Carlotta. April had been transfixed by Ivy's story of turning her old beach house into an inn and Carlotta's world travels. How they lived their lives was inspiring.

As if reading her mind, Deb nodded. "You can be anything you want now."

Turning back to Adrian, April said, "I've decided to stay on Crown Island. There's a local history project I'm working on." She didn't want to announce her plan about the historical society until she was sure she could make a living at it. Her plan had to be solid, or she'd have to return to teaching—and that meant a long commute. But now, she felt as determined as Junie.

"That's a great idea," Adrian said. "My dad and gramps told me a lot of stories, too. I think I have some old newspapers and stuff in my attic. Maybe you'd like to look sometime."

"Maybe so."

April paid for the bicycle restorations, then she and Deb wheeled the bikes outside onto the sidewalk.

A couple of kids on skateboards swerved to avoid them.

"Hey, watch it," Adrian called out, his voice gruff.

The boys took off, glancing back over their shoulders.

April laughed. "You sounded just like your dad then."

Adrian grinned. "That used to be me on a skateboard. Now I have to keep them in line, just like he did." He waved and went back inside his shop.

"He's interested in you," Deb said.

"What? No, not Adrian."

"Oh, honey." Amused, Deb shook her head. "'Come look at the old stuff in my attic' is like 'come see my etchings.' You have been out of circulation way too long. I can't believe you didn't keep up better with all the young people you taught."

"They shared a language I didn't know anymore. Somewhere along the way, I missed a memo."

"I have a lot to teach you." Deb motioned to her. "Before I deliver this bike to Junie, let's take a spin around town. Smoothies are on me."

"You're on," April called back. With her new outfit, freshly painted bike, and the sun on her shoulders, she felt much younger than the number on her passport indicated.

In the next block was City Hall, and she cruised along the sidewalk, circling the large, four-tiered Mexican fountain bubbling in front of the administrative offices.

The door opened, and a tall, dark-haired man walked out. *Ryan Kingston.*

Caught off guard, April gave him a bright smile and waved —really, what else could she do? She slowed the bike.

Ryan stared at her and Deb in what she could only describe as disbelief. Then, he merely nodded and stepped back inside the city offices.

That was that, was it? April didn't care. She looked good, and she knew it.

Ryan was the one talking about being neighborly. Well, she'd knock on his door later, she decided. Unless he was avoiding her. Not that she cared. The plant thief was on the loose.

She laughed and shook her hair in the breeze before turning toward Cuppa Jo's.

When she and Deb arrived, they parked the bikes outside and strolled inside.

"Did you see Ryan Kingston?" Deb asked.

"Sure did."

"I worked until midnight on my proposal for him," Deb said. "It's almost ready. I've done the interior design for several mainland hotels, but the Majestic would be a real coup."

"Hi, ladies," Jo called out. "What'll it be?"

"Smoothies," April said, feeling exhilarated after the ride and the fresh air. They ordered the mango-kiwi blend that Jo recommended.

As they sat at the retro bar, April turned to Deb. "I have two things on my mind. One, I'm working on a new plan so I can stay on Crown Island. My savings is small, and I can't expect much from Calvin. So, I just officially established the Crown Island Historical Society."

"A nonprofit?" Deb asked. "Do you think that's wise?"

"Nonprofit doesn't mean no profit. Crown Island has a fascinating history that can drive tourism. I can promote tours, pitch tour operators, and speak to the media about our history. I'm dreaming up angles to benefit the community."

Deb nodded, taking in the idea. "And the Majestic Hotel."

"It would be a beneficiary, too," April agreed. "I would also like to write a book about Crown Island. Maybe create souvenirs to sell in the historical society's shop."

Deb looked surprised. "A shop? Where would that be?"

"The city has a dedicated space. I never thought I'd be an entrepreneur, but then, I never thought I'd be in this situation."

"Listen to you," Deb said, breaking into a smile. "You have my full support. I'll help you make it look fabulous. Now, what's the second thing on your mind?"

April swallowed a surge of anxiety. "Seattle," she managed to say.

Instantly, Deb understood. "I'll go with you."

April put a hand to her forehead, dreading the trip. "I need to pack my things, talk to an attorney, and list the house for sale." And just like that, the life she'd known would be over.

"When?"

"The sooner, the better." She didn't want the past dragging down her future, whatever that might be. "I'll check flights right away."

15

From his balcony, Ryan saw a delivery van stop at the pink house down the street. A young man stepped out with a small plant and hurried to the front door.

"Is that it?" Ryan wondered. The plant had looked larger online. Usually, an assistant would have taken care of this, but Ryan didn't want any word of this getting around as it could give the wrong impression.

What about the impression he was making with that plant? While his plan was to stroll over after it was delivered, that puny plant just made him look cheap.

When he saw April open the door, he started down the stairs and toward the house. This was his chance to see how she lived and meet her mother again.

Surely there would be something that would turn him off. Maybe they were hoarders. Or the opposite. Perhaps it was the kind of pretentious environment where you were afraid to sit on the furniture. He would look for any signs or behavior that would signal trouble.

The rosy pink paint on the house might be an indication of what was inside. But here on Crown Island, the locals like their bright colors.

Personally, Ryan liked the tradition. It made Crown Island look like a happy fantasy land with palm trees swaying above the bright homes and picket fences. It also drew visitors who enjoyed looking at the variety of colorful houses and taking photos. He was considering an advertising campaign for the Majestic that would extoll the virtues of Crown Island, including photos of the more unique homes.

Besides, his parent's home was turquoise.

Maybe he was the one who needed color in his life. Ryan rapped on the front door. A few seconds later, it swung open.

"Hi," April said, clearly surprised. In her hand, she held the note card from the plant delivery. She wore the same short skirt she'd had on when she was riding past City Hall. She'd caught him off guard, and all he could think to do to keep from staring was to step back inside. That definitely wasn't like him, which is why this plan had to work. He couldn't afford the distraction.

"I wanted to make sure you received the delivery."

"That's from you?" April nodded toward the small pot of greenery and read the card. "Wishing you a happy retirement." She looked at him in confusion.

"The florist must have mixed up the deliveries. Maybe they'll be back." Though he doubted it. "For the record, my taste is a lot better than that. I know how much you like plants."

April raised her brow. "I wonder how you might have guessed that."

Embarrassed, Ryan pressed a hand to his forehead. "I didn't mean it like that. I simply wanted to check on you. To make sure you're alright. After that incident at the hotel," he added for clarification, fumbling his way through the English language. This was not like him at all.

"That's a kind gesture, and your neighborhood plant thief appreciates the thought."

An attractive older woman appeared behind April. "Who is at the door, dear?"

"Our new neighbor. Ryan Kingston."

Ryan nodded to April's mother. "We've met before, ma'am. It's been a few years."

"Why yes, I recall." She turned to her daughter. "April, let's invite the gentleman in."

April swept out her arm with a graceful motion, welcoming him.

Strike one against his plan.

Ryan stepped inside. This was one of many original bunga-lows on the street. And regrettably, it looked quite comfortable and well-kept. A faint scent of roses filled the air.

"Thank you for having me," Ryan said.

April's mother extended her hand to shake his. "What a plea-sure to meet you again. Please call me Ella. April told me how quickly you acted when she was in distress the other day. I'm thankful you knew what to do. How did you come by that training?"

Ryan hesitated. That wasn't information he usually shared. In fact, he hadn't talked about it for years. Yet, Ella's question was so earnest and heartfelt. "During college, I worked at a senior care facility. We learned several life-saving techniques."

Ryan waited for her judgment, feeling a little guilty about putting her and April to the test.

After his benefactor died in Ryan's last year of high school, he paid his way through work, scholarships, and government loans. While his college friends from wealthy families skied Chamonix, jetted to London, or sailed to Ibiza, he worked. He was embarrassed that he couldn't join them for movies and parties on the weekends, so he never discussed what he did.

In turn, friends called him the mystery man, a term that followed him throughout school and into his investing career.

"And did you enjoy working at the facility?" Ella asked pleas-antly. Her clear blue eyes held keen curiosity.

"As a matter of fact, I did." That question also threw him off guard, but he didn't mind telling Ella, who seemed genuinely interested. "The residents had fascinating backgrounds. One woman was a mathematician and had worked at NASA for the first moon visit. Another man was an award-winning documen-tarian who had traveled the world with *National Geographic* maga-zine. I enjoyed hearing their stories, and I learned a great deal from them."

Ella led him into the living room, which was decorated in a relaxed coastal theme. White-washed wood paneling and marine-blue slipcovers over sofas and chairs created an easy-care look. Accent pillows of navy and pink echoed the exterior, and tall plants anchored the room. French doors stood open to the ocean breeze. Outside, wind chimes softly tinkled.

Ryan chewed his lip. Though he tried, he couldn't find fault with any of it.

After easing into a chair, Ella smiled at him again. "When you say you learned from them, what do you think made the most impact?"

It was an intelligent question and one he hadn't expected. "I met a couple who were investors. They were still extremely sharp, and when they learned of my interest, they augmented my finance curriculum with real-world advice and guidance." He laced his hands and looked down, remembering them with fondness. "I might not be where I am today if they hadn't taken an interest in me."

Ella nodded thoughtfully. "I've never heard you tell that story in your interviews."

"I've never shared it because it's personal." Ryan had only given interviews on the business channel. "Do you follow the market?"

"My husband passed away when April was young," Ella replied. "A nursing salary only goes so far with a child. I learned to invest so I could make ends meet and put something aside for my daughter's and grandchildren's educations. I didn't want to touch the small inheritance her father left her. That was for her. Of course, I also wanted to have a worry-free retirement." Ella waved a hand around the room. "I might not have the largest house on Beach View Lane, but I'm happy it's paid for."

"Being independent is a good feeling." Ryan was impressed. This is not what he had expected. He half-hoped April's mother would be a problem, but she was quite the opposite. He liked and respected her. From the corner of his eye, he could see April studying him. He tried to avoid admiring her well-toned legs, which were casually crossed.

April leaned in, adding to the conversation. "My mother taught me that financial independence through your unique contributions to the world is a good recipe for life."

Ryan was pleasantly surprised. "I've always thought the same." This is not at all how he thought the conversation would go. His plan was sinking fast. "And what do you contribute?"

"Until recently, I taught history at the university level in Seattle. Now, I'm bringing my experience to the island." April paused. "We haven't offered you anything. Would you care for strawberry lemonade?"

And she had good manners, Ryan thought with a sigh. "Thank you," he said, holding her gaze perhaps a little too long. "Lemonade would be refreshing."

She went into the kitchen, and Ella motioned to him. "I'd like to show you what April is doing for me in the garden. Come with me. I believe she is working with your landscaper."

"Derek."

"That's right. A very talented man."

They stepped outside, and Ryan was struck by Derek's work. "It's going to look nicer than my yard."

"Different, I understand. I wanted a lush, tropical garden look. And spots for April's pottery and mosaics."

"She collects these?"

"April makes these." She gestured to a collection of pots and a mosaic birdbath. "She's talented in many areas."

Ryan gazed at the garden in progress. Paths curved around the yard, and flowers and climbing vines had just been planted against a pink-painted fence, which contrasted beautifully.

"This makes my garden and yard look awfully dull."

"You haven't been there much, but you can change that if you stay." Ella motioned to a lemon tree. "We retained these beautiful old citrus trees. Every morning, I squeeze a lemon or an orange into my water to start the day. Speaking of that, you can try our magnificent lemons now."

April brought a tray of drinks and placed it on the table. "This is our strawberry lemonade."

Ryan lifted a glass and looked closer. Even simple lemonade looked different on Crown Island. "With purple ice cubes?"

"April created that for her daughters," Ella said, smiling. "As the ice melts, the drink changes color. It's become a Crown Island tradition now." She sipped her drink, studying him. "And where did you say you were from, Ryan?"

He grinned. "I didn't. California, mostly," he replied, unwilling to share much, even with her. "I studied on the mainland."

Ryan saw a subtle glance pass between her and April.

Ella inclined her head. "You've picked up our vernacular very quickly."

"How's that?" he asked.

"Most visitors don't use that phrase," April replied. "On the mainland. Usually, only those of us who live here. Or were brought up here."

"Having moved so much, I adapt quickly." He almost wished he could trust them with his secret, but that wasn't why he was here, he reminded himself.

Ryan drank the lemonade, which was as good as she'd promised. To fill the awkward pause in the conversation, he turned to Ella. "As a nurse, do you have a treasured memory where you felt you made an impact?"

Ella smiled as she thought. "I'm retired now, but nurses care for their patients in so many ways. It's hard to think of just one example."

April turned to her mother. "What about that baby you delivered?"

"Oh, yes. That's what solidified my decision to remain in nursing. A young mother had gone into labor, not quite realizing it at first. You see, it was her first child. She was working and planned to have a natural home birth as women did for centuries. However, she had complications. I was there, so I did what I could. Unfortunately, the baby was in a breech position. It took a while, but I managed to turn the infant, and then I found the umbilical cord around its neck." Ella paused and shook her head.

Ryan didn't dare ask the question.

April must have sensed his discomfort, so she finished the story. "Both the mother and child lived. His parents called him a miracle baby." She took her mother's hand and smiled.

"I was a young nurse," Ella said. "That was my turning point, when I found true meaning in my work. We must all find that. Whether we're teaching, running a hotel, or tending to those in need."

"Thank you for sharing that," Ryan said, feeling moved by her story. He sensed how deeply devoted Ella was to her profession and how proud April was of her mother's commitment.

Ella sipped her lemonade and regarded him. "Though I am curious about your plans for the Majestic Hotel. As you know, our community is quite interested."

Ryan was prepared for this question. "I plan to retain as much of the original structure and interiors as possible. The Majestic is a landmark, and while she needs a renovation, I want to maintain her character."

Another look passed between the two women.

April began, "You might know that my mother started the petition to block the modernization of the Majestic. She spoke at City Hall against the plan. So, we're pleased to hear about your idea. We hope you see it through."

Ryan shook his head. "That was my partner Larry's plan. And it was part of the reason for our partnership dissolution." He didn't want to go into Larry's greed, recklessness, or addictions. Larry hadn't been a menace at the beginning of their partnership, but sadly, he turned out that way.

"I followed that, too," Ella said. "You have a large job ahead of you."

"The residents of Crown Island care about the Majestic; it's part of our history and is a major employer." April rested her hand lightly on Ryan's forearm and confided in him. "If your plan is really to maintain the character of the hotel, and you need community support, my mother can help. She knows so many people here. I would help, too," she added.

April's slender hand was whisper soft on his arm. "I will keep that in mind," Ryan said. "And I assure you, that is my intention." He turned to Ella. "I'll outline the plan at a special reception at the hotel for local VIPs. I'd like for you and your family to attend."

A smile bloomed on her mother's face. "How nice. We'd love to, wouldn't we, April?"

"We'll have to check our schedule, but thank you."

April was a little less enthusiastic than he thought she'd be. Then, Ryan surprised himself with an idea. "Would you ladies like to join me for dinner this evening at the hotel?"

April shook her head. "That's kind of you, but I'm packing for a very early trip tomorrow morning."

"Thank you, but another time," Ella replied.

"Of course," Ryan said. Sensing it was time to leave, he added, "I'm glad you're both well, and I should be on my way."

April walked with him to the door. Again, he detected the faint scent of roses in the house. As they passed the opening to the kitchen, a vivid shade of red attracted his attention. Glancing at the kitchen table, he noticed several red roses in a vase with a green ribbon wrapped around it.

"Thank you for the plant," April said, opening the door. "And for checking on me."

His plan having thus far failed—and no longer caring that it had—Ryan reached for her hand, unable to resist the feel of her skin on his any longer. "Will you join me for dinner when you return?"

April's eyes widened slightly. "I'm just separated from my husband. I'm not ready to date."

"I wouldn't call it a date."

"No? In my book, dinner is considered a date."

"And it's too soon, of course." Ryan recalled the scene by the ferry. "My mistake. You're welcome at the hotel anytime with your friends or family."

The smile returned to her lips. "I'd like that very much."

Grinning, Ryan tried again. "Is a bike ride a date? Because that's more like exercise or sightseeing."

April raised her brow. "Not usually a formal date."

"Or a trip to the nursery? I could use some suggestions."

Shaking her head, April allowed a small smile. "Enough with the plants. But no, that's not a date. I'd be happy to go shopping with you as your plant-thieving friend."

Ryan chuckled. "Alright then, it's a d—*not* a date," he said, quickly correcting his near slip.

"We're neighbors," April said. "People around here don't need appointments. We're fairly casual." She wiggled her fingers in a sweet little wave. "See you around."

With mixed feelings, Ryan stepped through the door. Never had he felt such joy to have failed.

Only after April closed the door did it register with Ryan where he'd seen roses like that. Every market sold roses, of course, and surely, most had green ribbons in stock. That must be a coincidence.

He gazed back at the house, questions suddenly racing through his mind. The threat of being exposed was now greater than ever.

Ryan walked toward his house, then continued toward the beach, weighing the potential outcomes of his choices. After years of careful concealment and becoming Ryan Kingston, his persona could be ridiculed and swept away with one careless slip. More than anyone, he knew how fast the gossip flew in a hotel. His parents didn't want the attention, and neither did he.

But then, April wasn't his usual type, which made her dangerous.

With a fresh breeze blowing sense into his addled brain, Ryan made the only practical decision he could. He had to get April Raines out of his mind.

16

"*Maileah*, honey, I'm leaving you another message. I thought I might reach you before you left for work." April hesitated. "I'm on my way to Seattle and want to see you. I know you're busy, but it's important that we meet while I'm there. I'm worried that you're not returning my calls."

After she hung up, she saw Deb heading toward her through the airport terminal. This morning, they wore jeans, T-shirts, and lightweight jackets. Today would be a work day for them, as April had arranged to meet with movers on their arrival.

She'd organized this trip to the minute because she didn't want to spend any more time than necessary in Seattle. She'd allocated one day to sort out what she wanted from the house, which wasn't much more than her personal items and mementos. The next day she would meet with her attorney to file a legal separation and with a real estate agent to discuss the house. There was sure to be pushback from Calvin on the sale, but she had to start the process.

Her eyes sparkling, Deb carried a bag of saltwater taffy. "It's nice to be adults so we can eat taffy for breakfast. Want one?"

"It seems like noon already." They had left long before sunrise to fly from the airport in San Diego. April eyed the bag. "I shouldn't, but that sure brings back memories." She fished in the bag for a strawberry one. "I lost a tooth in this gooey stuff once. It was a hot day in July."

Deb grinned as she chose a lemon one. "You were nine. And we were at that old candy shop on Orange Avenue." Deb spread a hand before her as she spoke. "One more chapter for your book. Saturdays and Saltwater Taffy. How's that?"

"You should be the writer."

"Not me. I just know how to pitch." Deb grinned. "Speaking of which, my proposal for the Majestic is almost ready. I think this could be my best work. A retro beach resort that our islanders and visitors alike can enjoy."

At the mention of the Majestic, April recalled Ryan's visit to her mother's home. When she opened the door, he took her breath away. She never believed he would check on her, as he mentioned at the hotel. She understood that as a pleasantry strangers might say but never followed through on. So surprised was she by his presence, she hardly knew what to say. Her mother even endorsed the idea of having dinner with him. *When you're ready.*

April was still shocked. While she couldn't deny the attraction, Ryan Kingston moved in a different world, even though he lived on her street.

No, she wasn't quite ready for dinner with a hotel-owning jetsetter. She wasn't sure about a bike ride or plant trip. Or, judging by her heart palpitations when he was around, spending any more than five minutes alone with him. Besides, when he could have any model he wanted, why her?

Deb threw the taffy wrappers away. "Hey, you're awfully quiet."

"Taffy." April pointed to her mouth, grateful for the sticky candy.

She wasn't ready to share anything about Ryan with Deb because she knew what her friend's response would be. She'd tell her to go for it, but April needed time. Was she having real feelings for Ryan, or would she fall into his trap? He could be like a cat with a toy, enamored at first, then bored and disinterested.

Deb put the bag of taffy away. "Did you reach Maileah? You can nod *yes* or *no*."

April finished chewing and swallowed the candy. "She's not

answering. I can't help feeling something is wrong. I tried to reach Calvin, too. Total radio silence on him."

She had to sweep her silly infatuation for Ryan from her mind for this trip. Everything she had to do in Seattle was serious.

"I'm not surprised he didn't call you back," Deb said. "Count yourself lucky."

"Not when I'm trying to find out if our daughter is still alive. Maybe I should check the local hospital. They could have been in an accident and admitted together."

Deb turned toward her. "While that could be remotely possible, it's a minuscule chance. Maileah is a brat—sorry, but she's acting like one, at least—and Calvin is—"

An announcement rang out. "Flight twelve-sixty-six to Seattle, now boarding."

April picked up her carry-on bag. "You're probably right. Junie checked Maileah's social media. She's been out almost every night, so I know she's very much alive, at least as of two nights ago. She's avoiding me."

"And probably hungover at work. When was the last time you spoke?" Deb followed her toward the flight gate.

"I called her right after the Calvin disaster." April hoped Maileah wasn't messing up at work, but she didn't have a good feeling about that either. "She was cool to me, saying that most of her friends' parents were divorced. She was only surprised it hadn't happened sooner."

Deb stared at her. "Seriously?"

"It hurts to think about what she said: 'Your marriage has been over for a while. I knew it, and Dad knew it. You and Junie have been avoiding it, hiding out on Crown Island.'"

Deb shook her head in disgust. "That was cruel. And completely untrue. Your mother needed you and Junie. May, excuse me, *Maileah*, would know that if she carved out a weekend to visit Crown Island."

"She won't. She has a new sophisticated attitude and looks down on me like I'm from the provinces."

"The provinces?" Deb raised her brow. "Was that from your French history lesson?"

"That's what she calls Crown Island." April was glad that

Deb was with her. "She thinks the marriage breakdown was my fault for letting myself look older. As if I alone can halt the progression of age in the human body. She said Calvin was naturally attracted to Olga because she was so much younger."

"That girl is in for a rude awakening in about fifteen years." Deb snapped her fingers. "Those went by in a flash."

April showed her boarding pass to the gate agent, who waved them on. "Evidently, several of her friends date much older men. Like their father's age."

"I thought they'd be going for the young tech bros in Seattle."

"These are the tech investors. Much older and wealthier. Yachts, planes, funny money to throw around." More like Ryan, April imagined with a pang.

Deb shook her head. "I can't keep up. I'll take my sweet, artistic, provincial little island over that one-upmanship madness any day."

Once on the plane, they found their seats and sat down. "So, we're on our own once we reach the airport. As a courtesy, I left another message for Calvin to let him know I'm coming."

"It's your home, too. Technically, you didn't need to do that. Say, didn't you provide the downpayment?"

"You remembered." April made a mental note to tell the attorney that. There was so much to sort out. "That money was from the trust my father set up for me in his will."

"How long will it take you to extricate yourself from Calvin?"

"If Calvin agrees to the financial division I drew up, about three months in the state of Washington, give or take."

"Free by New Year's," Deb said with a wink.

April buckled her seatbelt. "I'm not even going there yet." But the idea was intriguing.

"We could go to the Majestic," Deb suggested, her eyes lighting up. "I hope the hotel still puts on its New Year's bash. It's the grandest party on the island. You might meet someone there."

"Maybe," April said nonchalantly.

"I wonder who Ryan Kingston will bring. I've heard he's an actress-and-heiress kind of man."

April's stomach sank. "Where did you hear that?"

"It's been all over the gossip rags for years," Deb stated with an incredulous look. "He never seems to commit, but there's lots of speculation."

THE SKIES WERE gray over Seattle as the flight touched down on the runway. By the time they reached the taxi line, it was drizzling. And when they pulled in front of the two-story, red brick house that had been her home for more than three decades, fat raindrops pummeled her shoulders.

April pulled up the hood on her rain jacket. "Here we go." She didn't see Calvin's car in the drive where he usually parked it, so she pulled out her key and slid it into the front door lock.

"I wonder if he's changed anything yet," Deb said, looking up at the house.

"He didn't mention it. Since he's with what's-her-name now, he's probably not home much. I'll call him again from here. Maybe he couldn't reach my mobile phone when we were in the air."

April turned the key and pushed open the door. Everything was quiet. Her jacket still hung on one of the hooks behind the door. One of her plants was dead in the pot. With the window closed, the air seemed heavy and stale.

"He was never much on plant care," April said.

"Or kitchen care," Deb added, peeking into the kitchen. "What do you want to take?"

"I'll pack some personal items in one of the suitcases I left behind. We can sort through things until the movers arrive and put sticky notes on items for them to pack. I certainly don't need the Ikea furniture that's been through two kids. I never liked it anyway." Although she loved antiques, Calvin disliked anything old. "Maybe Maileah will need some things."

"How about this?" Deb pointed to a photo of April and Calvin on their honeymoon in Hawaii.

All at once, April felt overwhelmed. What should she do with mementos of their life together? "One of the girls might want that. I certainly don't." It would be too painful.

They crossed the soft carpeted living room, saying little.

"This is like looking at a corpse," Deb said softly. "And you're deciding what to pick off and what to let the vulture have."

The memories were almost too much for April. Thankfully, Calvin wasn't there. Still, she didn't want to take too long here.

"There isn't much I care about enough to transport and store. I don't need an ancient blender or servings for twelve that Calvin selected. I'd rather travel light and buy what I want if I need it."

Deb gestured toward a lava lamp on a coffee table. "Calvin's, I'm guessing."

"A gag gift from the holiday party." April blinked back tears that welled in her eyes.

Looking around, Deb said, "Your taste has changed anyway. When you find a place, I'll help you decorate. That will be a lot more fun."

The idea was a welcome relief to her. "You're right. The house doesn't seem like home anymore."

"Come on, let's go upstairs. Sorting through your closet will be easier."

April climbed the carpeted stairs, and Deb followed. The door to her bedroom was closed, and she pushed it open.

A bloodcurdling scream erupted. "How dare you walk in!" Olga shouted in her Russian accent, her blond hair whipping around her bare shoulders...and bare everything else.

"It's my house," April shot back, equally shocked. "What are you doing here, and where's Calvin?"

"At work. I live here." Olga snatched a silk robe from the chair in front of April's dressing table, where she'd strewn a vast assortment of makeup and accessories. Gaudy earrings, open tubes of red lipstick, lacy underwear on the floor.

April felt like she'd stumbled into a bad B-movie set. The air was thick with perfume; it was all she could do to keep from being sick.

Deb put her hands on her hips. "You clearly don't know whose name is on the deed."

"This is Calvin's home," Olga said, whipping the robe around her. "I have right to be here. He is father of my son." She cradled her flat stomach dramatically as she spoke.

"Oops, you dropped your articles," Deb said.

Olga looked down, perplexed, and April let it go. They had more problems than grammar.

Lightly tapping her stomach, April slid a glance toward Deb. The other woman didn't look very pregnant to her. At least, not enough to determine what she was having. But Calvin obviously hadn't remembered that. He was fixated on having a son.

Reining in her disgust, April took a step forward. "This is still my home, and we're staying."

She and Deb had planned to spend the night in the guest room while they worked here, and she'd left a detailed message for Calvin about that.

April was so angry she could scream. Didn't anyone check their voice messages anymore? She'd left at least four voicemails for him. And left a voice message with his assistant at the university this morning. That had been her last attempt.

Olga swept her long hair over her shoulder. "You do not stay."

"You heard my friend," said Deb. "What part of *this is my home* did you not understand?"

April folded her arms. This is where she drew the line. Calvin's girlfriend could go back to wherever she came from for one night. "You have to pack your things and leave."

"I will not," Olga spat out. "Calvin wants me here. I stay."

Although she was nearly shaking with anger, April pulled out her phone and mustered as much calm as she could. "Alright then. I'm calling the police to have you removed."

"I do not believe you." Olga stomped her foot. "Olga will not leave."

Deb wagged a finger. "Olga better, or Olga will be forcefully removed, charged with trespassing, and spend the night in jail."

Olga threw up a hand. "No, no. Wait. I call Calvin."

"Good luck getting through. I've already done that." April held up her phone and wagged it.

She was growing tired of this encounter and would call for help if needed—not the emergency number. Other people needed more help than she did. April just wanted this woman out. No telling what of her belongings this woman had helped herself to.

"Olga will be back," the other woman shouted, her eyes

blazing with anger. She stuffed a few garments into a Louis Vuitton overnight bag and swept her makeup in after them. Next, she stormed into the bathroom.

They could hear her throwing out words in Russian.

Deb clapped a hand over her mouth in mock shock. "Geez, I think that was an especially bad one. You're probably going straight to——"

"Shh. Be serious." Beside her, April could hear Deb snicker, fighting to hold in her laughter.

"Don't you dare laugh," April whispered.

"I can't help it. She's ridiculous. Who talks about themselves in the third person?"

April smirked at her. "Outside of Calvin, you mean?"

Deb's eyes widened in horror. "Oh, you poor thing. As if he's king. What madness is that?"

"Got you. Let's just say I wouldn't put it past him." April managed to lift one side of her mouth.

Deb jabbed her. "At least you haven't lost your sense of humor."

"As I wrote in an article for Calvin, humor in desperate situations is a coping mechanism and a sign of resilience and perseverance."

"You're through with that," Deb said, rolling her eyes. "If I were you, I'd be tempted to toss Olga from that two-story window. I still might."

"I'd like to toss this junk." April looked around the room. Clothes were strewn everywhere. Empty glasses, food wrappers, cigarette butts. "Calvin probably wanted out because of her habits. He hates filth." It was ironic, really. "What a mess he's gotten himself into. I almost feel sorry for him."

"Don't you dare." Deb gestured toward the closet. "See if your clothes are still there."

"Good idea." April opened the door. Instantly, her blood pressure shot up. "I don't believe this."

"What's wrong?" Deb flew to her side.

April stepped aside. Her clothes had been thrown onto the floor, and a dizzying array of garish garments hung on the racks in their place. "She's been here for a while. This is no weekend capsule wardrobe—this is the entire year."

Deb folded her arms. "I wonder where the maternity clothes will go. And since when do well-educated pregnant women smoke? Calvin doesn't, does he?"

"I noticed that, too. That's his problem, not mine. I'm through." Just then, her mobile phone buzzed in her pocket. "It's Calvin. At long last."

"You yell at him while I rearrange."

April stepped from the closet. "You finally decided to call me back? It's only been four days."

"Olga called me in hysterics. What are you doing there?"

"I already told your girlfriend. This is my house, too."

"You shouldn't be there."

"You shouldn't have moved in your Russian girlfriend." This time, April was not taking anything from Calvin. Not anymore. "The least you could have done was to tell me what you planned to do. Or return my calls. Or show me an ounce of respect for all the years I spent with you. Writing your thesis, your dissertation, and your articles. Having our children, keeping our home. Making your boxed lunch every day, for Pete's sake. Plus, making a sizable down payment on the house."

"Don't start on me about that," Calvin snapped. "You weren't working, and I was making the mortgage payment."

"That's right. While I was having babies and doing the work that paved the way for your career, Professor."

"Don't you ever tell a soul about that," Calvin said in a hoarse whisper.

"I have no doubt that someday the truth will finally set you free, if you know what I mean. It won't come from me, but I'm through covering for you. Now, how fast can you pick up your girlfriend, or have you called an Uber for her?"

"She already did. I don't know what's wrong with you, April. You were never this mean before. Deb is with you, isn't she? She's a bad influence, always was."

"Why, because she speaks her mind? I've learned how good it feels."

"I am not having this conversation," Calvin said. "And you'd better be gone by tonight."

"Why don't you stay with your girlfriend, like you should

have been doing. Although, you really shouldn't have been doing that either. Look where it got you." She clicked her tongue.

Calvin exploded, and she held the phone away from her ear.

Just then, Olga emerged from the bathroom. She dumped an ashtray in the trash and shoved it into her bag before she stormed downstairs. Moments later, the front door slammed, rattling the windows.

April brought the phone calmly back to her ear. "And while I have you on the phone, Calvin, since when does an educated pregnant woman smoke?"

Again, he went berserk, and she held the phone away. When he was through, she started over. "May we do this in a civilized manner? I came to pack my belongings, as you wanted. Tomorrow, I will talk to my attorney and a realtor. If we can remain relatively courteous, this will be behind us soon."

"Except for the house. The cost of housing in Seattle has skyrocketed. It's for my son."

"As it has everywhere. Your son can make do without a house, just as our children did before I drew out my inheritance. I will construct a document outlining an equitable division of assets, and you'll see that I am quite fair. I don't want to argue and run up a huge legal bill any more than you do. But I will not be a pushover, Calvin. You were in the wrong, so accept it. And don't think I won't defend my position. Goodbye, Calvin."

Deb stepped from the closet. "Bravo," she said, clapping. "I always knew you had it in you to stand up to that freeloading womanizer—sorry, but that's the truth. He never would've made it to where he is without you." She waved a hand behind her. "Come see my handiwork."

As April suspected, Deb had thrown Olga's clothes onto the floor and put April's back where they belonged, even though they would soon be packed.

"Come here, you." April folded Deb into her arms in a huge hug. "Thank you for coming with me."

"If you're about to say you couldn't have done it without me, you can stop right there." Deb grinned. "That woman I just heard is the one I grew up with on Crown Island. Watch out, world. April Raines is back, and the flood waters are rising!"

April laughed. "You bet I am. Now, the movers should be

here any minute." She looked around the room. "I don't care about most of this stuff, except for photos of the girls and my pottery wheel. This won't take long. After that, we'll check into the fanciest hotel Calvin can afford. The Four Seasons, I should think."

"You still have his credit card?"

April only smiled. "Now, how can I reach Maileah?"

"I have an idea, but you might not like it." Deb looked a little sheepish. "And I know she'll hate it."

"What?"

"I checked her social media." Deb pulled out her phone. "I know where she's going to be tonight."

"Deb, you shouldn't go sneaking around like that." April hesitated. "Okay, where?"

"At a dance club. Maileah is meeting some people at 10 p.m."

"On a work night?" April shook her head. "My daughter would die if I showed up."

"Our mothers did things like that, remember? It's a mother's prerogative. But if we're going to get into that club, we have to borrow some trashy clothes." Deb jerked a thumb over her shoulder. "Especially that strappy bustier dress that still has the tags. Looks designer to me."

"What am I letting you get me into?" April drew her hands over her face. "Still, I need to see Maileah. If I don't, she'll blame me for it."

"And if you do, same thing. Isn't Maileah a little old to be acting like this?"

"She's always been a Daddy's girl."

"And we know what a fine role model he's been."

April cringed. "I should give her a pass on that alone. Still, I know her. In my gut, I feel like something is wrong." She gestured behind her. "You'd better grab that dress."

17

"*I* can't talk," Junie said. "I'm getting ready for work." As soon as the words were out of her mouth, she braced herself for her sister's response. She hadn't meant to tell her she was working. Junie held her breath, bracing herself for Maileah's ridicule.

"You? A job? That's rich. Doing what?"

Junie mustered as much dignity as she could. "I'm managing the gift shop at the Majestic Hotel."

Maileah tapped on the phone. "Hello-oo, we must have a bad connection. It sounded like you said *gift shop*."

"That's right."

"Please tell me you're kidding."

Junie hated having to defend her choices to her sister. "I'm not like you, Mayday."

Maileah muttered something Junie couldn't make out. Then she added, "Come on, Junie. You don't have to punish yourself for Mark's death. If I had your money, I would never work again. Go travel and play."

"I thought you would be happy that I got out of my pajamas. Isn't that what you're always telling me?"

Maileah dragged out a tortured sigh. "I love you, Sis, but I can't believe we had the same parents."

"Neither can I. Mom's been trying to reach you. She's in Seattle."

"I know. But I just can't be around her right now. She's probably moping around about Dad like she always does. What she doesn't understand is that we all have to live our best lives. Olga is actually super fun. You should give her a chance."

"And I can't believe you've been cavorting with the enemy. You helped destroy our family."

"Now you've gone too far."

"You know what? I haven't even started," Junie said, jabbing the air as she spoke. "But I have to go, Maybelline. Good-bye." Junie tapped off the call and screamed at the phone.

"Everything alright in there?"

Junie opened her door and called back to her grandmother. "I was just on the phone with May. She's dodging Mom's calls." She stepped into her sandals and made her way into the living room.

"I have to go, Nana. Are you going to be okay by yourself?"

Ella smiled. "I have been for many years, dear. But if it makes you feel better, you can call to check on me. I always like to receive a real call. That texting just isn't for me. It's so banal."

Junie grinned at her grandmother's use of one of their Scrabble words from last night. "So basic. Ordinary."

"Unimaginative." Ella shrugged. "Derivative, one might say."

They laughed together, and Junie hugged her. "You're the best, Nana. I will give you a real call later. And if you need anything, reach out."

Junie smiled as she left. When they watched *Some Like it Hot*, Ella had pointed out the beach and hotel scenes in which she was an extra. Junie had stopped the movie so they could get a better look. Ella was a knock-out when she was young, though she was still very attractive now.

Junie often caught older men checking out her grandmother, which amused her. She couldn't wait until her grandmother began going out again. She and her mother were making sure Ella ate and slept well, and her cough was greatly improved.

Junie brought out the sparkly turquoise vintage beach cruiser her mother had surprised her with and climbed on. She was wearing the outfit Deb had given her. The skirt with shorts underneath was ideal for cycling around the island, which was small enough that many people rode bikes, walked, or sped around in golf carts.

When she arrived at the Majestic, she parked her bike alongside others in the employee area before making her way toward the shopping arcade.

Junie stepped inside the charming vintage shop that dated back more than a hundred years. Although the walls had been repainted and the wood refinished over the years, the original chandelier, rewired, still hung overhead. Whitley had told her the Majestic was one of the first hotels on the west coast to be built with electricity, which explained why she had so few outlets. Some of the wooden display cabinets were quite old, too.

The aroma of musky aged wood and fresh salt air was a combination forever lodged in her brain. She inhaled deeply, instantly recalling when her grandmother had brought her to the Majestic on spring breaks and summer holidays.

Glancing around, she took a visual inventory and imagined how she would change the shop. For the new look, she was considering a vintage holiday-by-the-sea theme, similar to the old inns that dotted the shores of Nantucket or the Eastern seaboard.

California had its unique flavor, too, with local artists and south-of-the-border influences. She wished her mother had her pottery wheel—she made beautiful pieces that Junie could sell here. Or she could play up the Golden era of Hollywood angle.

Whitley had given her carte blanche in reorganizing and merchandising the shop, within a budget they set. According to the other shopkeepers along the corridor, the general manager was overloaded with Ryan Kingston's new tasks. Whitley was leaving a lot up to her.

Junie looked up as a familiar face with short, tousled red curls appeared at the entryway.

"I'm from the spa shop, and I wanted to say hello again. I'm Faye with an e. Welcome to the neighborhood."

Junie extended her hand and introduced herself. "Whitley hired me as the new manager."

"I heard. The rest of the shopkeepers—including me—lease their spaces. We've been here a long time and have seen many changes. After the longtime gift shop manager crossed paths with the former owner about her budget slashes and left, Whitley hasn't been able to keep anyone in the gift shop very long."

Junie didn't like to speak badly of anyone, so she proceeded with caution. "Did you know the guy who's here before me?"

"He is my cousin." Faye rolled her eyes. "But he's always been lazier than molasses. I heard what happened, and it serves him right. Whitley was just doing a favor for his dad by giving him his first job." Faye gestured toward the merchandise Junie had been piling on a table at the front of the store. "What's all this?"

"I'm having a blowout sale to get rid of everything that doesn't fit my new vision. Most of it looks like it's been here a long time." Junie picked up a bottle of moisturizer and found a sell-by date on it. "This is so old I can't even sell it." She tossed it into a trashcan.

"You sure have a lot of work to do. Let me know if you need any help."

"Thanks." Junie paused. "I'm glad you came by. I don't know many people on Crown Island."

"I didn't think you were local. Where were you living, and what are you doing here?"

Judy told her the abbreviated story of visiting her grandmother and deciding to stay, leaving out the part about Mark's death. Whenever she brought that up, she saw the instant pity in people's eyes. For a change, she just wanted to be one of the girls like she'd once been.

"I couldn't imagine living anywhere else," Faye said. "The mainland is so crowded and busy—just not my scene at all." She tipped her head toward the pile of shopworn merchandise that Junie hadn't sorted. "Need help organizing that?"

"Sure, but don't you have work to do?"

"Most of us are friends here, and we help each other out. Besides, I have a part-timer who can cover for me. And I can see if anyone goes into the shop from here."

"I think I'm going to like it here," Junie said. She turned to the cheap candy counter. "All of this can go."

"There's a local chocolatier you should meet. Her line would work well here. I carry some at the holidays, and people love it."

"Like a taste of Crown Island," Junie said as ideas whirred in her mind. "A unique point of view."

"Exactly."

Junie had traveled enough with Mark on buying trips that she knew people liked to buy things they couldn't find anywhere else. In this case, items that remind them of their vacation. She recalled the unique shoes she and Mark had discovered—the traditional *avarca* leather sandals in Spain, or the woven huaraches in Mexico. They loved them so much that they'd added them to their online store, then sent samples to fashion magazine editors and online influencers. After they were featured, those had become among their top summer items.

She knew there were plenty of local artisans on the island whose work she could curate and feature here. Suddenly, the idea of white monogrammed shirts paled, and her thoughts were alive with the colors of Crown Island.

"One thing you might want to carry are tiaras," Faye said. "You know, this being Crown Island and all. We do a big business in bridal showers. Many women ask for tiaras and crowns."

"I thought you carried some."

"I do, but you could carry a different style. For what it's worth. People love the whole royalty angle. Especially because of Princess Noelle."

"Who's that?"

Faye's eyes sparkled. "More than a hundred years ago, she fled her country and came here. It's rumored she left treasure worth millions here with her lover for safekeeping. But it's said that as the country was invaded, she left to aid her deposed family and never returned. He waited for her but eventually ran out of money, so he took a job here. It's said he stayed to guard her inheritance, certain that she would return someday."

"Why wouldn't he just sell some of the loot?"

"I guess it wasn't the honorable thing to do back then."

"And did she ever return?"

"Who knows? But the last owner, that nutcase Larry, tore apart a guestroom looking for it. As if he didn't have billions already. But supposedly, there was a rare Burmese ruby in the lot. Personally, I think it's a story some former owner made up to fill rooms. I hope the new guy isn't as weird as the last one."

Junie could have shared the story about how Ryan Kingston had saved her mother, but something stopped her. She realized that the people who worked at the hotel were like family. Gossip wafted through the hotel like the scent of old wood.

By noon, Junie had already sold quite a bit of the merchandise she'd marked down. She would have to work on a new merchandise assortment quickly.

She turned over the sign that read, "Gone to the beach. Back soon." She moved the hand on the cardboard clock, giving herself half an hour, and made her way to the employee lunch area. Eager to eat quickly and return to work, she'd brought a simple salad she'd made last night.

When she arrived, she was startled to see a police officer talking to Whitley, who was hard to miss in a lime green jacket today. They held bottles of orange juice that Junie had discovered were provided free to the staff. Whitley turned around.

"Blue, I'd like you to meet our latest staff addition, Junie Raines, who is managing the gift shop for us. This is Officer Blumenthal, who usually responds to handle minor domestic disputes that erupt here at the hotel."

Junie stared at the officer. "It's you," she blurted out. "You're the one who stopped me for rolling the stop sign by our house."

While Officer Blumenthal rubbed his jaw, others in the break room looked up, clearly amused.

"What's this?" Whitley asked. "Have we hired a criminal?"

"I can explain. We're not a bunch of scofflaws," Junie began before she realized the general manager was jesting with her, as her mother would say. Now she had her mother's historical vocabulary running through her brain. She paused, feeling self-conscious.

"It's okay," Blue said. "Even though Junie had an emergency, she was still driving responsibly."

Heads swiveled to her in anticipation of an explanation. "Thank you for helping," Junie said, grateful that Blue didn't elaborate. She recalled how kind he'd been to help her mother into the house.

"Glad I could be of service," Blue said in a deep voice that resonated with her. "I hope you'll be happy here at the Majestic. She's a lovely old place. Nothing like her."

"I'm making a lot of changes in the gift shop. You should stop by." As soon as she spoke, she regretted her words. What a silly thing to say.

Blue held her gaze a moment longer than necessary. "I will." Touching his hand to his hat, he nodded to her and Whitley before leaving.

"He's Crown Island's finest," Whitley said when Blue was out of earshot. "I never worry with Blue on the job. He's seen a great deal of action, and we're lucky to have him here. Today, he quickly diffused the situation, and we asked the husband to leave."

"What happened?" Junie asked, intrigued.

"A guest called security on a couple in the next room. They'd been arguing, and the guest was concerned about the woman's safety. When our security guard arrived, the man refused to open the door. He barricaded it, so that left us no choice but to call the police. We can't risk the safety of our guests."

Junie had never thought about that. She couldn't help asking, "Has anything really bad ever happened?"

A couple of people at the tables looked down quickly, and Whitley sighed. "The Majestic is generally quite safe. But any hotel of this age has its storied past. I'm sure others will be all too happy to enlighten you." He turned to the other employees and wagged a finger in warning. "Don't frighten her."

Junie made a face. "Now I'm scared."

"Not to worry. Our security, or Blue, is a short call away if you ever need assistance."

That thought was comforting. In fact, seeing Blue here—as much as he'd annoyed her the other night—was reassuring. She had a different insight into the officer. Whitley thought highly of him. Maybe she should, too.

18

"*I* feel ridiculous," April whispered to Deb as they approached the line snaking around a trendy night-club in Seattle called Blast. "I'm the same age as these kids' parents. Last spring, I was a respected university history teacher, and now look at me."

The club's thumping music spilled outside, where a string of twenty-somethings with short skirts, tattoos, and vivid makeup were swaying to the beat and ready to party.

April shivered in the autumn night air. She'd forgotten her jacket—a clear indication she was accustomed to Crown Island, where it was still warm and sunny.

Turning to Deb, she asked, "Did we actually do this when we were younger?"

"Don't you remember clubbing on the Sunset Strip in Los Angeles?" Deb grinned. "I'm sure I have some incriminating old photos from the Roxy and the Rainbow. It was glam rock, big hair, and skin-tight jeans. That was so much fun."

"I've blocked a lot of that from my memory bank."

"Trust me, you had a great time. The Whisky A Go Go really rocked. We used to wear strappy tops with jeans and high heels. Remember all those sequins and retro crocheted hippie stuff we found at thrift shops? We thought we were so cool. Just like these kids."

"You still fit right in." Deb had poured herself into one of Olga's skinny strap dresses without remorse, but April couldn't bear touching anything belonging to that woman.

Deb let her gaze run over April's outfit, which she'd fashioned from one of April's old denim dresses she was leaving behind anyway. Deb had taken scissors to the skirt and sleeves, and now she felt like one of her students.

This was a mistake. April felt silly and out of place. "I wish we could've caught up with Maileah at her apartment."

They had tried, but a neighbor said Maileah had been away for several weeks—and she'd been seeing someone new. That news struck April hard because she didn't even know who her daughter was dating. For all intents and purposes, they were living together.

Even though Maileah was a grown woman, April still wanted to know she was safe. That was only being smart and cautious.

Although the worrisome feeling still churned within her, April was having second thoughts about barging into her daughter's personal life. "Maileah will be mortified to see me here, especially in this costume. I should keep trying to reach her on her phone."

"You can't. She's dodging you. I vote for the element of surprise. This might be your last chance to see her for a while. If your gut is telling you something could be wrong, listen to that. Your mom instincts are good." Deb pushed up a pair of tinted sunglasses on her nose.

"Do you need those?"

"They're good for hiding my lines," Deb replied. "I've been watching that doorman. He's choosy, and we have to get in."

April scanned the line. "Maileah might be waiting in line. Let's look for her."

As they strolled along the queue of bright young things in barely-there club wear, clouds of designer perfume and men's cologne wafted into the air. When a light rain began to fall, hoods went up, and umbrellas unfurled.

Just then, April grabbed Deb's arm. "I see Maileah. She's going in now."

"Let's go."

"Wait. If I run up there, I'll only alienate her."

Discomfort tightened April's shoulders. Her daughter was with a group of other young women. A muscular man with multiple piercings and an attitude to match had a burly tattooed arm wrapped around her. Who was this guy? He didn't look like her daughter's type. With his haughty attitude, he looked like he could be dangerous.

Her senses went on full alert.

April wasn't out of touch. She had taught plenty of intelligent students who had all sorts of tattoos, piercings, and multicolored hair. Youth styles were about rebellion, being cool, or emulating their favorite singers. But this guy had a menacing look about him.

April rubbed her neck, irritated that she didn't know much about Maileah's life anymore. Yet, she desperately wanted to talk to her and make sure she was safe.

April chewed her lip as she considered her options. "I can't embarrass her, especially dressed like this. Just look at me. A middle-aged woman masquerading as a young hipster. What was I thinking?"

Deb threw her a look. "You had me squeeze into this designer costume, and now you're backing out?"

"That was your choice." April was drained from the day's ordeal of flying to Seattle and sorting out her belongings with movers. Not to mention the shock of discovering her husband's girlfriend in her private quarters.

April turned away from the line. "My relationship with her is tense enough. If I flounce in there in this get-up, I'll destroy whatever speck of trust might remain between us. She's old enough to do what she wants. I guess I should grant her that freedom and back off."

The prospect of losing her daughter was almost physically painful. If Maileah was making a mistake, April hoped she would come out safe and learn from it. This is where she needed Calvin's help, but he'd be more likely to encourage Maileah's behavior.

A rain cloud swept overhead, pelting them with fat droplets. They'd forgotten an umbrella. Rain splashed April's face. Brushing it away, she pulled her phone from her purse. "That's it. I'm calling an Uber."

Deb caught her arm. "You're right about one thing—you shouldn't go in there. But I can. I'm just her eccentric Aunt Deb —or whatever she wants to call me. An old friend."

"Very old friend. No one here looks over thirty." Even Maileah was looked like a twenty-year-old with a short leather skirt slit high to the hip and a plunging top.

Deb turned a compassionate gaze on her. "Let me try to bring her out. You can talk here."

"I don't have a good feeling about this anymore."

"That's why we're here. And you're right to be concerned." Deb backed away. "Find an awning or share someone's umbrella. I'll be back with Maileah, I promise."

April watched Deb charge toward a group near the front of the line. She brushed away tears of gratitude mixed with rain. Deb was so much more than a friend; she was the sister she'd never had. They looked out for each other. April had taken countless middle-of-the-night calls from Deb, despondent over her latest breakup. To have her best friend sticking up for her now meant more than April could put into words.

Thunder cracked, sending bolts of lightning flashing through the blackened sky. She hugged her arms around her torso, folding in on herself.

At that moment, all April wanted was to go home. Except she didn't even have that anymore. At her age, she never thought she'd be living in her old room at her mother's home. She'd thought that would be temporary, but now, her life was in shambles.

She couldn't afford a home until the house in Seattle sold, and Calvin was likely to fight her. Without a regular job and paycheck, she couldn't even qualify for a rental.

She was far too old for this. If not for her mother, she'd be in real trouble.

A pair of young women motioned to her. "Hey, you're getting wet. We'll share our umbrellas."

April hurried toward the two women, who looked about college-age. "Thanks," she said, shivering.

One of them checked out April's ripped denim outfit. "Cool dress. Vintage, right?" Then she peered closer, and her mouth opened in surprise. "Oh, my gosh. Professor Raines?"

The courtesy title was commonly used, but that struck a nerve. "I was a lecturer at the university. Were you in one of my classes?"

The two young women nodded. "We had you for World History last semester. I'm Hailey, and this is Jordan. We always thought you had such a great name. April Raines. I can't believe you're here."

April nodded. "I'm kind of out of place, aren't I?"

While they grinned at that, April recalled Calvin's issue with her professional use of her maiden name. That had been another source of contention. April had always liked her name. Even if it was a weather description, it was memorable. The real reason was she didn't want her relationship with Calvin to be so apparent at the university. She preferred being recognized for her work, not her husband.

April smiled at the two young women. "I remember you two. You always sat near the door. I hope I gave you a good grade."

They giggled again. "You did, thanks. And you made history sound interesting."

April had heard that before, but she always appreciated it. "That's because I believe it is." She arched an eyebrow at them. "Are you two even old enough to drink?"

The pair grinned sheepishly. "Our IDs say we are," Jordan said. "You won't give us away, will you? I only have a couple of weeks to go. Besides, my older brother is in there, and he looks out for us. Especially Hailey." She jabbed her girlfriend, and they exchanged a private look.

Just like she and Deb used to do.

"I won't say a word." April pressed a finger to her lips.

Hailey glanced shyly at her from beneath her thick false eyelashes. "We're surprised you know about this club. Or like the music."

April leaned in to confide in them. "It's fun for you, but I have to admit I'm not crazy about it. I'm here because my daughter is in there. We're having a...family emergency."

Jordan's eyes widened. "I hope no one is hurt."

"Thankfully, no. It's a different kind of emergency."

The two girls nodded.

"Whatever it is, I hope it works out," Hailey said. "You were one of the coolest teachers we've had. I had a conversation with my parents about one of your lectures. The one about the French Revolution. They listened to me like I was an adult for a change. I remember you said, 'those who cannot remember the past are condemned to repeat it.'"

April was pleased Hailey had retained that. "Santayana said that line, and Churchill also used it, along with a few others. History is a touchstone among people. It must not be forgotten."

"I was surprised how much I liked the subject," Hailey said. "I'm thinking of changing my major. Do you teach advanced history classes?"

April would have enjoyed teaching Hailey and Jordan again. "Unfortunately, I'm no longer teaching at the university."

Uttering those words was painful. At heart, she was an educator and a historian. That was all she had ever wanted to do. Without that, who was she?

"That's too bad," Jordan said. "I gave you a good review and told my friends to take your class."

"I appreciate that," April said. "That means a lot to me, especially now."

"What are you going to do?"

"I've started a historical society on Crown Island. You should visit sometime if you like sun, beaches, and history. The Majestic Hotel is a treat to stay in."

"I've been there with my parents," Jordan said, her eyes widening. "I love that hotel."

A tiny voice nagged at her. Could she really make a go of the historical society to offset her income as a lecturer? Not that she was paid nearly as much as Calvin.

Just then, Deb emerged with Maileah, and they hurried through the quickening rain toward April. "There's my daughter now. But I'm so glad we ran into each other. Have fun and stay out of trouble tonight."

April ducked out from under the umbrella.

"Wait, take this." Hailey handed her the red plaid umbrella she held. "I found it anyway."

"That's very kind of you." She held out the umbrella to Deb and Maileah.

As usual, Maileah had a scowl on her face. Her arms were crossed over her short black outfit that fit her like a band-aid.

She looked April up and down, clearly disgusted with her attempt at blending in. "What do you want?"

"Did you get my messages?"

Maileah shrugged. "I don't have time for your pity party, Mom."

"Fair enough, but I'm doing just fine. Deb helped me arrange my move from the house today."

"Yeah." Maileah rolled her eyes. "I heard."

April tried again. "I wanted to see you before I left because I don't know when we'll have another chance. We'll have to work out the holidays."

"I'm staying here. I already made plans with Hawk." Before April could ask, she said, "You don't know him."

"I'd like to. How did you meet him?"

Maileah's eyes darted to one side. "Somewhere. He's just a guy I met, okay?"

Her daughter wasn't giving her any consideration tonight. "I know you don't think much of me right now, but if you need anything, I am always here for you."

"On Crown Island?" Maileah sneered.

"Whatever you need, how's that? We always have room."

"Don't expect me to run over there. I have a life here, Mom."

"I realize that." April yearned to say more, but Maileah's mind was closed to her. "I just wanted you to know that I love you. And if there's anything at all—"

"Yeah, yeah. I gotta go back inside."

April stepped toward her for an awkward hug. "Love you, kiddo."

"Mom, really." Maileah squirmed out of her embrace. She started back toward the club.

Deb put her arm around April. "We did all we could do. At least she knows you love her."

With a long sigh, April rested her head on Deb's shoulder. "Thanks for that. What was Hawk like?"

"Full of himself. You know the type. Nothing he did would surprise me. He had the audacity to watch us from the door as if he couldn't trust me." Deb hesitated, suddenly appearing reluctant. "And I should probably tell you that—"

"Maileah, wait up." An impossibly long, bare leg with a jeweled stiletto reached out from a black car that had pulled up in front of the club. A tall, familiar blond woman emerged.

Her daughter spun around.

"Olga?" April was shocked they were that friendly.

At that, Olga whirled around. "You two again—you're following me."

Deb laughed. "We were here first, toots."

"What is 'toots?'" Her horrified gaze took in Deb's dress. "Is that mine? Why, you—"

"Ignore them," Maileah said, tugging the Russian woman's hand. "Come on, everyone's waiting for you." She threw a look at April. "Dad got here early and has a table for us."

"But she has my dress," Olga cried. "It is Versace."

Deb shrugged. "Guess he made more than one."

"We're through here." April slid her arm through Deb's, and they hurried down the street. When they were far enough away, she stopped under an awning. "You didn't tell me Calvin was in there."

Deb's face fell, and she clasped April's hand. "I was about to." She opened her arms. "Come here, you."

April collapsed into her friend's arms. "Thank you for helping me with this disaster here."

"It's a mess, alright. You've done the best you could. And you're going to do much better from here on."

"I'm still so worried about Maileah."

"At least Calvin is in there to look after her."

"I suppose." That was only a little comforting. "Let's go. Our reservation at the Four Seasons is waiting for us."

And after that, the rest of her life. Whether she was ready or not.

19

The next few days passed in a blur for Ryan. His renovation plan for the Majestic was taking shape, and he'd hired a general contractor. Work would commence in phases, beginning with roof repair, windows, and exterior painting. Other trades would tend to the electrical, plumbing, and heating systems inside. He planned to roll the renovation across the hotel during the slow winter season and finish by spring with a fresh look.

As he sat in his office finalizing the contract for the renovation, his thoughts turned to how he could broadcast the changes underway to the hotel's most important clientele. While the VIP reception was a start, the hotel needed a multipronged campaign.

With that in mind, Ryan stood to open the windows. The sound of the surf in the distance was calming. Inhaling, he filled his lungs with fresh ocean air. The breeze felt unusually tropical, but then, it was monsoon season. While they didn't expect anything more than a few thunderstorms on the island, the muggy air drove up the air-conditioning cost as guests retreated to the cool sanctuary of their rooms.

Ryan scanned the horizon, where fluffy white clouds gathered. The reception was planned for the terrace. They'd been monitoring the forecast, and the weather would likely be fine. The view overlooking the ocean was spectacular. They'd planned the reception for sunset, so the terrace would be bathed in a warm glow.

Returning his attention to the strategic plan, Ryan drummed his fingers. Ordinary marketing would not be sufficient to increase occupancy as much as required by next summer. The Majestic needed more reservations before the high summer season arrived, and people often made those months in advance.

Ryan took pride in succeeding against the seemingly impossible, but he'd had his share of failures, too.

Not this time, though.

His plan would commence with the reception for local VIPs. The community's support would be critical. The publicist he'd hired had arranged mainland news crews to cover the event and disseminate the story to nationwide broadcasters.

The media had followed the feud between Ryan and Larry during their partnership fallout as Larry took to social media and resorted to name-calling. He had tried to oust Ryan for blocking his raid on properties. If Ryan could follow up with a success story for the media, that would be a win.

After all, the Majestic Hotel was a national treasure.

Footsteps sounded outside the door, and he rose from his desk. "Whitley, is that you?"

"Yes, sir?" His general manager stopped at his threshold.

"What did you just say?"

"Mr. Ryan," Whitley corrected himself.

Ryan shook his head. "Is that as casual as we can get?"

"I'm afraid so. Old habits die hard." Whitley smiled and stepped inside. Today, his jacket of choice was a vivid peacock blue. "What can I do for you?"

Ryan laced his fingers behind his neck and stretched. "Give me a good report on the reception plans."

"Everything is ready," Whitley said, beaming, "The buffet, entertainment, florist, and photographers. The staff is very excited, too. Judging from the RSVP list, we can expect a crowd on the red carpet, which we'll roll out for them. Everyone is curious about plans for the hotel, and they're eager to meet the new owner."

"Well done." Ryan gestured to the contract on his desk. "As to the renovation, the contractor will begin as soon as we have permits from the city, which shouldn't take long." Even without bribes, Ryan thought, satisfied with the progress. "We'll stagger the renovation schedule so we can manage guest reservations. Do you foresee any problems with that?"

"We'll manage," Whitley replied. "I'll instruct my team to set guest expectations in advance. We'll be prepared to extend special perks to those who might be inconvenienced." Whitley stroked his chin. "As long as we adhere to a strict schedule and accurately project our available room inventory, we can still accommodate guests."

"No one better to execute than you, Whitley." Still contemplating his plan, Ryan shared his thoughts. "Here's the deal. What we do now will drive our summer season. We have a great opportunity this holiday if we can work fast enough."

Whitley raised his brow. "That's not long. What do you have in mind?"

"Hear me out. The holiday season, from Thanksgiving to New Year's, is when locals gather at the hotel for family dinners and parties. How are reservations going, by the way?"

"Not good. Likely due to the quality of our cuisine last year. Larry also fired some of the favorite servers and bartenders here."

Ryan ran a hand through his hair. At times, it seemed he was plugging a leaky vessel, but he would not allow it to sink. "First, see if we can get them back. Locals like familiar faces."

"I'll reach out today," Whitley said, nodding his approval.

"Next, ask Giana how she's doing on the new holiday menu. We'll need to publicize that." Only on Crown Island did a new menu make the news, but that's how ingrained the Majestic was in the hearts of locals.

"It's ready."

"Good. We'll start the holiday campaign early."

"I'll make sure you have what you need." A smile grew on Whitley's face. "Guests are commenting on the flowers lining the entryway. People can see the changes under your new management, even though they're small."

"We'll have more changes soon." Ryan ticked off his mental list on his fingers. "To kick off the holiday season, I want Stafford throwing the switch on brand new lights and decorations on the front lawn. Update or replace the candy house and menorah. Decorate that old pine tree to the hilt and bring in the faux snow. We'll give people a Majestic Christmas and holiday season they'll never forget."

"Yes, *sir*," Whitley exclaimed.

Ryan chuckled, letting it go this time. "The New Year's Eve ball is the social event of the year for Crown Island. This year, it will be spectacular."

At that, Whitley frowned. "That's different. The New Year's Eve party draws many out-of-town VIP visitors, but we've received few reservations after last year's disappointing event. We can put out all the press releases and throw a huge party, but those guests are less forgiving than locals. Word will spread that the Majestic is still tired. You can't put paint on a pig, Mr. Ryan. You said yourself that we won't complete the remodel until spring. We might consider canceling the ball unless we begin to receive reservations."

Ryan shook his head. "I respectfully disagree. This is our chance to unveil the new Majestic Hotel, and I have an idea how we can pull it off."

Pacing the office, Ryan continued to outline his thoughts. "Rather than starting work on half the guest rooms, the contractor agreed to split the work. The public rooms will be completed first to showcase changes and give guests a preview. A good designer can manage that."

"Have you engaged one yet?"

"Today." Ryan paused by his desk and tapped the proposal he'd received. It was sound, reasonable, and most of all, the designer could start immediately.

"We'll pitch Deb Whitaker to the media as a rising design star of the west coast, carefully selected to bring the Majestic Hotel into the current century. By Christmas, we can unveil the new lobby décor, and by New Year's—with the help of special lighting—the ballroom will look magnificent."

Whitley raised his brow. "Are you sure we can do this?"

"I know we can. Deb has a reputation to maintain, and she's hungry for this job. She's the right one for it. And you have a carte blanche budget for this. We don't succeed by going halfway."

Ryan wasn't going down without giving the Majestic Hotel his best. That's the least he could do for the grand old lady.

Whitley broke into a smile. "That's the attitude we've needed at the Majestic."

"Let's get to work." With deliberate nonchalance, he added, "And Whitley, if you see April Raines on the property, please let me know." He'd been thinking about her but hadn't seen her at her mother's home. His balcony had a good view of the front of the pink house.

"Of course. Might I ask why?"

Ryan wasn't prepared for that. "Since she choked on that lumpy strawberry smoothie, I've been concerned about the hotel's liability. I want to make sure she's well taken care of when she's here."

"I don't think she's the type to sue."

"We can never be too sure, can we?"

"I've known her mother, Miss Ella, a long time," Whitley said, springing to the defense. That's not the way April was raised."

Ryan detected the change in his general manager's demeanor. "I don't think I've ever heard you speak about Mrs. Raines like that," he said lightly. "Is there something I should know about?"

Whitley's face turned red, and he struggled to maintain his composure. "Miss Ella is a fine woman, and she's done a lot for the community, including the Majestic. She went up against Larry, rallied the community, and got his half-baked modernization plan blocked. I wish you'd seen her in action."

Ryan folded his arms, listening.

"This summer, I worried we might lose Ella," Whitley said, his eyes blazing with emotion. "I believe the tireless effort she put into the hotel case brought on her pneumonia. Thank goodness April came when she did." He ran a finger around his shirt collar and composed himself. "That's what I think. But if I see April, I will let you know. As long as you don't intimidate her."

"Well, I deserved that." Ryan raked a hand through his hair. "It seems you're fond of her mother."

Whitley allowed a small smile. "I suppose I am."

"They're a good family. How is Junie working out at the gift shop?"

"She's taking charge. Junie came with a great deal of experience, not like other applicants we would have had."

"You made a good decision." A sudden gust of wind blew papers from Ryan's desk. As he scooped them up, he noticed the high, fluffy cumulus clouds growing on the horizon. "Any news on the monsoon weather forecast?"

"This is normal this time of year," Whitley replied. "The unstable, humid air carries moisture from the sub-tropics. A little uncomfortable, but the large monsoonal clouds usually dissipate quickly."

Ryan knew the odds were low for anything more than sudden showers. "In any case, make sure we're prepared to move the open house party inside."

His general manager left his office, but thirty seconds later, he was back.

"She's here."

"April? Where?"

Whitley led him to the bank of windows across the hall. He peered down from their second-story vantage point. "On the beach, talking to Sailor, who runs our bike concession. His father Adrian owns Regal Bikes in the village."

Sailor was a fit surfer type with blazing blond hair, but he was far too young for April.

"I'll take an early lunch." Ryan clapped Whitley on the back and rushed downstairs, weaving through the cafe and slowing when he reached the sand.

Sailor had turned to help a family with their bikes, and April was walking along the beach.

Ryan trotted toward her, not caring what the staff thought. He felt an urgency to talk to her again.

When he was within earshot, he called out, "April, welcome back."

As April turned around, the breeze caught her hair, and he resisted the urge to brush it from her face. With her short, blue cotton sundress and sand shoes, she looked at home on the beach. A delicate gold heart pendant twinkled at her chest, and he wondered who it was from. Not her husband, he decided. "How was your trip?"

She turned her face up to his. "Eventful. I'm glad to be back. I went back to Seattle to settle some personal business."

"I hope it went well." Ryan's dress shoes slipped on the sand. "I was just taking a break on the beach. Would you like to walk together?"

"Sure." She seemed surprised.

"I understand Junie is working out well at the gift shop."

"She loves working there. I'm so happy she found something she enjoys."

"That's important for all of us." Ryan put his hands in his pockets. He hardly knew what to say. "I saw you talking to Sailor."

"His father is an old friend. I've known Adrian since child-hood. If you need a bike, you should stop by his shop. He's been repairing our old models." She snapped her fingers. "But you must have a bicycle, right? You mentioned going for a ride."

"I figured I'd buy a nice one to have here."

"I see. Well, I suppose you can."

Ryan felt a little foolish. The way she said that sounded like she thought he bought his way out of everything. In a sense, maybe he did. To him, money was a tool to achieve his goals. But it hadn't always been that way.

April's gaze dropped to his feet. "Those are awfully nice shoes to wear on the beach. They might get ruined if the water—"

Just then, April screamed and pushed him away from a wave that rushed toward them. Ryan took her hand and leapt away from the water.

Laughing, they staggered onto higher ground together. After stumbling to her knees, April grabbed Ryan's arm. He lifted her to her feet in a swift motion. For a few seconds, they held each other's gaze. Ryan hardly dared to breathe, and then April laughed, breaking the tension.

"That was close," she said.

As April brushed sand from her legs, Ryan ached to help.

"There," she said, shaking off the rest. "We can walk in the street."

"Let's stay here. Hang on." Ryan eased onto a boulder, slipped off his Italian loafers, and stuffed his socks into them. The sand under his feet felt good, connecting him to nature. He'd missed this.

April motioned toward his trousers. "Might want to roll those up, too."

"I'm all in." While shorebirds squawked around him, Ryan cuffed his slacks and rolled them up to his knees. He picked up his shoes and spread his arms, drinking in the smell of the ocean and the scenery around him. Instantly, his spirits lifted. "How's that?"

"Much better," she said, her green eyes blazing. The sun flashed on the golden streaks in her hair. "Have you been to the beach since you arrived?"

Other than when he'd walked to the edge of the sand, he couldn't say he had. "I hate to admit it, but I haven't. We've been working on the VIP reception and renovation plan. We'll see you at the reception, I hope?"

"My family is looking forward to it," April replied. "You must be awfully busy with the new plans for the hotel."

"We all are," he said, confiding in her. "I have a good team, but it's a stressful project."

"Then it's good for you to take a short break." She drew a breath and swung her arms. "I love to walk on the beach and listen to the waves. They remind me that life goes on regardless of our challenges. That helps me put things in perspective, especially now."

He longed to know everything about her. "What sort of things?"

April raised her chin. "I filed for a legal separation in Seattle and moved out of my home. I am now a full-time resident of Crown Island."

Inside, Ryan was rejoicing, but he realized she had just gone through a major upheaval. "I'm sorry. You lost a lot of years."

"There were some good ones, until they weren't." She shook it off, brushing her hands.

"Do you think you'll be happier on the island?"

"I love it here." April looked up at him with a playful smile on her lips. "Now let me see you squish your toes in the sand."

"Excuse me?"

"Squish, like this." She slipped off her sand shoes and smoothed her toes into the wet sand. "Try it, and tell me what you feel."

Ryan did as she instructed. The sand was cool under the top layer. Feeling more relaxed, he wiggled his toes, recalling how much he liked to run and play on the beach as a boy.

"That feels good." He gazed down the beach. "As a boy, I used to spend hours on the beach building sandcastles, tossing balls, and racing the waves. I'd forgotten how much fun it was."

What he didn't share was that it was this beach. Before she could ask, he said, "Tell me about growing up here. What was it like?"

"Most of all, I remember being outside a lot. Beach barbecues, building sandcastles, beach volleyball. When my father was alive, we used to sail. We biked all over the island, of course. We'd pitch in to help people paint their houses or have art projects and plays in the park. Sometimes we'd help rescue wildlife after a storm. There was never a shortage of things to do."

Ryan listened, recalling some of the same memories, though on the other side of the island, a world away.

He slowed, taking in the island through April's fresh lens. The colors around him grew more vivid, and the air seemed sweeter. The sound of her calming voice against the mesmerizing surf was the music he'd been missing from his soul. She was so full of life he could listen to her for hours.

When he finally looked away from her lovely face, he realized they had walked all the way back to Beach View Lane. A stark white house on the corner stood out, unfinished and unloved.

"I never saw my house like this. From a fresh angle, I mean. It looks…"

"Like a blank canvas," she finished.

"That's right. Do you think there's hope for me?"

April laughed. "Nothing a little sunny yellow paint can't fix. Or, are you more of a periwinkle blue type?"

"How about both?" Ryan smiled. He'd been enjoying her company so much that he'd forgotten to look for cracks in her façade. Worse, he was beginning to realize she didn't have a façade.

He touched her hand as he spoke. "You remind me of someone I used to know as a kid."

"Who was that?" She turned to him with a curious look.

"A little girl I used to see around."

"On the beach?"

"Sometimes. She had your eyes. And even your laugh, now that I think about it."

"What was her name?"

Ryan shook his head. "I never knew. I was too shy to talk to her."

"You, shy? I find that hard to believe."

"It's true. I wasn't always Ryan Kingston, master of the universe." He was only half kidding, but he was enjoying their banter.

"No? Then who were you?" She turned her sunny smile up at him. "Who are you really?"

Her words struck him. He dropped his shoes and took her hands in his, mesmerized by the feel of her skin on his. "It's funny you should say that. I thought I'd forgotten, but he's starting to come back to me."

April didn't pull away. "It must be the magic of Crown Island."

Ryan gazed into her eyes and bent his head, leaning in to do what seemed entirely natural. Savoring the anticipation, he could almost taste her kiss. He closed his eyes.

Suddenly, someone called out, "April?"

With the spell broken, Ryan took a step back.

Deb Whitaker had been running on the beach with a dog, and now she stopped near them, jogging in place. "And Ryan. Oh, hello." Surprise was evident on her face.

The fluffy dog, some sort of collie or shepherd mix, jumped to greet April.

"Down, Duke, sit," Deb said, pulling his lead.

April tucked her hair behind her ears and bent to pet the dog behind the ears. She seemed self-conscious, too.

"I wanted to ask you about something." Deb's gaze slid toward Ryan.

"Go ahead," Ryan said. Giving them some space, he walked to the surf to rinse off his feet. As the two women spoke, Ryan looked back at April, weighing the situation.

She wasn't a supermodel or an heiress to a fortune, but he no longer needed that puzzle piece to complete his image. April was a lot like him—the real Ryan Finley. A scruffy beach kid from the island. Maybe she'd had a few more advantages in the beginning, but life had kicked her around, too. He had an overwhelming desire to be there for her, to prove that she could have a second act in life.

Because that's what he wanted, too.

If Ryan Kingston were to survive, this relationship would not work. Talking to April was the easiest, most natural conversation he'd ever had with a woman. He almost slipped when she talked about growing up on Crown Island.

More than that, he wanted to slip. He had an aching desire to unload and tell her everything. That's how his parents lived, sharing the minutia of each day, laughing, and reminiscing together—and that's what he wanted now. Maybe it wasn't too late.

Maybe he could start again.

And then Ryan remembered who he had become. He remembered the responsibilities he shouldered at the hotel and the many whose livelihood depended on his success. If he revealed himself to April and the relationship soured, he also stood to lose Ryan Kingston, his carefully crafted image trusted by his valued investors and banking partners. If he ever really existed at all, that is. And that character owed Ryan Finley everything.

Without his alter ego, the Majestic wouldn't stand a chance. If he failed, investors would pluck the Majestic from bankruptcy, likely raze the old hotel, and build a soulless resort on the ashes of its bones.

April finished talking to Deb, and her friend continued her run along the beach.

Turning back to April, Ryan took her hand again. He wished they'd had that moment, at least. Quickly bringing her hand to his lips, he did the next best thing, only this time, he lingered, savoring the warmth of her skin on his lips. And then, he released her.

"I have to go, but it was good to see you," Ryan said, his voice sounding hoarse, even to his ears. "And I mean that. Don't ever forget that."

"Wait," she cried. "Who are you?"

It seemed as if she were staring into the essence of his spirit, searching for the answer. He didn't even know if it was still there, although she'd given him a glimpse today.

Overwhelmed, Ryan hugged her, then stepped away. "I have work to do," he said, his voice cracking with emotion.

And then he turned, leaving the heart of Ryan Finley with April while he made his way back to the hotel.

Near the hotel, he stopped to dust sand from his feet and put his shoes on. A sense of loss left him hollow, but he couldn't dwell on it. He wondered how many people might have seen him leave with April. It didn't matter. Gossip blew over, and everyone would forget soon enough.

Ryan strode toward the rear entrance that opened onto the beach. The cafe looked busier than usual today, probably due to the new menu. He nodded toward the servers.

Whitley stood to one side, just outside the cafe entrance, where a few women waited to be seated. "Excuse me, Mr. Ryan. The contractor has arrived. He's looking at the lobby now."

Before Ryan could answer, a voice cried out.

"Why, Ryan Finley, as I live and breathe. It is you, isn't it? I couldn't work out if you were the same fellow with a new name."

As heads swiveled in his direction—guests and staff alike—Ryan felt his dignity torn to shreds. First April, and now this.

"Very nice to see you," Ryan said. At a momentary loss for words, he leaned on pleasantries. The woman seemed familiar. He couldn't place her, but she must have known his family. She was among the group waiting for a table.

Whitley swung into action. "I believe your table is ready, ma'am. This way, please."

With a courteous nod to the group, Ryan strode toward the lobby, but he could already hear whispers. It might not be long before people put it together.

"Not only that," the woman was saying in a loud voice. "He was born in this hotel. I have it on good authority."

That didn't take as long as he'd hoped. Ryan steeled his emotions. He could see the headlines shouting the news now.

Impoverished baby, born at the Majestic Hotel, now the owner! Or, *Ryan Kingston, millionaire investor unmasked!*

Staving off his emotional turmoil, Ryan clenched his jaw. He had come full circle. But he didn't want the notoriety, and such gossip might very well damage the hotel. Not to mention his relationship with his investors. And then, a sickening thought occurred to him.

He'd have to call his parents right away to warn them.

20

*A*pril jiggled the key in the old lock on the storefront door, trying to avoid getting years of grime on her new white shirt. "Come on, open." The unusually muggy afternoon wasn't helping her frustration.

This morning, she put on a new pair of jeans she bought at Beach Babes, pairing it with what Babe called the perfect white shirt. With her wedge shoes and a new pair of vintage 1950s Trifari earrings she'd found at a yard sale, she felt very put together.

Yesterday, she visited the Miller family, and they gave her the key to the building their grandmother had, along with local historical projects Ruth had identified—many of which April knew about. She was thankful that Ruth had negotiated with the city for the right to use this space to house a historical society before she passed away. April was committed to continuing this legacy.

She tried turning the key the other way, wondering when the last time anyone had been inside.

She could hardly wait to see inside—if only the lock would cooperate. April had already started work on a fundraising plan to support the historical society. In her work at the university, she often met with historical societies to conduct research. By bridging the past and present, these organizations and their committed volunteers furthered the understanding of history in their communities, provided educational opportunities to schools, and helped future generations appreciate their heritage. She was eager to make this contribution to Crown Island.

April tried the knob again, then turned the key the other way. She understood how historical societies raised money. Events that added to the quality of life were important, as was cataloging historical details about Crown Island. She was growing more confident, and this was just what she needed. She knew she was uniquely qualified to do it.

Just then, a golf cart pulled into a parking spot in front, and Deb stepped out. Wearing navy slacks with heels and a striped mariner sweater, she looked like she was going somewhere. "You're not answering my calls?"

"Only because I know what you're going to say. What happened on the beach...I didn't expect any of that."

"You don't waste any time," Deb said, sauntering toward her. "Every unmarried woman on the island will soon be gnashing their teeth at you when they find out you've snatched Ryan Kingston out from under them—even before the official VIP reception."

"It wasn't like that." April wasn't sure she wanted to attend, although her mother and Junie wanted to.

Deb stopped in front of her. "Most of them didn't even stand a chance, myself included. Not that Ryan is my type. I'm happier with landing the design job at the Majestic. That's what I really wanted to tell you. I'm on my way to pick up the retainer check now. Before it rains."

"That's wonderful, Deb. Congratulations. Now I feel guilty for not calling you back." April brushed her hair out of her eyes and looked up at the monsoonal clouds above. High humidity and a chance of thunderstorms had many people on edge. Herself included.

April stepped back. "Do you want to give this lock a try?"

"Sure. Let me see that." Deb took the key from her. "I really have to hustle with this job, though. Ryan wants new furniture in the lobby in a matter of weeks."

"Can you manage that?"

Deb grinned. "You bet I can. I have good sources, and I'll

figure it out." Deb twisted the key with all her might until the lock clicked. The door creaked open. "Did you bring a flashlight?"

April shook her head. "We can pull up the shades over the front windows, and I have a light on my phone. That should be enough."

With great anticipation, April stepped over the threshold. The space was dark, dank, and dirty, but to her, it held tremendous promise. Despite that, she wrinkled her nose at the musty odor. A good airing would eliminate most of that.

"I'm so surprised to have found this space," April said. With the shop fronting busy Orange Avenue, the location was excellent for foot traffic. "The Miller family told me this building was part of the original Majestic Hotel compound. The retail shops on the street were laid out later and attached to this building."

Deb followed her inside. Gingerly, April rolled up the shades, and sunlight streamed into the space through the smudged windows. Wooden floors and a finely crafted wood ceiling were clear evidence that this had been one of the original hotel buildings. She could just imagine the parties that took place here. Perhaps she could locate some old photos at the hotel.

"It's dusty in here." Deb paused to sneeze. "I wonder if Ryan is aware of the city's agreement for this building. He didn't mention it."

"I confirmed that the historical society has a long-term lease on it." April gestured toward the rear. "The back of this building should open onto the Majestic Hotel grounds. I could have two entrances, one from the street and one from the hotel side."

She had noticed another wide door on the side, as this was built on what was now the corner. In her mind's eye, the years fell away, and she could imagine how the space might have looked more than a hundred years ago.

She nodded toward the side door. "That was probably used for carriage deliveries."

"By horse and buggy?"

"The Majestic was built before automobiles. I can hardly wait to piece together old plans and photos." Doing this work, April would be in her element again, and she could hardly wait to begin. "I'll study the old photos in the hotel. Perhaps they have old records as well."

"I'm under strict orders to retain all photos used throughout the hotel. I'm designing around them."

April nodded in relief. "I was worried about what would happen to them during the renovation. I would store them here if I had to."

"You won't have to," Deb said. "During my first meeting with Ryan, he made it very clear that no expense would be spared to preserve the original architecture. That extends to the furnishings and artwork as well. He has great respect for the history of the Majestic and Crown Island."

"I'm glad to know that." That meant a lot to April. After living with ordinary furniture for years, she looked forward to a home she could fill with meaningful antiques and artwork.

Deb pulled out her phone and began to snap photos. "I'll send these to you. What would you like to do with this space?"

April spread her hand in the air, laying out her vision. "I plan to construct a timeline from the ancient era to the indigenous Chumash era, then to early European settlers and the hotel and village development. I'd like to enlarge and post photos with the timeline around the room. In the middle, I'd like displays of local artists and jewelers, particularly those employing old methods or vintage styles. Works will be for sale, with a portion going to support the Society."

She turned on the light on her phone, illuminating the space and giving Deb more light. Dust particles floated in the air.

"Skylights would make a huge difference," Deb said. "I'll talk to my father about donating labor and materials. That won't be a large job."

"I'd appreciate that." April would need all the help she could find.

"We'll figure out what to do with the windows, too." Deb ran her hand along the wainscoting, inspecting the old architectural trim. "The proximity to the hotel will help. You could open the rear door to attract hotel guests. Once the hotel is underway, I can help you with this space. You'll need an army of volunteers to make it habitable."

"Hazel at the city is already rallying residents for me," April said. "She knows several retired people who could use something to do. Their family memories and skills will bring value, so we can help each other. I'll start cleaning this place right away."

"I'll bet Ella will love spending time here," Deb said. "Having you and Junie return was a stroke of luck for her."

April smiled at that. "Mama loves the idea." Deb regarded her mother as an aunt, and the two were close.

Deb paced off a rough measurement, her heels clicking on the old wooden floor. "How do you plan to divide the space?"

"That's where I'll need your help. In the front, I envision an educational space for children and adults." April walked to the door. "I want to open this up to showcase and promote events like walking tours, benefit dinners, and auctions. Even though the rent is free, I'll need to raise funds for utilities and event programming."

"Larger windows will help sidewalk visibility." Deb brushed the dust from her hands as she spoke. "And those are great ideas. I can just imagine an annual benefit ball in period costume."

"That's a good idea." April put her hands on her hips, surveying the empty room. "I wonder why the hotel stopped using this space?"

"I wonder about a lot of things, too," Deb said, arching an eyebrow. "Like why my best friend didn't tell me she was seeing the most eligible bachelor in town."

April's heart thumped. She had been holding back, but not for the reason Deb thought. "What you saw...I don't know if it was real. We had such fun and a great conversation. Then, for a split second, I thought Ryan was going to kiss me. Until you came charging across the sand with Duke, that is."

"If I had known, I would have turned around. I hope I didn't ruin your chance with him." Deb slid her gaze toward April. "Is that something you wanted, though?"

April thought about that. She was certainly old enough to know what she wanted by now. And what she didn't. Yet, she'd been thinking about little else these past few days.

Finally, April nodded. "I would have liked that. I don't know why, but we have a strong connection." She hesitated, searching for the right words. "It's as if he has something important to tell me but can't bring himself to do it."

Deb threw up a hand. "That's never a good sign, trust me. It's usually a wife or fiancé in the background."

"I don't think so. I know what that's like. No, it's something else."

"Money laundering, drugs, gambling?" Deb reeled off the possibilities. "Nothing surprises me anymore."

April shook her head slowly. "None of that. Ryan is quite private. But the day before we left for Seattle, he visited me at the house."

"What? And you are just telling me this?"

"I didn't know what to think of it myself. He even sent a plant. Well, not the one that actually arrived, but another one. There was a mix-up."

Deb waved her hands in confusion. "Wait, I'm lost. Why would he send you a plant?"

"The day I had lunch at the Majestic with the Bay family, I choked on a strawberry."

"You told me about that. That's why he sent you a plant?"

April knew how odd it sounded. "That surprised me, too. But he told me he'd check on me. I think that was his way. Nevertheless, he and my mother spoke at length. Did you know my mother believes he might have saved my life?"

Deb swept her hand through the air. "I'm trying to get back to the almost-kissing part."

"So am I," April said, quirking a corner of her mouth. Her heart ached at the thought, and she wondered if they would ever have another chance.

"Look, I'm sorry," Deb said. "How can I fix this?"

"I don't think you can." Ryan's last words floated into her mind. "He told me it was good to see me, and then he said, 'Don't ever forget that,' as if he didn't plan on seeing me again. And I haven't heard a word since. I'd like to know Ryan better, but is that how dating is now?" She was beginning to feel foolish. He had awakened a long-dormant part of her heart.

Deb put her arm around April's shoulder. "I hate to break it to you, but ghosting is common. Many men just aren't serious about a relationship. Unless, at my age, they think they might need a nurse."

"You're way too young for that, but my mother says the same thing. And she is one."

"I'm only half kidding," Deb said. She snapped a few more photos.

"Part of me wishes this encounter with Ryan hadn't occurred," April said. "It's awkward with Junie working at the hotel. She asked me to stop by today to see the shop. Junie is so proud of what she's accomplishing. And the Majestic is my mother's favorite place to dine on the island. Besides that, Mama is determined to go to the reception."

"You have to visit Junie's shop," Deb said. "Getting a job was a huge step for her. As for your mother, it's her first time out in months. She wants to go to the Majestic, so do what will make her happy. I'll be there with you for moral support."

"I'm not sure if I'm ready to face Ryan again." April sighed. "I'm also surprised I have feelings for someone already. Maybe Ryan sensed that, so it's just as well. Besides, we're from two very different worlds. I don't even know where he's from, except that he grew up near a beach in California. He was probably raised at some beachfront mansion. Way out of my league, right?"

"It sounds like you're trying to talk yourself out of your feelings for Ryan."

"Maybe it would be easier."

Deb was quiet for a long moment. Finally, she said, "It's been a long time since you and Calvin had a real marriage, so I wouldn't be so concerned about the timing. You've been on your own for a while. You just didn't want to admit it."

"I suppose that's true." April recalled all the nights she had spent alone. "I never knew you could be so lonely in a marriage."

"Plus, you're legally separated, and the divorce is in progress."

"I meant to tell you that Calvin had a change of heart," April said. "He signed off on the property division. He agreed to everything, so we only need the court's approval. It might be faster than my attorney originally thought."

Deb pressed a hand to her chest. "Thank goodness for that."

Preparing to leave, April checked the lock on the side door. Yet, Ryan was still on her mind. "Do you want to know the irony of all this? I would advise any friend in my situation against a rebound affair."

"Been there," Deb said, raising a hand. "I would say that, too. Except that I know you, and I know how selective you are. And you have to start somewhere."

As they spoke, April raised her phone light to the ceiling, illuminating a pair of vintage chandeliers. If only she could somehow shed light on this dilemma. "It's awkward when he lives a stone's throw away. And my mother is besotted with him."

Deb's eyes widened. "No kidding? Now there's a discriminating woman."

"I know, right? After Dad died, my mother dated a little, but no one measured up to her standards."

"You can't avoid Ryan," Deb said. "Just let your friendship—or whatever it is—unfold. Crown Island is a small place. Unless you move in completely different social circles, you're bound to see him."

"I suppose you're right. Still, he seemed close to a breakthrough. It's hard to explain." April walked toward the back door to make sure it was locked before they left.

"Why don't you come with me to the hotel now?" Deb asked. "While I'm picking up my check to start working on the project, you can visit Junie."

"Sounds good. I'll check the back door."

Deb followed her. "I wonder where it leads to on the property?" She drew the deadbolt lock and turned the knob. Nothing happened. "It's stuck."

"My turn to try." April put her shoulder against the old wooden door and shoved it. "Oh," she cried. The door pitched open, sending her sprawling into a row of shrubs surrounding the rear entry. Several guests looked in her direction. She picked her way through the shrubbery.

"Are you hurt?" Deb asked.

Before April could answer, footsteps sounded on the walk behind her. "April?"

The single word pierced her heart. Slowly, she turned around. "Ryan." Her chest tightened at the sight of him.

Then, she looked closer. Ryan's hair was disheveled as if he'd been running his hands through it. His eyes were bloodshot, and his jaw had an unshaven shadow. Had he been working all night?

Ryan's eyes bore into hers. "What were you doing in there?"

"That's the historical society offices."

Ryan raised his brow in surprise. "That's part of the hotel."

"And the historical society has a long-term lease on it," April said. "Evidently, it was part of a tax concession negotiated with the city several years ago." April yearned to reach out to him, but she didn't. He seemed distracted; something was weighing on his mind. She'd never seen him like this.

Ryan pinched the bridge of his nose. "And who is in charge of this historical society I've never heard of?"

"I am now," April replied. "You can confirm it with the city."

He ran a hand across the back of his neck. "I will. Just not today." He turned and walked away.

Deb pulled her back inside. "Let's lock up and go around the front."

Devastated, April decided that whatever fleeting connection they had was definitely over.

21

*J*unie was with customers when April arrived at the gift shop. While she waited, she strolled around the gift shop, admiring the changes her daughter had already instituted. Art glass sculptures, pottery, and jewelry from local artisans were displayed on antique fixtures. Baskets overflowing with local delicacies, including chocolate and wine, sat on another antique table. Displays of soaps and essential oils filled the air with an airy beach aroma.

The customers were curious about the new items they saw, and Junie patiently answered questions. When they decided, she rang up the sale and wrapped their purchases.

April thought Junie was a natural at retail. She was so pleased her daughter had found something to do that made her happy.

After guests left with purchases, Junie hurried across the shop. "I'm glad you're here. It's been a wild morning with all kinds of craziness in the air."

"It's monsoon season," April said. "Everyone is on edge."

"Why is that?"

"It could be a change in barometric or atmospheric pressure linked to the release of certain chemicals in the brain. That wasn't my field of study, but if so, weather patterns could have contributed to some of our world events." April thought that might be an interesting comparison.

Junie arched an eyebrow. "Whatever it is, people are talking about you. And Ryan. We need to talk."

April's heart sank. The last thing she wanted was for her family to get involved.

Customers slowed in front of the store. "Just a minute," Junie said. She flipped the Open sign to the Closed side. It was near the end of the day anyway.

"Let's go into the back." Junie led her to the storage area and gestured toward a small table. Partly organized shelves of merchandise surrounded them. "I've been cleaning back here and finding all sorts of things." She moved a box of papers from a chair so April could sit down.

Her mother folded her hands on the table. "I assume people saw us walking on the beach the other day."

Uncertain how to proceed, Junie drew a breath. "Mom, now that you and Dad are legally separated, what you do isn't any of my business until it's in my face."

"Honey, it was just a walk. People exaggerate."

"Someone said he kissed you."

April shifted in the small chair. "Oh, that. Well, not quite."

"That's what they're saying," Junie charged, hurt evident in her tone. "You didn't prepare me, and people don't know that you and Dad are separated, so it looks especially bad."

"I can't stop people from talking, but I hope you set them straight."

Junie twisted her mouth to one side and nodded. "I hadn't planned on discussing our personal business with the staff."

"I'm sorry, but it will blow over. Ryan is single and well-to-do. I won't be the only person linked to him. And I assure you, nothing is going on between us."

"Then what was it that people saw?"

April hesitated. While she could unload on her best friend, being that vulnerable or blunt with her daughter was another matter. "Ryan had some concerns that he needed to unload. What people saw was him thanking me for listening." An element of truth was in there somewhere. Guilt tightened her shoulders.

"That's not all." Lacing her fingers, Junie leaned in. "People say Ryan Kingston has always had a mysterious background. The day you saw him, a guest at the cafe outed him when he returned. An older woman called him by a different name. Ryan Finley. Whitley whisked her to a table while Ryan fled to his office."

"He goes by another name?" April was surprised, but in a way, this made sense. He had been so vague that she thought he was hiding something.

"That woman must have known him from a long time ago. People think he might be a criminal. Maybe he killed someone or swindled money from investors. They're speculating that's why he's here on Crown Island." Junie paused, frowning. "Do you think any of that might be true?"

"I highly doubt it." April reached for her daughter's hand. "But people will talk. Try to ignore gossip." This explained why Ryan looked like he'd been up all night.

"We're still going to the VIP reception, right?"

April hated to subject her family to a potentially awkward situation. "Under the circumstances, do you still want to?"

"More than ever now." Junie jutted out her chin.

"Then we'll go." April might regret this, but she would keep her promise to her family.

Junie looked relieved. "We should tell Nana, so she won't be blindsided by people's comments. She's looking forward to the event, but she should be prepared."

"Of course, we'll tell her. Still, your grandmother can certainly take care of herself." In tense situations, Ella was the one colleagues at the hospital had counted on. "I'll meet you at the house."

While April waited, Junie gathered her things. As she unlocked the door to the gift shop, a nice-looking man approached the shop. He looked familiar, but April couldn't place him until he greeted Junie. It was Officer Blumenthal, out of uniform.

His focus was on Junie. "Adrian is jamming with some other local musicians at Cuppa Jo's. Want to come along? Jo's making specialty burgers tonight. A bunch of us are going now."

"Hello, Blue," April said. "Have you arrested any more cyclists?"

Immediately, color rose in Blue's face. "Always doing my job, Ms. Raines. Would you like to join us?"

Junie brightened. "Sure, Mom. Want to go? Everyone says how much fun it is."

"I'm sure it is. Not tonight, but Junie, you should go."

April was glad to see her daughter making friends. Junie had not been out with friends since Mark died. Even though April had a run-in with Blue, he had helped her into the house the day Calvin had asked for a divorce. She would reserve judgment for now.

Junie's eyes were sparkling with happiness. "I won't be late."

"And I'll make sure she gets home okay, Ms. Raines."

April suppressed a smile. "That would be a good idea, Blue."

When April arrived at the house on Beach View Lane, she saw every light in the place on, which wasn't at all like her frugal mother. She opened the screen door.

April walked through the house, but she couldn't find Ella. Growing worried, she called out, "Mom, where are you?"

The door to the guest room burst open. "We're in here, April."

"We?" Why would her mother be in Junie's room? April hurried there.

Inside, Maileah was sprawled on the bed, sobbing. Her hair and clothes were in complete disarray. Ella was rubbing her back, comforting her.

Instantly, April recalled Maileah's treatment of her in Seattle, yet this was her daughter. She yearned to fold her in her arms and comfort her—if Maileah would let her. April eased onto the bed. "What's wrong?"

Ella rested a hand on April's shoulder. "Before you say anything, I told Maileah she's welcome to stay here."

April reached out to her daughter. "Whatever happened in Seattle or between us, I want you to know we're all here for you."

With a gut-wrenching sob, Maileah rolled over and flung her arms around April. "Oh, Mom, I'm so ashamed of what I said to you." She sniveled on April's shoulder. "I'm a complete disaster. I got fired, and Dad won't let me move in with them. I didn't have anywhere else to go."

April stroked Maileah's tangled hair. She looked like she'd been crying for days.

"What about your apartment, honey?"

"I did something so stupid. Hawk wanted me to move in with him, so I gave the landlord notice."

"Hawk is the one I saw you with at the club?"

Hanging her head, Maileah nodded. "He wasn't as bad as he looked, and he needed me, or so I thought. But when I found out Hawk was having an affair with Olga, I broke up with him and moved out. But my landlord had already rented my place. I only had two days to get out."

"Are we talking about the same Olga who is with your Dad?"

Maileah drew her sleeve across her eyes and curled into April's embrace. "How could they do that? They cheated on me and Dad. And that's why he won't let me stay there. Dad said that he and Olga need to work on their relationship now for the sake of the baby, and it's not a good idea for me to be there. And you know what? That might not even be Dad's kid. But he's still choosing them over me. How messed up is that?"

"Did your father offer to help you until you can get another job?"

"Dad said he can't spare any money to help me get another apartment. I know where it's all going. You wouldn't believe how much Olga is running up on Dad's credit cards."

April had a pretty good idea. Versace dresses, Louis Vuitton luggage. That explained why Calvin agreed to the financial settlement so quickly. After hearing this, April was thankful she'd proceeded with the legal separation on the advice of her attorney. She hoped she wouldn't be responsible for Calvin's bills, but she would talk to her attorney about the financials. With this new information, they might have to change their original agreement.

April also had doubts about whether Olga was even pregnant. The woman was definitely playing Calvin, but that wasn't her concern anymore. Maybe Hawk was in on it, too.

As Maileah erupted with another heartbreaking wail, April held her close, rocking her. Her independent eldest child had been knocked down hard. While she'd made some extremely poor choices, April couldn't throw that in her face now.

After all, learning from mistakes was a necessary part of life. As April thought about Calvin and now Hawk, she gritted her teeth. All Maileah wanted was to love these men, yet they'd ground that love under their heels and left her in shambles.

April pressed Maileah to her chest. "I'm glad you came here, sweetheart."

"I was so scared to tell you after what I did to you. But Nana said you would understand."

Meeting her mother's compassionate gaze, April nodded. "More than you know."

LATER THAT EVENING, after getting Maileah settled in her old room, April collapsed on the sofa. She could sleep here if she had to, but Ella had been talking about getting a new couch. Given their circumstances, a sleeper sofa might be a better idea.

April was looking at a local shop's assortment online when Junie arrived home. With a broad smile on her face, Junie was in high spirits.

"Did you have a good time at Cuppa Jo's?"

"It was so much fun, Mom. Many people who work at the hotel go there, and I met a lot of Blue's friends, too."

April detected the beginning of a relationship. "How much do you know about Blue?"

"Oh, Mom, really," Junie replied, bristling slightly. "It's not like we're dating. We're just friends. But if you want to know about Blue, you should ask Nana."

Judging from the way Junie replied, April could tell Junie was beginning to think about dating. She should, April thought. Her daughter deserved to have a life again.

"I've been thinking about something," Junie said. "Now that Nana is feeling better and you're staying on Crown Island, it might be time for me to find my own place."

April was relieved to hear Junie say that. With Maileah here now, she didn't want Junie to feel pushed out.

"I met the owner of Cuppa Jo's tonight. Jo seems to know everyone's business here, and she said there might be a cottage for sale on her street soon."

"Where is it?"

"On Sunshine Avenue. With such a happy name, I think it might be good for me. I still have work to do on myself, but Mark would have approved. I hope Nana won't mind."

"I think she'll be pleased. Actually, this couldn't have come at a better time." April touched her daughter's hand. "Junie, if you don't mind, I'd like to share your room until I can buy a sleeper sofa for the living room."

Junie looked confused. "What about your room?"

Just then, Maileah shuffled in. "I'm taking Mom's room. No one wants to share with me."

Staring at her sister in surprise, Junie cried, "What are you doing here?"

"It's complicated," Maileah replied. She stopped, taking in Junie's upbeat demeanor and new outfit. "You finally got dressed."

To her credit, Junie ignored the dig and patted the cushion beside her. "Come tell me what happened."

While Maileah unloaded on Junie, April went into the kitchen. Her mother was sitting at the table with a cup of tea. The color had come back to her face. April knew she was looking forward to the reception at the Majestic.

"Sounds like you should put on another kettle," Ella said, nodding toward the living room. "Those two have a lot of catching up to do."

April filled the kettle with water and placed it on a burner. "If Junie and Maileah don't sort out their differences, this house will be a battleground." She adjusted the flame and turned to her mother. "Junie mentioned a house on Sunshine Avenue that might be available soon."

April told her mother about the conversation they'd had tonight. "I'd also like to know everything about Blue. I didn't like the way he pulled me over on my bike, but he was nice enough to help me into the house after Calvin's episode."

Ella flicked her eyes to one side. "Why do you ask, dear?"

"Junie went to Cuppa Jo's tonight with him. I don't want her getting involved with another man like Maileah's Hawk. Do you know what he's like?"

Ella sipped her tea thoughtfully. "I was afraid of that. Blue has a good heart, but he's complicated."

22

S tanding by the bank of windows in the executive offices, Ryan gazed out to sea, thinking about the last couple of days as he watched high clouds hugging the horizon. If his emotions hadn't been so raw after his walk with April, he would have reacted differently to the guest who had called out to him at the cafe. *Ryan Finley. It is you, isn't it?*

He should have approached the woman and diffused the situation. He could have told her she was mistaken, perhaps.

But she wasn't, and that probably would have become even more obvious. Still, he would not have been viewed as running from the accusation. He could have embraced it and laughed it off.

His reaction had set off a firestorm of gossip that blew through the hotel, then leapt to the local news and continued straight to the peak of gossip empires.

Bad news always spreads faster, he thought, opening the window for fresh air. The sound of laughter from the beach filtered up. But even that didn't make him smile today.

Whitley appeared at the doorway, his orange jacket catching Ryan's eye. "What now, Whitley?"

"Calls are still coming in for you. Do you wish to return any yet?" Whitley held a stack of message slips from the front desk.

"Not until after the reception. If then."

Whitley shifted on his feet. "Will you address this situation today?"

Ryan shook his head. "Where I was born, what my parents did, or the name chosen for me has nothing to do with the Majestic Hotel. However, it seems my past is all people want to talk about." He clenched his jaw. If only it hadn't been a slow news day.

He had no desire to be the topic of media commentator jokes. *Millionaire Majestic Owner Hides Past.* And social media was worse. *Crown Island Cradle of Sordid Secrets.* The island community couldn't be happy about that. It took him about five seconds to shut off the television and his new feed this morning.

The business was another matter. Ryan had already spoken to his investors and assured them his background gave him more experience in running the Majestic. However, he didn't know if he'd gotten through to them. His financial returns were solid, yet he knew better than most that old money could be cliquish. Even though Ryan was the majority shareholder, they could still suggest he step down from management based on morals clauses in their agreement.

No one would run the Majestic Hotel but him. Investor greed had landed the Majestic in its current mess. Before him, investors had drained its coffers for quick quarterly profits without reinvesting for the long term. And if the hotel had failed? They would have torn it down to build a resort made of concrete. That's what his ex-partner had planned.

Ryan checked the time. "Let's review the reception area." He picked up his jacket.

THE TERRACE WAS BUSTLING with staff setting up for the reception. Vivid tropical floral arrangements with orange and blue birds of paradise, pink ginger flowers, and red anthurium stood out against the blue sea beyond. Lights were strung overhead. The bulbs would cast a warm festive glow after the sun set. Chairs and tables filled the center area. A band was set up under an awning in case of rain.

Ryan could just imagine the terraced filled with people laughing and talking. It wouldn't be long now. The fate of the

Majestic Hotel depended on how well the media and local people received his message.

The chef looked up as Ryan and Whitley crossed to the buffet. Giana wore a colorful island-print chef jacket, and her dark hair was pulled back under her white chef hat.

Ryan greeted her with a handshake. "Your new menu is being well received. Thank you for that, and for the holiday menu.

"It's been a joint creative effort with my team," Giana said. "I brought in several special dishes from my hometown in Amalfi, so I was glad we could switch suppliers. That made all the difference to guests. We did the best we could before, but none of us liked having food sent back to the kitchen."

"The numbers are up in all the restaurants on the property," Whitley said. "People are talking about the improvements."

At that comment, Giana looked uncomfortable. She glanced down at a cheese platter her staff had assembled, intent on rearranging the garnish.

Without much effort, Ryan could read her mind. This new revelation about his background had sprung up like a wall dividing him from the staff. They were acting awkward around him, sneaking glances or avoiding eye contact like Giana.

He needed his team on his side, and there was only one way to do that.

"That's not all they're talking about, is it?" he asked with sincerity. "The cafe was ground zero. I should have faced that woman."

The noise level on the terrace instantly subdued.

Giana looked up, surprised. "In Italy, you know what we say to people like that? *Basta!* Enough." She gestured as she spoke. "Or in America, get a life."

Nervous laughter rippled across the terrace. Ryan lifted a corner of his mouth. It was easy to say but difficult to implement, especially since this was so personal. "Sometimes, that's all we can do."

Yet, in business, Ryan had no problem facing down those with opposing views. He'd even gotten the best he could out of his bombastic ex-partner.

This was different.

"Excuse me." A young man working beside Giana leaned in. "I just want to say that knowing you're one of us makes me…" He glanced at three or four other servers and kitchen staff, who were gathering around them to listen. "Makes us all feel proud."

Ryan was surprised and touched. "I appreciate that. What's your name?"

"People call me Nacho. I'm a cook." He grinned, then hesitated before a young blonde woman prodded him to continue. "And this is Sofie, a pastry chef from Poland. We understand why you wouldn't want to talk about it."

Hearing that saddened Ryan. "Actually, I'm very proud of my parents. They sacrificed a great deal for me." His parents had always made sure he had the right clothes for school. While he didn't have many, what he had was nice.

"That's true." Another woman who had delivered freshly ironed tablecloths spoke up. "I worked with Mary and Patrick before they retired. Finest folks you'd ever want to know."

"That means a lot to me," Ryan said, putting a hand to his heart. "And you are?"

"I'm Maddie, sir. Housekeeping." She whipped out her hand, and Ryan shook hands with her. "Some of us knew their son had gone away to school and worked in real estate, but we didn't know you were the same person." Maddie shrugged. "Can't say as we blame you for keeping it quiet. Folks are snobby, they are."

Ryan looked around at the small group that was nodding in agreement. All of them had stories, hopes, and dreams—if not for themselves, for their children. Family was what mattered most.

"I've been where you are." Ryan spoke to them from his heart. "What you've probably heard is true. I was born here in the staff quarters. And I owe everything I am now to my parents. I wish they could be here tonight, but I'm afraid the attention would be too much for them."

He had asked them again, but of course, his father had refused. He couldn't blame them and wouldn't want to see them humiliated anyway.

Ryan continued talking with the staff for a few more minutes, learning about them as they worked. Knowing he had their support touched Ryan. They were the heart of the Majestic

Hotel—those who showed up every day and cared for the property. All so that guests could visit and make memories that would last forever.

Where would he be without any of them?

Ryan considered the formal speech he had planned to make. But there was one major issue with it. That was the speech of Ryan Kingston, not the man he truly was. Now that his secrets had been revealed, it was time for the two to coexist. He shrugged out of his custom-tailored jacket.

Leaving Whitley with the staff, Ryan strode into the hotel. Their VIP guests would arrive soon. But he still had time to make changes.

23

*W*hile Junie and Ella were getting dressed, April checked on Maileah in her room. "Are you sure you don't want to join us at the Majestic Hotel?"

Maileah rolled over on the bed, her blonde hair a mass of tangles. "I don't want to be around people. But could you bring me some food back?"

Before answering, April smoothed a hand on her daughter's shoulder and thought about her request. Even though April's first inclination was to rush in to help Maileah, she had to let her daughter reflect on her mistakes and learn to take charge of her life. That started in small ways and would benefit her in the long run. "There's plenty here for you to eat."

"I can't make it to the kitchen."

April kissed Maileah's forehead. "Unless your legs are broken, I'm sure you can."

This was the beginning of Maileah's new journey. When April was too young to know better, she had fallen into the trap of enabling Calvin's behavior, so he never changed.

Now that April knew better, she would not do that to her daughter.

Maileah sat up, hugging her knees. She blinked as if seeing her mother with fresh eyes. "You look nice, Mom. Different."

"Thanks. I'm trying out a new look." She'd gone to Deb's

hairstylist, who had given her a new cut and suggested a different makeup technique. It was subtle but enhanced her natural look. Deb had also given her a Tori Richard tropical print dress she'd never worn, saying it was too short on her.

The dress was perfect on April, especially for today's muggy weather. Crown Island represented a chance to recreate herself from the inside out.

When April walked into the living room, she saw that her mother and Junie were similarly dressed in island-inspired outfits. Ella wore a long, sunny floral dress that brushed her ankles, and Junie had on wide-legged pants with a modest crop top. Junie stood in front of the mirror, trying to clasp a necklace.

"Almost ready?" April asked.

"Sure. Can you help me with this, Mom? I'm having trouble with it."

April swept Junie's hair to one side. Her reddish highlights glinted in the late afternoon sun. "This is an old piece, but I haven't seen it before."

"I found it while I was cleaning out the store room at the shop. There were boxes back there that hadn't been touched in years. I'll show it to Whitley, but I thought I'd wear it just once because it goes so well with this outfit."

April snapped the clasp. "Let me see."

Junie turned around. "With this big amethyst-colored stone, it looks like one of your old Miriam Haskell costume pieces." The pendant sparkled at her chest, accenting the lavender and coral floral print outfit she wore. "Can you tell anything from it?"

April lifted it for a better look. The fine craftsmanship sparked her intuition, and on the back were tiny hallmarks. Barely visible was a crown imprint, often found on antique pieces.

"I'll have to look at this with a jeweler's loop, but it might have real value. Be careful with it."

Ella touched April's arm. "We should go. I'd like to be there early to find a table before it gets too crowded. And on the way, Junie wants to show us the little cottage on Sunshine Avenue she's interested in."

"Of course, we'll drive by it." Even though her mother was going out, she still needed to pace herself. Though April had mixed feelings about attending the reception, she wanted her mother to have a wonderful evening. There would be people Ella hadn't seen in months. And others that April should talk to about the historical society.

FROM THE MOMENT April entered the Majestic Hotel, she was enchanted. In the lobby, a local jazz band was performing, the staff wore new aloha shirts, and floral decorations filled the air with a heady aroma. Flowers lined the walkway to the terrace, and the mood was festive.

"How delightful," Ella said. "And what a good turnout."

April was glad to see that Crown Islanders had turned out to support the hotel—or maybe they were curious about Ryan Kingston. She drew a breath, steadying her heartbeat, which still quickened every time she thought of him. She had to get over that.

"The staff has been working so hard to make this a success," Junie said. "I was afraid the rumors about Ryan would have an impact on attendance."

"Everyone likes drama, as long as it's someone else's," April said. "Although I can't imagine how he's taking it." If the way he looked when she'd seen him outside the historical building office was any indication, it wasn't good.

A woman stopped her mother. "Why, Ella Raines. So good to see you out."

April and Junie waited as the two women spoke.

Junie leaned in to look at an old photograph of the restaurant. An attractive young couple, surrounded by others, was smiling for the camera. She touched the vintage pendant she wore. "Mom, look at this."

"What is it?"

Junie gestured toward the young woman in the photo. "Doesn't that necklace look like this one?"

April studied it. "It's uncanny, but it looks identical."

"I wonder if that could be Princess Noelle?" Junie's eyes glittered with excitement.

"It could be," April said. "Whitley might be able to tell us."

Junie broke into a wide smile. "If that's her, then the legend might be real." Quickly, she shared the story.

Ella turned back to them. "What's this about Princess Noelle?"

"We're wondering if that's her in the photo, Nana. If it is, then this is her necklace."

"Good afternoon, ladies." Whitley greeted them, and Junie repeated her question. "Who is in that photo?"

"This is what we call our regal row of photographs. The presidential series is on the other wall. So that would be…ah, yes. Princess Noelle."

Junie gasped and held up her pendant. "I found this in the storeroom, but I thought it was an old costume jewelry piece like my mother collects."

"She planned to give it to you," April added.

"Well, I'll be," Whitley said slowly, awe lighting his face. "I think you might have found a missing link."

An idea formed in April's mind. "This would be a fascinating project to delve into—as it relates to the Majestic and guests of note. We could plan a showcase for the new historical society."

"Ah, that," Whitley said, stroking his chin. "Mr. Ryan mentioned a possible agreement with the city for that space. I investigated, and it appears you are correct. Would you like to look through our archives? They haven't been tended to in some time."

"I'd appreciate that," April replied, excited at the prospect. "And I would be happy to organize the archives and plan a retrospective of the hotel from the past to the present. I could give you a proposal for the project."

Whitley inclined his head in thought. "That might work well with the planned renovation and unveiling. Yes, we'd like to see that proposal. We might have some real treasures here."

Ella beamed. "My family is the real treasure."

"Because they take after you, Ella." Whitley offered his arm. "Would you walk with me to the reception?"

"I can think of no one I'd rather make an entrance with than you." Ella slid her hand demurely into the crook of his elbow.

Junie nudged April and raised her brow. "Do you think…" she whispered.

"Who knows?" April replied, smiling. Her mother certainly had an avid admirer in Whitley. She and Junie walked behind the pair, who made quite the entrance at the outdoor terrace reception.

The setting by the sea was spectacular, particularly when the sun set, April knew. Twin buffets overflowed with a cornucopia of delicacies, from artisan cheeses and a charcuterie station to tropical fruits and crudité. Roast pork and beef carving stations already had lines of guests waiting. Others were chatting near the bar, where bartenders were mixing tropical-inspired cocktails.

Many people turned to welcome Ella, asking about her health and commenting on how well she looked.

"She grows more beautiful every day," Whitley said as Ella smiled up at him. He walked with her to a table in the front with a reserved sign on it. "Here's your table, my dear."

With rounded eyes, Junie nudged April again. "How did we not know about this?"

"I guess we're all entitled to some secrets." April could hardly wait to ask her mother. Whitley was right, though. Her mother was a lovely, vibrant woman.

"Is Whitley married?" Junie whispered.

"Mama said he was widowed," April replied. "Shh. We'll grill her later."

Junie was quickly swept into the crowd by her new friend at the hotel, Faye. She turned to April. "Do you mind?"

"Go ahead, have fun." April watched her daughter go. Others quickly surrounded her, welcoming her into their group. Blue and Sailor immediately vied for her attention, with Sailor getting a glass of wine for her while Blue brought her a plate of hors d'oeurves.

Grinning in surprise at the attention, Junie turned back to her mother. April winked and blew her a kiss. Junie deserved to have fun again.

April turned, gazing at the lively crowd around her. The only person missing was Ryan.

Over the next few months, these were the people she would contact about supporting the historical society in terms of artifacts, memories, and donations. From listening to her mother and

Deb, she knew most were kind and engaged, although every community had its share of difficult people.

And they liked to gossip.

April picked up snippets of conversation about Ryan and his family. Likely, people didn't mean harm. He was a newcomer with a mysterious past, and now they discovered he had roots on Crown Island. Who wouldn't be interested in that? Yet, some of the speculation was less than kind.

April made her way toward the edge of the crowd, where several renderings had been set up on easels with sample boards of colors and fabrics.

Deb appeared by her side. "What do you think of my concept boards?" She wore a long coral-colored dress that showed off her curves and a long strand of coral beads around her neck. Simple, yet elegant.

"Very impressive. So, this is what you were working so late on —a preview of coming attractions for the hotel." Grinning, April added, "You're not just a pretty face after all."

Feigning shock, Deb poked her. "You're the only one who can say that and get away with it, shortie."

Laughing, April hugged her. "It's good to be back on Crown Island and hanging out with you. It's feeling more like home every day."

"I had to wait long enough for you to come to your senses."

April had to share her news, too. "I just spoke to Whitley. I'm going to pitch a proposal for a historical retrospective of the hotel. Along with working on the old archives." She had a vague memory of them in the basement, if they were still there. The prospect was exciting and would be a welcome source of income.

"Well, look at you go." Deb wrapped her arm around April's shoulder and lowered her voice. "Have you seen you-know-who?"

April shook her head. "And I'm not looking for him."

"Plenty of fish in the sea, that's for sure." Deb glanced back at the crowd. "I need to talk to a couple of people here about furnishings for the hotel. Mind if I leave you?"

"I'll be fine. I'll join my mother in a moment."

Deb lifted her chin toward Ella's table, where a crowd had gathered around her mother. "If you can find a seat. I don't think you have to worry about Ella being left alone. And she looks so happy. I'm glad to see her feeling so much better."

After Deb left, April lingered by the concept plans, enjoying the expert detail of her friend's work. Presently, the sun dipped beneath the horizon, bathing the terrace in golden hues. Overhead, strings of lights twinkled on, casting a romantic glow across the venue.

April was immersed in the new vision for the hotel when a shadow fell across one poster, and she turned.

"Deb brought my vision of Majestic to life," Ryan said, offering her a glass. "Sparkling water with lime. I don't even know what you like. Wine or a cocktail, perhaps? Or maybe an apology for how I've been acting. Whitley confirmed the use of the old dance hall for the historical society."

April accepted the sparkling water. "This is refreshing, thanks. And I understand that you've had a lot on your mind." Still, she appreciated his apology.

Something was different about him. Instead of his usual tailored jacket, he wore an aloha shirt with his trousers.

April took a step back, surprised at his casual attire. "I've never seen you dressed like this."

A slight smile crossed his face. "I was due for a change. In several areas, it seems. Do you think this works?"

April touched the edge of his shirt. The subtle, reverse-printed patterned shirt felt like a fine blend of linen and silk. As opposed to the bright prints marketed to tourists, this was a finely crafted aloha shirt like islanders often wore, even for business.

"The blue brings out your eyes," she said thoughtfully. "You look like you belong here now."

"I'd like that. And it's much more comfortable in this humidity." Ryan gestured toward the horizon in the dimming light. "Looks like the monsoons will pass us by."

"Which is good with this turnout."

"We have more than expected," he said. "In the last few days, we had people asking to be included on the guest list."

April parted her lips, surprised. "They all want to meet you and learn your plans for the Majestic."

"We both know it's more like curiosity now. I assume you've heard the talk around town?"

April wasn't sure if anything Junie had told her was true. "Whatever your reason, I'm sure it made sense at the time."

He rocked on his feet. "Sometimes we cover up details that other people probably don't even care about. I should have set the record straight a long time ago. But I was afraid to."

April was surprised that he would have any insecurities. "Well, they're all here for you tonight." Sipping her water, she saw heads swiveling in their direction.

Ryan stepped closer and lowered his voice. "Maybe you've heard talk about us, too. I'm sorry if my carelessness on the beach has cost you."

"I don't care about that." She'd been through so much with her marriage that idle gossip paled in comparison. "You'll be the topic of conversation one day, and a month later, they'll forget all about it."

He touched her hand lightly. "I hope you don't."

"No, I won't." April pressed her lips together, afraid of what she might say.

One corner of his mouth turned up, and Ryan seemed to search her soul with his gaze. And then, blinking, he took a step back. "I need to say a few words to our guests before my presentation."

While April sipped her cool drink, she watched him move through the crowd, greeting people. Whispers followed in his wake. Finally, he reached the podium close to where Ella sat.

Her mother had a few friends with her, but there were still seats at the table. She would join her mother in a moment, but she wanted to observe people's reactions to Ryan.

An older couple approached the concept boards, and April stepped aside to let them see better.

"Why, would you look at this," the man said, inspecting Deb's renderings. He spoke with a faint Irish accent.

The woman's face held a sense of awe as she admired the color scheme. "The Majestic will be a real beauty again, like when we first arrived on Crown Island."

April glanced at the silver-haired couple, but she didn't recognize them. From what they said, she assumed they'd lived on the island a long time, but she'd also been away.

"He's speaking now," the man said, sounding eager.

"Hello," April said, greeting the couple.

They responded in kind. "What a special evening," the woman added. Her eyes glittered with excitement.

April saw them acknowledge several staff members. She assumed they were well known.

Ryan tapped the microphone for attention. "Welcome to the soon-to-be new Majestic Hotel. I'm Ryan Kingston."

The noise level subdued, save for a few whispers. Beside her, the couple clasped hands and beamed.

Who were they? But April's attention was quickly drawn to Ryan, who was speaking about his plans for the hotel. The renovations, upcoming holiday season, New Year's Eve ball, and the summer season ahead.

"I have the best team in the business," Ryan said, sweeping an arm out to the staff standing at attention. He introduced key members of his team, including Whitley and Giana, who stood to one side.

"They care for the Majestic Hotel as if it were their own. And as of tomorrow, it will be. I'm instituting a new profit-sharing plan to award not only a few but all who contribute to making this a legendary hotel."

Beside April, the couple looked at each other with pride. And then it struck her. Were they Ryan's parents? That couldn't be. They lived on Crown Island, and he...

No, that wasn't quite right. What was it she had heard again?

April was trying to sort it out when a red-faced man from the audience spoke up. He wore a gaudy shirt and was swilling a cocktail. "Mr. Kingston, would you address the rumors that have been circulating about you?"

Ryan hesitated, flicking a look in April's direction. "There is no shortage of rumors."

Heat burned in April's cheeks as she recalled their walk on the beach. But when the couple beside her nodded to him, April realized Ryan wasn't necessarily looking at her, but at them.

"Go on, son," the man said so softly that no one else could hear him.

The man in the crowd swirled his cocktail, clinking the ice cubes. "Specifically, the rumors that might impact your investors' confidence. Can you address those tonight, Mr.

Kingston?" The man shot a grin at his friends. "Or shall I say, Mr. Finley?"

Murmurs swept across the room, and April watched Ryan closely. He seemed composed, but she sensed a torrent of emotions running beneath the surface.

The woman next to April gripped her husband's hand. As Ryan looked at her, she nodded her support, whispering, "It's alright now."

Gripping the podium, Ryan continued, "Though my surname at birth was Finley, Kingston is my mother's maiden name. Times being what they were back then, it was the name my father used to enroll me in school. I was a scholarship student, and he wanted me to have every advantage."

The woman beside her leaned on her husband, and he wrapped his arm lovingly around her.

"Excuse me," April said. "My mother is seated at a table, and there are several open seats. Would you join us there?"

"We couldn't impose…" the man began.

April touched the women's shoulder. "I'm April Raines, a friend of Ryan's. Please?"

The woman hesitated, then gave her a small smile. April led the way and seated the woman next to her mother. April sat on the other side of the man she presumed to be Ryan's father.

When April looked up at Ryan, he gave her a small smile of appreciation that touched her heart.

At the next table, a woman piped up, "It is true that your parents worked here?" Another woman next to her suppressed a laugh.

Ryan flexed his jaw. "That is correct. They spent their lives working to make sure every guest had an excellent experience, caring for this hotel as if it were their own home. My father helped keep the hotel clean and in good repair, and my mother tended to guest rooms."

"A janitor and a housekeeper are what I heard," the woman said in a derisive stage whisper loud enough for others to hear.

Next to April, Ryan's parents stiffened.

Ryan stared at the woman. "That is also correct. A janitor and a housekeeper. And they never wavered in their support of me and my career. Even standing in the shadows so that I would have a better chance than they did. As the son of immigrant ancestors, I am thankful for their sacrifices. I'm proud to represent them and their vision for what could be accomplished in this country."

Ryan stretched a hand toward his parents. "And I am deeply honored that they could join us tonight."

With tears of pride and gratitude shimmering in their eyes, his parents clasped each other's hands.

April blinked back emotion as well. And then, from a far corner, someone began to applaud, and then another, and another, until a wave of applause swept across the terrace. Several people around them rose to honor the Finleys, and others followed suit.

April turned to them. "Would you like to stand and be recognized?" When they agreed, she helped pull out their chairs.

Ella gazed up at them, smiling. When April caught her eye, she nodded her approval.

"Thank you, thank you," Mr. Finley said, looking self-conscious but filled with pride.

Once the applause died down, Ryan went on.

"You might have heard other rumors. For example, that I was born at the hotel." He allowed himself a slight smile. "You might say that I am a true child of the Majestic Hotel. So devoted was my mother to her job that she worked up to the day I decided to make my way into the world. She gave birth in the employee's quarters below. Had an off-duty nurse not been here that evening, it's highly probable that my mother and I would have both died. We owe a debt of gratitude as well."

At that, Ella let out a small gasp and turned to Ryan's mother. "That was me," she said, and the two women embraced each other.

"I'm also proud to employ others like my parents who have a dream of a better future." Ryan gestured to two of the kitchen staff standing beside the buffet. "Like Nacho and Sofie, a skilled cook and pastry chef who've joined us from Mexico City and Poland, respectively, and are part of our multilingual guest team as well."

As people turned toward the couple, Sofie smiled shyly and

clasped Nacho's hand. April was touched by their affection for each other.

"Those two are practically engaged," Mary said. "They remind me of us."

Ryan held out his arms and continued, speaking passionately, "The Majestic is more than a hotel. It is, and always has been, a family. And all of you here are part of it."

His words touched April, and when she glanced around, she saw others nodding in agreement now. Ryan was reaching them, and she was so relieved for him.

As she listened to him speak, her perception of him shifted, and the questions she'd had were resolved. Slowly, she realized that they were more alike than not, despite his success.

Ryan caught her eye and smiled. "As for the other rumors that I might have robbed a bank or killed someone, I can honestly attest to one fact—that those stories are pure nonsense."

He paused and pressed a hand to his heart. "And I assure you of another fact—that you will never find an owner more dedicated to the Majestic Hotel, its employees, and the future of the hotel's service to the community. Hard work doesn't scare me, and my standards are high. As my parents did before me, it is my deepest privilege to serve. Thank you for coming, and enjoy the evening." Ryan turned off the microphone and left the podium amidst another round of applause.

April was truly impressed. His love for the Majestic rivaled her own, and he had swayed his most ardent detractors.

Ryan strode toward his parents and embraced them. Turning to April and Ella, he said, "I see you've met my parents. This is my mother, Mary Finley, and my father, Patrick."

Mary's eyes sparkled with happiness. "Ryan dear, this is the lovely woman who delivered you. Ella Raines."

A look of surprise and wonderment filled Ryan's face. "We've already met, and she shared a story about delivering a baby at the hotel. But I had no idea that I was that child. She and her daughter April are my neighbors."

Patrick exclaimed, "Why, you don't say?"

"Since we live so close to your son, I'd love for you to visit sometime," Ella said. "All of you," she added, gesturing to Ryan.

"He usually comes to see us," Mary said. "But we'd like that."

April noticed Ryan looking at her. A smile twitched at the corner of his mouth. Just as he was about to speak, a sudden gust of wind swept across the terrace, toppling several of the floral arrangements.

"Oh, my goodness," Ella cried.

People screamed as raindrops swept across the terrace. Staff members rushed to fling plastic coverings over food and wheel in carts. The rain quickly intensified.

In no time, a swift sheet of rain followed, and guests raced for the hotel entrances.

"It's the monsoon," Ryan called out, gesturing toward the doors. "Everyone needs to go inside now."

"Let's go," April cried, reaching out to her mother.

Ryan led his parents inside. "Right behind you."

As they were helping their parents to safety, April saw Deb hurry inside. Junie's friends raced toward a doorway, but Junie was searching the crowd. Blue and Sailor were trying to get her inside.

April and Ella reached the corridor just inside the door. Behind her, screams rang out, and she turned around. Another gust swept across the terrace, bending the palm trees overhead. Spiky fronds ripped loose and cartwheeled over the tables. People ducked to avoid them.

April's heart leapt. "Watch out," she yelled. A giant fond was whipping right toward Junie.

Sailor swept Junie into his arms and slid under a table. Blue dove under, too, just as the palm frond hit the table, tearing off the tablecloth and dragging it away.

"Over here," April shouted. "We're okay." She gestured for her daughter to go on.

Watching overhead, the trio crept out and scurried to safety.

With his parents safely inside, Ryan raced out to help others to safety. As April watched, her heart thumped. She was on her way to help him when a strong arm pulled her back.

"Stay with your mother," Whitley said. "We'll tend to the others."

Ella was shivering, so April draped her arm around her mother's shoulders and pulled her close.

The man who'd been questioning Ryan was behind them.

"Look at those two out there," Ella said. "Now, those are real men. The Majestic is in good hands with that pair and their staff."

Within a couple of minutes, Ryan and Whitley had brought the stragglers into the hotel to safety.

Ryan ran his hands through his wet hair and turned to address everyone gathered in the wide hallway. "Looks like that monsoon staged a sneak attack from the other direction after sunset. I suppose this is no surprise to those of you who've been living here for a while."

"You'll learn to run for cover," Deb called out, laughing. Everyone chuckled and nodded in agreement.

"I'm sorry we were caught off guard, but we did have contingency plans," Ryan said. Throughout the corridor, staff members were passing out towels for people to dry off. He gestured toward a ballroom. "We have more libations in the King's Salon for you, the band is setting up, and our chef and her team will bring the dessert course in a few minutes."

Deb waved a hand for others to follow. "What's a little rain? Let's go."

Cheers and applause coursed through the damp crowd, and they began to make their way forward. April saw Junie and her friends heading inside.

Whitley approached Ella. "I have a table for you and the Finleys reserved. Will you come with me?"

"How nice, thank you," Ella said. As she tucked her hand into the crook of Whitley's damp jacket, she looked back at April. "We'll see you in there."

Ryan draped a towel over April's shoulders. "Will you wait here for a moment? I need to speak to the chef, but I'll be right back. I want to talk to you before we join the group."

April lifted an edge of the towel and blotted her cheeks. "Take your time. I'll dry my hair."

"You look just fine with it wet." He lifted a damp strand from her cheek.

She smiled up at him. "So do you." With his dark hair wet

and plastered back, he looked like the first day she'd met him. Only this time, he was fully clothed.

April watched him walk away, thinking again about how much her perception of him had shifted. She wondered what he wanted to talk about with her. Taking the towel, she moved to a corner and perched on a chair under a potted palm blotting her hair and dress.

Just then, the young couple Ryan had introduced rushed inside, laughing. They had been moving equipment into the kitchen and were soaked, but they didn't seem to care. And they didn't notice April in the corner.

Quickly, Nacho glanced around. "We're alone." He cupped Sofie's lovely face in his hands.

"Shh, not here," Sofie said, giggling.

"I can think of no better place." He kissed her lightly on the lips. "I'll ask you again. Will you marry me?"

"Well, now that you've been properly recognized by Mr. Kingston, how can I say no?"

"Is that all it took?"

"I had to make sure you had prospects."

Nacho's smile dimmed. "I have plenty of prospects, but no ring to offer you right now."

Sofie shook her head. "I don't need one. Let's just get married."

"How's next week in Nevada on our time off?" His face bloomed with happiness. "We'll get people to cover a couple of extra days so we can have a proper honeymoon. My sister works at a hotel where she can get a rate we can afford during the week."

Sofie gazed at him with love in her eyes. "I'd like that very much."

After the sweetest of kisses, they rushed toward the kitchen, giggling as they went.

April leaned back and smiled. Young love was a beautiful thing to witness. And then she thought about her mother and Whitley. He was clearly smitten with her, and April wondered if her mother had deeper feelings for him.

Ella certainly seemed to come alive in his presence. But her mother was comfortably set in her ways.

Still, Ella loved to travel. It might be nice for her to have a traveling companion. April smiled to herself. Whatever that meant, she thought. That was her mother's business.

April had lived away from Crown Island for a long time. She didn't know if her mother had dated more recently. But now that Ella was feeling better and able to go out, maybe she would be open to it.

While April waited for Ryan, she rose and strolled along the corridor, looking at the vintage photos on the walls. She leaned in toward one, making out President Franklin Roosevelt and his wife Eleanor, a powerful woman in her own right.

Ryan hurried toward her. "There you are. I thought I'd lost you. I'm sorry I kept you waiting."

"That's alright. I was entertained."

"Hotels are good for that. You can people-watch for hours. And each of these old photos tells a story, too."

Recalling the pendant Junie found, April said, "Whitley will have some news for you about that tomorrow." Teasing him a little wouldn't hurt.

Ryan ran a hand over his damp hair and grinned. "I'll wait. But now, I have a confession to make." He reached inside his pocket. "One evening, I was at the Ferry Cafe waiting for take-out when I overheard an argument. I wasn't eavesdropping, but I couldn't help it."

A memory came rushing back, and instantly April knew what he was talking about. She drew a hand across her brow. "So, you heard it all?"

"I got the gist of it. And then, I saw you throw something." He brought out a small black pouch from his trouser pocket. "You both left, and I don't know why, but I picked this up. I can't keep it."

April shook her head and pushed her hand out. "I don't want it."

He studied the pouch, clearly torn over it. "It has value. Maybe one of your daughters would like it."

"It would only have bad memories for them." April turned away from it.

And then, she recalled what she'd just witnessed. A smile grew on her face, thinking about how much it might mean to the young couple. "Whitley might know of someone on the staff who would like it. Maybe Nacho and Sofie."

Mentally, she bestowed all her best wishes and memories on the ring to bond two people. This time, she had a good feeling about it.

Ryan's face brightened, and he stashed the pouch in his pocket. "I'm glad that's settled. About tonight…before the reception, I was concerned. And when that jerk started questioning me…"

"That was rude of him," April agreed. "But you handled it well."

"I'm glad you think so. At least it's all in the open now." Ryan rested a hand on her arm. "I'm glad you met my parents. They seemed to like you and your mother."

April smoothed her hand over his, enjoying the warmth of his touch. "I think they're lovely people. And they are so proud of you."

Ryan dipped his head with modesty. "My parents changed my life. A frequent guest from Ireland befriended them. He'd done well for himself and wanted to pass on his good fortune, so he paid for my education. I'm not the blueblood people thought I was."

"But you have more character," April said, realizing why he'd seemed reticent with her before. Now, he spoke with ease.

Ryan glanced around. This time, they were alone. "About my speech…I'm not entirely sure how it was received."

April inclined her head. "People love to talk, and there was some of that going on tonight. But you were so sincere and appreciative of what your parents had done for you. You brought people into your world, helping them see it through your eyes. As for the dedication you have for this hotel and the staff, it really came across. You're the perfect person to care for the Majestic. I'm sure people understand that now."

"It's more than that," Ryan said. "The Majestic is home to me. It had such an influence on my life. So many important moments occurred here."

"Beginning with your birth." April slid her hand into his. "It's incredible how our mothers are connected." She let her gaze linger on an old photo on the wall. "I understand how you feel. This hotel changed the course of my life, too."

Ryan turned to her with interest. "How is that?"

She led him toward the old photo. "In elementary school, my class took a field trip here." She gestured to the photo of grinning children. "This is us, in our idea of period costumes. After visiting the Majestic and learning about its past, I became enthralled with history. It was the first time the subject had come to life for me."

Ryan was staring at her in awe.

"I talked my mother into bringing me back so I could explore," she said. "I even wrote school papers on what I discovered here. This hotel is why I became a historian."

Ryan touched her cheek with tenderness. "Your eyes... The first time I saw you, I was transfixed. But now, I'm not sure when that was." Turning toward the photo, he tapped the glass, pointing out one of the girls. "Is that you?"

"That's Deb," April replied.

Ryan's smile faded. "Are you...sure?"

"Which one again?"

He pointed again.

"Oh, you're right. That was me. We had matching gingham dresses in different colors."

"Yours was green. To match your eyes."

April laughed. "That's an easy guess. But true." She leaned in. "I don't think I look anything like that now."

Ryan pressed a hand to his chest. "Inside, you're still the curious girl I fell in love with. But I was too shy to talk to you." He brought her hand to his lips and kissed it. "You were my first love, April Raines."

As memories came back to her, April's heart filled with warmth. "And you're the fascinating boy who was always here. I used to watch you, too. I wondered why you were here, peeking around corners at me."

Ryan laughed at that. "Since both of my parents worked here, I used to do my homework in the service area. I would explore the hotel and run errands. That's how I came to know it so well. The first time you walked through the hotel, the wonder on your face was so beautiful. I'd never seen anyone look at my home the way you did."

"It was like being transported through time."

"That's exactly what I thought." Ryan laughed at his memories. "You wanted to explore and touch everything and asked everyone a million questions. Whitley had just started working here. You drove him nuts."

April stared at him in amazement. "I can't believe you remember all that."

"I can't believe we're both here again. Some might call it fate." Ryan leaned in and kissed her forehead.

Fate. April considered the idea in her mind. She didn't believe in that, but she couldn't deny the coincidence, or her growing feelings for him. "Our past shaped who we are," she said. "Could it shape our future, too?"

"I'm willing to give it a try if you are. Would you like to get to know one another again? We can take it slow."

"I'd like that very much." April lifted her face to his, feeling a delicious sense of things to come.

As her lips met his, the future seemed to open to her in ways she had never imagined. She threaded her arms around his neck, sinking into the warmth of his body through their still-damp clothes.

"Thank you for coming back to me," he whispered, tightening his arms around her.

"We've both come home," she said, kissing him again.

BONUS! Thank you for reading *Beach View Lane*. Want to read a little more about April and Ryan? I have an extra first date scene that didn't quite fit, and I thought you might enjoy it! Visit my website at www.JanMoran.com/BVLbonus. Enter your email address to receive your bonus scenes by email. (If you don't have access to a computer, ask a friend to print these for you.)

Can't wait to find out what happens next on Crown Island? Read Junie's story in *Sunshine Avenue* and continue following the whole family. Is Junie ready to choose between Sailor and Blue?

Keep up with my new releases on my website at JanMoran.com. Please join my VIP Reader's Club there to receive news about special deals and other goodies. Plus, find more fun and join other like-minded readers in my Facebook Reader's Group.

Want more beach fun? Check out my popular *Summer Beach* and *Coral Cottage* series and meet the boisterous, fun-loving Bay and Delavie families, who are always up to something.

Looking for sunshine and international travel? Meet a group of friends in the *Love California* series, beginning with *Flawless* and an exciting trip to Paris.

Finally, I invite you to read my standalone family sagas, including *Hepburn's Necklace* and *The Chocolatier*, 1950s novels set in gorgeous Italy.

Most of my books are available in ebook, paperback or hardcover, audiobooks, and large print. And as always, I wish you happy reading!

STRAWBERRY LEMONADE & COCKTAIL

Strawberry lemonade is a lovely, pink-hued version of a summer cooler. In Southern California, my lemon trees often produce for nine to ten months of the year, so lemonade is a staple. Adding strawberries creates a tasty, pretty variation.

For a fun, color-changing effect, try adding purple ice cubes. As they melt, the drink will change shades, deepening from pink into the purple spectrum.

The type of lemon you use can affect the level of sweetness. Meyer lemons, which I prefer for lemonade, have a naturally sweeter taste profile.

In this recipe, you can adjust the tartness by adding a sweet counterpoint, but it might not be needed with sweet strawberries. A few drops of stevia or another sweetener is all you would need if you like your lemonade on the sweeter side.

This lemonade can be made ahead and enjoyed for a few days. It's also easy to whip up if unexpected guests arrive. With a dash of alcohol, a sugared rim, and a garnish of fruit, you'll have a fancy summer cocktail in a flash.

Read on for this recipe.

Make 4 to 6 servings
Ingredients:
1 cup (240 g) fresh strawberries, halved
1/2 cup (120 ml) freshly squeezed lemon juice (about 3-4 lemons)
Liquid stevia sweetener to taste
4 cups (1 l) water
Sliced strawberries and lemon wedges for garnish (optional)
Sugar for rim of glasses (optional)
Optional alcohol: 1 1/2 (45 ml) ounce of vodka

Instructions:

1. In a blender, puree the strawberries until smooth.
2. In a pitcher, combine the pureed strawberries, lemon juice, and water. Stir well.
3. Taste and adjust the sweetness by adding liquid stevia.
4. Fill glasses with colored ice cubes and pour the strawberry lemonade over the ice.

Serve with Royal Purple Ice Cubes for a color-changing experience. Garnish with sliced strawberries, lemon wedges, and mint if desired.

Royal Purple Ice Cubes

Here's a natural recipe for vividly colored ice cubes that will add a beautiful pop of color to your drinks. The secret is purple cabbage. You won't be able to taste the cabbage in your drinks. As the ice cubes melt, the color with drift into the drink. With strawberry lemonade, the pink tone deepens into purple.

No cabbage on hand? If you don't mind food coloring, you can add a few drops of red and blue.

Ingredients:
1/4 head of purple cabbage, chopped
Water
Ice cube tray

Instructions:

1. Rinse the chopped purple cabbage and place in a bowl with enough water to cover the cabbage.
2. Pour boiling water over cabbage to cover it. Let stand 5 minutes or until purple.
3. Strain the liquid into a container, discarding the cabbage.
4. Pour the tinted water into the ice cube tray, filling each section about 3/4 full.
5. Place the ice cube tray in the freezer and let it freeze completely, usually about 4 hours.
6. Add the ice cubes to your glass, pour in your beverage of choice, and enjoy.

ABOUT THE AUTHOR

JAN MORAN is a *USA Today* and a *Wall Street Journal* bestselling author of romantic women's fiction. A few of her favorite things include a fine cup of coffee, dark chocolate, fresh flowers, laughter, and music that touches her soul. She loves to travel, and her favorite places for inspiration are those rich with history and mystery and set against snowy mountains, palm-treed beaches, or sparkly city lights. Jan is originally from Austin, Texas, and a trace of a drawl still survives, although she has lived in Southern California near the beach for years.

Most of her books are available as audiobooks, and her historical fiction is translated into German, Italian, Polish, Dutch, Turkish, Russian, Bulgarian, Portuguese, and Lithuanian, and other languages.

If you enjoyed this book, please consider leaving a brief review online for your fellow readers where you purchased this book or on Goodreads or Bookbub.

To read Jan's other historical and contemporary novels, visit JanMoran.com. Join her VIP Readers Club mailing list and Facebook Readers Group to learn of new releases, sales and contests.

Made in the USA
Monee, IL
05 September 2023

42153123R00135